Tom Vowler is an award-winning writer living in south-west England. His short story collection *The Method* won the inaurugal Scott Prize in 2010 and the Edge Hill Readers' Prize in 2011. This is his second novel.

Praise for Tom Vowler:

'Thoughtful and engrossing . . . Much of the fiction peddled as "psychological suspense" weighs heavy on the suspense, with the psychology aspect feeling flimsy at best. Not so here' Kirsty Logan, www.thelist.co.uk

'*That Dark Remembered Day* is one of the most absorbing novels I've read in years. Brilliantly crafted, impeccably researched . . . Written in Vowler's beautifully cadenced, poised style, I was, appropriately, captivated' Ray Robinson author of *Jawbone Lake*

'A rewarding, if disturbing read' www.literatureworks.org.uk

'A compelling story about damage done, a touching exploration of the possibility of forgiveness and recovery' Alison Moore, author of *The Lighthouse*

'Dark and shocking' *Herald* (Plymouth)

'*That Dark Remembered Day* is a fine achievement. One vividly imagined and intensely realised scene follows another, each one ratchetir and deeper into Stehe stranger next to y" Anthony McGow

'Sensitively written and beautifully crafted . . . hard to put down, impossible to forget' Graham Mort, author of *Cusp*

'Much more than crime fiction, *What Lies Within* is unique not just for its sharp psychological insights but for the moral engine that drives the plot' Melissa Harrison, author of *Clay*

'Tightly spun, atmospheric and unsettling' *Lancashire Evening Post*

'A dark modern thriller' *Western Morning News*

'A powerful and unsettling book' Jen Campbell, author of *Weird Things Customers say in Bookshops*

'Deeply psychological . . . A devastating story, staying with the reader long after the last page' www.shotsmag.co.uk

'Taut and compelling, you won't just read this book, you'll devour it' Alex Preston, author of *In Love and War*

'An absorbing, thought-provoking novel about past pains resurfacing, brought to life through prose that is both compassionate and clear' Jonathan Lee, author of *Joy*

'An accomplished literary creation, truly a gripping, outstanding first novel' *Tavistock Times Gazette*

'*That Dark Remembered Day* is an intense and contemplative novel . . . beautifully written' www.andthenireadabook.blogspot.co.uk

'Dealing with difficult themes . . . the story is utterly absorbing . . . deeply affecting' Kate Wilson, www.literatureworks.org.uk

'Engrossing and intriguing . . . Dark and harrowing . . . Superb' www.novelheights.wordpress.com

Also by Tom Vowler

The Method
What Lies Within

That *Dark* Remembered Day

TOM VOWLER

headline

First published in 2014 by
HEADLINE PUBLISHING GROUP

First published in paperback in 2014 by
HEADLINE PUBLISHING GROUP

1

Cataloguing in Publication Data is available from the British Library

ISBN 978 0 7553 9224 7

Typeset in Giovanni by Avon DataSet Ltd,
Bidford-on-Avon, Warwickshire

Printed and bound in Great Britain by
Clays Ltd, St Ives plc

Headline's policy is to use papers that are natural, renewable and recyclable
products and made from wood grown in sustainable forests. The logging and
manufacturing processes are expected to conform to the environmental
regulations of the country of origin.

HEADLINE PUBLISHING GROUP
A division of Hachette Livre UK Ltd
338 Euston Road
London NW1 3BH

www.headline.co.uk
www.hachette.co.uk

For victims of violence, be it arbitrary
or state-sponsored.

Acknowledgements

The generosity of people in such matters never fails to astonish me, and this book would not have been written without the help and support of the following people: Mark Appleton, John Martin, Jack Harris, Lynne Hatwell, Charlie Brotherstone, Claire Baldwin, Anthony Caleshu, Lytton Smith, Moira Briggs, Gerard Donovan, Alison Smith, James Walkley-Cox, Simon Withers, Jane Miller, Margaret Bonnett, Hilary Payne and Martin Smith. As ever, any failure to correctly distil their proffered knowledge lies with the author alone.

Thanks also to the Centre for Humanities, Music, and Performing Arts at Plymouth University for a PhD studentship.

I am also indebted to two texts in particular, J. A. Baker's inimitable book, *The Peregrine* (Collins), and Tony McNally's account of the Falklands War, *Watching Men Burn* (Monday Books). Adriana Groisman's hybrid project, 'Voices of the South Atlantic', also provided much inspiration.

The words 'nothing but the wild rain' on p.220 are taken from Edward Thomas's poem 'Rain'.

The past beats inside me like a second heart.

John Banville, *The Sea*

Spring 1983

In those last moments of childhood, before everything splintered for ever, he watched her disappear along the lane. They'd got off the school bus together, made plans to meet later in the woods behind his house, nervous and exhilarated at what might occur. Their fumblings of the last few weeks, gloriously ardent explorations of one another that had so far been contained, now longed for a crescendo, a progression to unknown, untasted delights. He assumed it would be her first time too, although when he'd asked, she'd just smiled and pulled him closer. It irritated him that his own bedroom was ruled out for such a momentous occasion, his father, with the exception of walking the dog, home all day since his return from the war, ghosting between rooms, ever present, albeit in a vacant approximation of himself. There was enough to contend with – performance, the mechanics of the thing – without the fear of someone walking in, though the woods hardly guaranteed privacy. He'd wanted so badly to ask his friend for advice, a sense of what to expect, but of course the one person he could ask about such matters was now the one person he couldn't.

Once she was out of sight, he caught up with his friend – a

friend he'd replaced in the girl's affections – hoping the awkwardness between them, the sense of betrayal, would recede a little in the days ahead. More than anything, he wanted his friend to punch him, to lash out in a rage that would see them sprawling on the ground, bloodied but with the tension broken. Anything but this silence. He wanted to say sorry, how neither of them had meant it to happen, that you couldn't help your feelings, that he hoped the three of them could still hang around together.

Instead he kicked a stone along the road, watching it skim and buck, hoping his friend might join in, before the hedge claimed it. Passing the gate they sometimes climbed over for a smoke, he suggested a fishing trip at the weekend, if the weather held; he'd found a new spot, miles upriver from the old iron bridge. There would be chub and roach, even a barbel if they got lucky. They could get up at first light Saturday, pack some food, make a flask of tea, then meet by the oak tree in the top field and walk down to the river with their rods. 'How about it?' he said, looking at his friend's back. Still the silence, the unspoken allegation of theft, his friend striding on in anger.

Reaching the houses on the outskirts of town, he saw a car on the brow of the hill, sideways on so that it blocked the road, and they stood staring at it for a moment. One of its doors was open, the engine ticking away. Beyond the car, the town's lone traffic lights passed through their silent cycle, the roads leading off them empty as a Sunday morning. Someone was shouting, perhaps half a mile away, the pitch of the words rising, the sound just carrying to them on the breeze.

They walked on, around the car and up to the crossroads, where several dogs barked in a discordant choir. A hundred yards or so along Cross Street, they could see a bicycle abandoned on the pavement, the groceries from its basket spilt on to the side of the road, a trail of fruit strewn along the gutter. Opposite the bike, outside the newsagent's, a pushchair was upended as if it had fallen from the sky, its contents long gone, and he realised that that was what was missing: people. To the north, beyond the town, they could hear a siren now, distant like white noise.

At the fork in the road, the two of them separated without speaking, and a few seconds later he found himself running past the churchyard and out of town, over the humpbacked bridge, where finally he stopped to catch his breath. Hands on knees, puffing, he looked ahead, seeing by the side of the road a mound that looked both ridiculous and commonplace. Still as a rock, it had been covered almost entirely by an old grey blanket, and as he passed it, as his mind processed what it was, he felt his heart quicken, da-dum da-dum, as if it were dancing.

Part One

Autumn 2012

One

Grateful to emerge from the violence of his dreams, he prepared for the hangover awaiting him. Somewhere in the fog of his sentience Zoe left for work, the front door if not slammed, then closed with scant consideration. She'd have made their daughter's breakfast, got her ready for school, but with nothing of significance to fill his days now, the school run had become his alone. Reaching for some painkillers in the bedside drawer, Stephen knocked over the glass of water, the last of which trickled in a rivulet into the paperback he'd yet to start. A pallid light bled through the curtains and he winced at the emptiness the day promised, as if all its moments had already been glued together with inertia. The steady build-up of traffic on the road into town could be heard, an insidious taunt from those with routine in life, whose days were a series of edifying events.

Downstairs, Amy was finishing her cereal, her lunchbox standing proud in the middle of the table. She looked at him standing there in his underwear, unshaven, her face full of concern that they'd be late again.

'Hey, you,' he said, offering a reassuring smile as he made

himself a strong coffee. There was a note from Zoe: some groceries to get if he went into town, a suggestion of what to cook tonight, that she would be home late again. She'd signed off with *This can't go on*.

He too wondered how long it could be endured. Initially, for the first couple of weeks, he'd savoured the leisurely rhythm of his days, filling the mornings with long-put-off jobs around the house, the afternoons with fishing for pollock or bass off the harbour wall, perhaps a few quid on one of the afternoon races before congregating by the school gates. But the absence of structure gave his mind space to lurch into darker realms, turning in on itself and sabotaging the quiet progress, bringing into relief the 'episode', as Zoe now referred to it.

She had tried to draw him into an exchange about his recent transgression – the hows and whats, if not the why – something he'd resisted for now. And whereas her instinct was to show support, to be, as they said, there for him, her face could barely hide the incredulity at the situation he'd brought upon them.

'What made you do such a thing?'

'I've tried to tell you, I don't know.'

They had made love last night, a frantic scramble he'd initiated once she had stopped reading. There was something about his enforced idleness that lent the passion, on his part at least, additional vigour, perhaps desperation, as if impotence, real or symbolic, could take root in such times. Once he'd finished, she'd rolled over, patting his thigh with her trailing hand in felicitation, sleep coming for her in seconds.

After walking Amy to school, he took the binoculars and trekked out of town, along the coast path, hoping the brackish air would calm him as he stopped to watch cormorants skim over the water, tight to the surf, their elongated necks cleaving the air like arrow shafts. If he was lucky, a kestrel would hover at eye level, out over the cliff edge, scanning for small mammals or nesting birds. At this time of year the sea could be black as ink as it roiled beneath a flinty, turbulent sky. He looked out beyond the headland, picturing the rusting hulks of wrecked ships that ghosted the sea floor, forests of kelp slowly claiming them. In the distance, out in the Channel, sheets of rain slanted downwards as if smudged from the cloud, while on the horizon a vein of sunlight divided land from sky. If he made good time, he could be near Helford by lunchtime; he'd stop for a pint, warming himself by the fire. The beer would be honeyed, a pint would become two, his hangover almost forgotten. Later he would time the walk back to pick Amy up from school.

The terms of his suspension, although anticipated, felt ridiculous. None more so than the mile radius of campus he was to remain beyond until the hearing. He'd held on to the vague hope that a resolution could be reached informally, his apology, if sincere enough, accepted. But the lecturer had lodged his complaint with unambiguous expectation: he would settle for nothing less than the full disciplinary procedure. HR had written to him, stressing that he should seek representation – a friend, someone from the union – that he would remain on full pay, but a return to work was out of the question. A link to the university's constitution was provided, should he wish to read it.

The day in question had unfurled in benign fashion for the most part. As a senior technician in the marine biology department, his job was a varied one. One day he could be collecting plankton for student research, the next mapping seagrass meadows on the ocean floor, or, more prosaically, feeding and monitoring fish stocks. Colleagues came to him with all manner of requests, whether practical or scholastic, his knowledge respected throughout the faculty and beyond – an encyclopedic familiarity with his subject that had emerged from a private passion rather than formal schooling. If this led to accusations of arrogance, he was unaware of them, though some probably regarded him brusque, even rude on occasion, his emails lacking the deferential etiquette required. But nothing had ever spiralled beyond the occasional tetchy or sarcastic exchange.

In recent months, however, small pressures had built up following a departmental shake-up. As their workload increased, resentment was cultivated. Talk of cutbacks laced conversations, rumours that they'd have to reapply for their jobs. Tensions between teaching staff and technicians could flare with minimal provocation as goodwill was slowly withdrawn. Lecturers, though, while often ignorant of how much work their requests involved, were generally courteous, his relationship with all but one productive and, at least superficially, egalitarian.

But David Ferguson had never warmed to him. Not since they'd clashed several years ago over conditions of an experiment into the immune systems of trout. Not since

Stephen had confronted him with suspicions that a mass mortality among the fish was his fault. And not since Ferguson's fellow lecturer, Zoe Wheeler, had moved in with Stephen. This last was conjecture, but Ferguson was certainly fond of Zoe and had barely hidden his surprise when she got together with a technician rather than a member of the academic staff. Stephen had once suspected the man of being one of her former lovers, but this seemed unlikely on a campus where extracurricular pursuits between members of staff rarely went unnoticed.

And so for years the two men had allowed a tacit feud to steadily gather, its impetus bolstered by each barbed email, every point of conflict exploited or stored for future vitriol. The fact that Stephen suspected he knew more about his subject than Ferguson only served to intensify the ill feeling. And perhaps on some level Ferguson sensed this too, his behaviour a defence against a perceived inadequacy: that for all his academic prowess and stature in the field, when it was stripped down, he knew less than the technicians he regarded as serving him.

The escalation had occurred in the weeks before, midway through a six-month feeding trial. Part of Stephen's role was to look after the automatic feeders, check the power to the pumps, change the filters when necessary.

In a hurry to get away one evening, he had inexplicably forgotten to set one of the internal alarms. Overnight, oxygen levels had depleted, and with no intervention, most of a tank of fish lay floating on the surface by morning, meaning the whole trial would have to start again. It was his first significant error in the job, the blame his alone. Ferguson, perhaps mindful of Stephen's past criticism of him, didn't hold back, despite the presence of two technicians and several research students.

Stephen took the rebuke without reply, his own sense of guilt fuelling the admonishment as Ferguson left with a disdainful shake of his head. But in the hour that followed, a sensation made itself known in his chest, a tightness of breath as if his own ribs were compressing him. As the agitation grew, nausea rose from his stomach, his head pulsing with a quiet rage. Even now, he couldn't remember the walk to Ferguson's office, who he might have passed and ignored on campus. What he could recall was the man's expression of astonishment as Stephen pushed open the door, walked steadily across to the desk and brought a fist down hard into the side of Ferguson's face.

After the incident, he was told to go home, a phone call from the senior technical manager later that day informing him that suspension was inevitable. The offence was a serious one, of course: the physical assault of a colleague, a facial injury that, although not requiring stitches, bled significantly. There would be bruising, a black eye that passed through the spectrum of hues in the days that followed, whispered outrage from all who saw it. The police had not been called, though Stephen was advised that this remained an option for the complainant.

There were three disciplinary levels he could be subject to. An oral warning would be normal for a first offence, but unlikely given the severity of the incident. Even a written warning would be lenient, the woman from the union had advised him in their brief telephone conversation last week.

Either of these would stay on his record for a year before, in the event that no repetition occurred, being wiped clear. Or, quite reasonably, the committee could decide that the offence warranted dismissal, which he could appeal against if he produced some mitigating circumstances.

And what form might these take, beyond the vague sense of his unravelling? Of the appalling crisis building inside him, the likely cause of which he'd managed to keep from colleagues, from his wife, all these years? No, better not to resist whatever punitive squall they unleashed his way. Better to ride it out, hunker down, try for once not to pick a fight with life.

The hearing itself was in three weeks, enough time for witnesses to be called, written submissions to be made. A supreme arbiter would be appointed, likely the Vice Chancellor, a brute of a woman whose sermonic emails displayed a level of corporate jargon Stephen could rarely fathom. He could expect little sympathy from her.

He'd waited until after dinner that evening to tell Zoe, who'd been off campus and hadn't heard. She spoke of the embarrassment, of colleagues' reactions, of what would happen if he lost his job, checking every few minutes that it had actually happened, that a mistake hadn't been made, or that she wasn't the victim of some ill-judged practical joke. And later, when her inquisition petered out, she'd looked hard at him, scrutinising his face as someone might a stranger, disquieted and appalled, perhaps a little frightened even.

The wind was gusting now, a fine rain blinding him if he looked into it. Herring gulls and fulmars rode the thermals in long, graceful arcs, the easy rhythm of their flight soothing him. The gulls on the beach below issued proud, barbarous cries as they delved into the seaweed or jabbed at stranded cuttlefish. Beyond them, groups of sanderlings gathered on the tideline in search of sand shrimps, scuttling comically back and forth with each breaking wave, froths of foam eddying around them. As he rounded the headland, a couple of walkers passed him on the path, a genial nod and half-smile exchanged, their dog scampering back and forth, nose to the ground. Inhaling deeply, he felt that the briny air had imbued him sufficiently now, dulling his headache to a faint pulse.

Did it mean anything? Beyond the fact that his temper could flare these days with such small provocation? A fuse that, while never being interminable, had now barely any length at all. When, a couple of months ago, the technical manager had called him in, asking if there were problems he should be aware of, mentioning that Stephen seemed uptight, often curt, he'd tucked it away in the part of his mind that resisted enquiry. Last week Zoe had even suggested he seek help.

'The union know,' he said. 'They'll help me prepare for the hearing.'

'I didn't mean that sort of help.'

He took a few seconds to catch up. 'That's a bit overboard, isn't it?'

'If you won't talk to me . . .'

'We do talk.'

'Apparently not about this, though. Not about your childhood.'

'What do you want to know?'

'I don't understand what's happening to you, why you did it.'

'I've told you why.'

'You don't hit someone because they're an arsehole.'

'It was a one-off, an aberration. I don't know, stress of work.'

'I'm scared.'

'Of me?'

'Of it all.'

This they shared, for the manifestation of violence had left him shaken at this new capability. Beyond childhood scrapes and a scuffle in a pub a few years ago, he'd avoided any physical run-ins, despite a contrary personality, one that shifted easily to aggravation after a few drinks. He'd always known both when to stifle the antagonising of others and how to stop his own temper rising. The incident with Ferguson was inexplicable. It belonged to the realms of fantasy, one you let play out in glorious retrospect in your mind, while acknowledging gratitude for decades of social mores and evolving civility that prevented you from punching colleagues you loathed.

Again he tried to recall details of the seconds leading up to it. There was a hangover, as was increasingly the case these days. There was general resentment towards aspects of work. He'd argued with Zoe the night before. Amy had been difficult over breakfast. Yet none of this excused what he'd done, the terrible person he was apparently becoming, the origin of which didn't bear thinking about.

He looked out to the open water, its irregular surface

specked with half a dozen fishing boats. A tanker sat sombrely on the horizon. For a moment he thought he saw the dorsal fin of a basking shark cutting through the swell a few hundred yards out, but by the time he found the spot with the binoculars, it had gone. Most, if not all of them, would have left for the warmer waters of the south by now. On the tip of the promontory ahead, sea heaved at the rock, slamming into its coves, the water forced up a blowhole with each wave, spuming into the wind.

Inland the cloud had opened, just a crack, allowing the sun to wash briefly over the fields, chased by a surging line of shadow. A pair of choughs squabbled in the gorse that flanked the path. Ahead, through the drizzle, he could just make out the bone-white walls of the pub a couple of miles along the coast, and he pictured himself sitting by its fire indefinitely.

Two

Clouds scudded in from the south, low and sombre, winter held among them. As his car left the main road, the fringes of the town could be seen, its lights pulsing like sodium lamps a mile or so away. How long had it been since he was last here? A couple of decades, perhaps a little longer. Enough time to allow a fantasy to flourish in which the place ceased existing.

The phone had rung as Stephen served dinner last night. He told Zoe to ignore it, that they were about to eat, but she was never able to, her curiosity or assumption that it wouldn't be some trivial matter triumphing.

'It's for you,' she said. 'Someone called Peter. Says he's a friend of your mother's.'

The man's voice was gentle, old-fashioned, with traces of a stammer riding the occasional word. 'I'm sorry to bother you,' he said.

'It's fine. You know . . .'

'Mary, yes.'

'Is she OK?'

'Yes, I think so. I don't want to worry anyone. It's hard to put into words. I suppose you'd say she's not really herself at the moment.'

In his mind, he'd held on to the idea of never returning, of keeping the distance between him and the town considerable; his coming back was probably as unpalatable for those who lived here as it was horrifying for him. His mother had stayed with them in Cornwall a couple of times, awkward visits, Zoe trying hard but failing to make a connection. In the coming years there would, he supposed, be issues of care, decisions on location to be made. But this was some way off: for all her eccentricity and diminishing lucidity, his mother was a hardy woman, capable of enduring the physical and mental challenges that living alone bestowed. And yet the man on the phone, a friend his mother had never mentioned by name, had hinted at something being wrong.

'I don't know what. Just that, even for her, she's behaving oddly – forgetting things, clumsy even.'

Keen to emphasise that their friendship was no more than that – something Stephen would have assumed anyway – the man explained that he helped her around the house and garden, fixing things, bringing her firewood at this time of year.

'We play canasta once a week, share the spoils from my allotment. I feel disloyal calling, but I thought a family member would want to know. I saw your number on the noticeboard in the kitchen.'

After a series of bends, the town's sign welcomed him. Years of dirt from passing traffic had encrusted around the letters so that they bled into one another, while the hedge, listing and neglected, had entwined itself between the sign's posts, reaching up to the words. As children, they had sat on the wall across the road, hurling stones at a nominated letter between passing cars. Or a bottle would be balanced on top of the sign, and once smashed, they'd amble home through the field of rapeseed and along the river. Back then, the place's name had been insignificant, denoting nothing more than arrival at an unremarkable market town in middle England.

Time unspooled in slow motion then, skewed as it was by childhood, days without end, lives barely begun. Their world, a few square miles fringing the town, was small yet felt gargantuan. He tried to picture the faces of friends, half-feral boys bound by some inexplicable force, but the years had dulled them to amorphous forms, the detail diminished, pushed beyond memory's grasp. Even Brendan's face could barely be recalled now, and the more he tried, the less he trusted the image. Returning here as an adult gave the illusion that none of it was real, that perhaps it had been read about or imagined, all aspects blurred by the years, like a fading photograph or a childhood nightmare.

Lost in thought, he had to swerve to avoid the half-eaten, half-run-over carcass of a badger. He imagined carrion crows pecking at its eyes and guts, a bird of prey swooping down between traffic, picking clean the bones.

Although he had kept to modest speeds, the drive here had taken less time than he remembered. He would have preferred the cover of darkness, the anonymity it brought, but any thoughts of interrupting the journey in one of the pubs he passed had been undone by a compulsive dread to witness the town again after so long.

The cloud now yielded some drizzle, the car's wipers issuing a rhythmic mewl. On the outskirts, where the old petrol station had once been, there was some new housing, twelve or so homogenous units packed together, their diminutive gardens manicured and featureless, incongruous against the town's more traditional buildings that rose beyond them. Perhaps they were termed affordable, built to accommodate those who didn't move away when adulthood arrived. And there would be new residents, eager to take advantage of the slump in prices such an event afforded. Add to this the second-home-owners picking up a bargain, impervious to the town's legacy, their contact with the community perfunctory, pragmatic.

The newspapers, mistaking aloofness for camaraderie, always termed it a close-knit community, as if this had somehow insulated the people who lived here, left them better prepared for that day. But there were factions here like any small town, schisms that divided one street from the next, regardless of their shared history. Neighbours who passed one another in decades-long silence.

He eased the car around the last bend before the road straightened, the town square now visible up ahead. A few people, the first he'd seen, went about their business, their pace skittish as the rain, harder now, slanted down. In the distance, towards the hills, the sky was still open a crack, a shaft of silvered light falling on to the valley's slopes as if beaming someone up. He strained to catch a glimpse of the house on the hill, the place where it had all begun, unable to resist in spite of himself, but the clouds soon fused, the higher ground lost to the rain.

Of the cigarettes he'd rolled before leaving, one remained, and he lit it, opening the window an inch. Beyond the mini-roundabout the traffic had slowed to a chunter, and he joined the end of the procession as it edged forwards. To his left, the low stone wall of the cemetery flanked the road before cutting in towards the town's Methodist church. Rows of gravestones lay along the mildly undulating ground, stopping abruptly in fallow space assigned, he assumed, to those the town had yet to give up. Some of the older slabs were listing badly, the granite weathered, garbed in patch-works of lichen. Further along, by contrast, the more modern headstones gleamed despite the murk, the rain glistening on the burnished marble. Without the rain it might have been possible to read the inscriptions from the car, surnames that resonated, their echo catching in the throat like an acrid vapour. Epitaphs began to form, unbidden, at the edge of his mind, and he pictured a stone-mason at work, carefully carving words that families had agonised over, attempts to capture a life in a sentence or two.

Up ahead a car sounded its horn, the driver remonstrating with an arm from his half-open window. Stephen watched, waiting for a retaliatory burst, but nothing came. He pictured the other motorists hunkering down, a generation wary of confrontation, happy not to give conflict its fuel. As his car inched past the gates of the cemetery, a coldness passed through him, a convulsion that was gone in an instant, someone treading on his grave, he might once have termed it.

Apart from half a flavourless sandwich on the motorway, he hadn't eaten today. Zoe would be making Amy's dinner about now, his absence perhaps enquired about for the first time. He imagined the awkwardness on his wife's face as their daughter asked whether Daddy would be home tomorrow. In truth, no timescale had been discussed, just a vague acknowledgement that he would come back when he could, that he'd use the time to reflect on his suspension, consider what he'd do if dismissed.

He thought about what his wife knew of the town. He'd kept her – and now his daughter – away from the place he'd grown up, his family home, giving her an airbrushed version of the truth. A version in which key players had been appropriated, names changed, his family's part in it all downgraded, though not so as he'd lose all sympathy. Just enough ambiguity to his backstory to resist scrutiny. What had he feared would be Zoe's reaction? Disgust? Fear? Or perhaps her judgement would have been more considered, benevolent even. But why risk it? Why parade your shame to those you met? Better to allow them time to know you in isolation. And after the initial months, it had seemed easier to go along with this version, to continue its propagation, tweak it on occasion, apologise to his wife for the estrangement of his family.

As he neared the town centre, he was reminded of a game he used to play with his sister. As children, returning from seaside holidays, almost drunk with torpor, they'd summon the last vestige of energy to peer out the back of the car, the winner the first to spot someone they knew. Their mother would tell them not to stare, his sister asking how they were supposed to see people if they didn't. Sometimes Jenny would announce a teacher's name, or a friend's parent, claiming to have seen them up a side road, insistent that it still counted.

'It's not proof,' he'd say as she grinned knowingly. 'I have to see them as well.'

The game was different now, played from the front seat, where, despite the drizzle distorting everything, he was as much on show as the people who passed by. Occasionally a face would spark some small beat of recognition, before morphing into something unfamiliar. And while he expected someone to fix on him, to cease their business and stare with quiet recognition, nobody did.

He turned into a side road, a short cut that bypassed the heart of the town, where a cat darted out from beneath a parked van, causing him to brake hard, the car skidding to a halt. Houses rose up like battlements on either side of him, their walls oppressive, darkened windows eyeing the car as he sat there, inert, listening to the idling of the engine. He realised that this street was where Brendan had lived. During the final year of school, they would siphon off alcohol from their parents' stocks and meet in the park on Friday nights. Stephen, looking marginally older, would sometimes manage to buy cigarettes, and they'd sit in the old fort, smoking ostentatiously, swigging vodka or gin or whatever from a plastic bottle, faking bravado as they talked about girls in their year that they'd ask out one day. In truth, the two of them shared an abundant diffidence when faced with a girl up close, though neither liked to admit it. So when Suzanne entered their lives – pretty, a little awkward herself – they could scarcely account for it, the two of them falling for her in the same moment, Brendan's charm opening that particular door ahead of Stephen. He tried to grasp more of the memory, but it retreated.

The last time he'd seen Brendan was shortly after the inquest. Stephen had been given permission by the board to take his exams separately, so it'd been months since they'd spoken. He'd passed him down by the river, at one of the spots they liked to fish together. Stephen had stopped and stood behind him, Brendan continuing to focus on the float that bobbed on the water. He'd said his friend's name, asked how his exams had gone, whether he'd caught anything, but the silence only deepened.

Scanning the line of houses now, he looked up at what had been Brendan's bedroom window, remembering staying at the house once, passing Brendan's mother on the landing in the middle of the night, entertaining his adolescent fantasy that she might come into his room, his virginity taken by a woman almost three times his age.

The cottage was a mile or so beyond the town. Built in the mid nineteenth century to house local miners, there were four or five rows of them, running at right angles to the road, the end ones with gardens backing on to the river.

He parked a few hundred yards along the road and walked back to the gate in the incipient darkness, the scent of woodsmoke lingering in the drizzle. He rehearsed a greeting – a courteous half-smile, cordial but scant – should any of the neighbours emerge from their doors as he passed. Outside the end-but-one cottage a faint orange glow issued through the curtains of the living room, and he paused, thinking that he might turn around, drive straight home.

His first knock was tentative, almost apologetic, so he followed it with something more purposeful. There were two hanging baskets he didn't remember, the cottage perhaps painted recently. Ten seconds or so later, he knocked again. Eventually a light came on at the back of the hall. She opened the door slowly, warily, as if expecting some cold-caller or the cackle of children as they ran away. Seeing him, there was barely a flicker of emotion on her face, as if his arrival was both expected and cause for indifference. She had aged, the skin around her eyes puffy, her forehead appreciably furrowed. Standing in the doorway, she appeared smaller; not merely thinner, but as if some height had been lost to a stoop as the heft of life had accumulated. Apart from a glance along the path, her gaze was floor-bound after making initial eye contact. Behind her he could hear the utterances of a radio play.

'Hello,' he said.

Perhaps forgetting herself, the beginnings of a smile formed at her mouth and for a moment he thought she might hug him. As he stood there in the drizzle, one of the cats appeared between his mother's feet, coiling itself around her legs in a figure of eight.

'You must be cold out there,' she said.

Leaving the door open, she picked up the cat and returned in silence to the lounge.

Three

The fire was little more than a tendril of smoke rising from damp wood. His mother tended to it with patience, adding more kindling, blowing from the side until it caught. She muttered something about the logs being wet, how Peter was supposed to be bringing round some drier ones. The fact that they didn't hug or kiss by way of greeting had always felt unremarkable until Zoe commented on it the first time she'd met his mother.

'It's not something we do,' he'd said, though he supposed they once had. He'd wondered whether the birth of his daughter might not give their bond a prevailing warmth, ushered in beneath their defences, but if anything, it rendered the prospect more absurd. Zoe, with little tolerance for such awkwardness, had wrapped her arms around his mother within seconds of meeting.

He put his bag down and looked around the room. The other cat was coiled asleep on the armchair. Above the fire sat his grandfather's mantel clock, the hands unmoving. To the left of it there was a framed photograph of him and Zoe, one he'd sent several years ago, and next to that one of Amy in the garden, her smile slightly forced for the camera. To the right of the clock his sister looked out at them.

Little had changed by way of furnishings, second-hand pieces bought hastily to fill a home in that other time, the mahogany's lustre dulled, the fabric of the chairs cloyed with the scent of woodsmoke, damp and cats. The only picture to survive Highfield – an oil painting of hills to the north – retained its brooding quality, the distinction between the colours in the gloom of the lounge barely perceptible. There seemed to be more paperbacks in the bookcase, some they'd sent as presents over the years, and he was curious to see if they'd been read. His mother had tried, with little success in his case, to get Stephen and his sister to read more as children. After school one day she'd announced that there was an account for them in the town's bookshop. They were allowed, the owner had been told, up to two new books a month – anything they liked – and their mother would settle up on payday. Perhaps it was hoped they'd return with some classics of children's literature, that the lure of choosing whatever they desired, rather than being told what to read, would set them on some gloriously edifying literary journey. Jenny, more than he, had taken the gesture seriously, spending hours in the shop, planning meticulously which books to acquire, which to save for future months. Often she would just buy a notebook to draw or press flowers in, but her most prized purchase was an audio book of *Peter and the Wolf*, which came with two accompanying records that narrated the story. She listened to it again and again, thrilled as each character's instrument in the orchestra was played. Within weeks the vinyl had several scratches across it, meaning that she had to lift the needle and gently lower it into a subsequent groove. She never tired of the French horns that signalled the wolf's entrance, her face rich with fear and excitement as if hearing it for the first time. Stephen would tease her, saying that Sonia the duck didn't really survive in the wolf's stomach, and Jenny would well up until he was proven wrong, whereupon she'd scowl at him, her face somehow both angry and forgiving.

The owner of the bookshop, a chubby, florid-cheeked man for whom even the slightest movement induced a diabolical wheeze, would always forget their mother's arrangement as he awaited payment from them. Each time they reminded him he'd affect weary resignation, as if regretting the agreement that had been reached, or somehow doubting their mother's ability to pay. In the end, when their financial difficulties worsened, their mother approached him, explaining the problem, how it was temporary, and asking whether he could see his way to continuing the understanding until such time as their situation improved. Perhaps he'd heard how bad things were for them, or just saw the chance to rescind his earlier generosity, for they were never allowed books on credit again. A few weeks later, as if to prove a point, Stephen and his sister were taken to the shop one Saturday morning. Once inside, their mother announced proudly that they were to choose anything they liked (she'd told them before going in that they could only have one book each). The whole shop seemed suspended in time as they gingerly browsed the shelves, their mother standing proud, daring the owner or any of the few customers to meet her eye. Stephen tried to remember what he'd bought that day, but couldn't. Likely some fantasy adventure book he didn't even read. After that, they never went back to the shop.

His mother, content that the fire had caught sufficiently, replaced the guard and returned the poker to its hook. Her hands still had the strength of someone who'd used them throughout life, although the skin had parched considerably. Her hair, previously flecked with grey, was now silvered throughout, its lustre gone, making it impossible to picture the once glossy strands that had spooled down. Years ago Stephen had discovered that she still cut it herself – a hangover from their money problems or just another aspect of her seclusion, he wasn't sure. The result was an irregular profile, with one or two mutinous clumps flaring outwards like peaks on a chart. Kneeling there by the fire, she looked tiny, the line of her spine visible beneath her jumper like that of an abandoned dog.

She eased herself up from the grate and went into the kitchen. It was to be expected, the sudden ageing of a friend or relative you saw only occasionally, rather than the trickling, imperceptible plunder of their vigour in your ever-presence. Perhaps she regarded him similarly, her once-little boy, awkward and sickly, now approaching middle age, a family of his own, a steady if unremarkable career, though this last part likely needed qualification now.

'Did you manage to get a space?' she called through.

Originally the cottages had been assigned parking spaces, but over the years the lines had faded, the system abused, becoming first come, first served. His mother had sold the car long before moving in, and, as far as he knew, had not driven since.

'Got lucky,' he said. 'There was one at the end.'

The tea was insipid, his mother using one bag for both cups, he assumed. He'd thought to ask if she had anything to drink in the house, but suspected she remained faithful to her temperance. The fact that this extended to denying her occasional visitors anything seemed churlish. If he was here more than a day or so, a pub would have to be chosen, perhaps the one on the edge of town, where he'd played pool with Brendan as kids. He would wear the cap that made him look a little ridiculous, find a spot in the corner, keep himself to himself.

'I didn't think you'd come back here again,' his mother said as she sat down on the settee.

'It's not by choice. Peter contacted me.'

'He needn't have bothered you.'

'It's hardly bother. It was good of him to call. He said you'd had some tests.'

Before speaking, she dismissed his words with a sweep of her arm, a petulant tut. 'Tell me, how's Amy? She must have started school now.'

He thought to press for more but decided against it, see what was offered in the coming days.

'She's good. Has her mother's brains.'

'She got lucky, then.'

'I thought I might stay for a bit, if that's OK. A day or two, perhaps a little longer.'

'There's really no need,' she said, before softening a little.

'But yes, stay as long as you like. Will Zoe manage without you?'

'Amy's at school most of the day now. And Zoe can work a little from home.'

'Won't work miss you?'

He wondered whether there was any sense in mentioning his suspension, but decided not to for now, fearing the connection she'd make. 'They'll manage.'

'What will you do? There's nothing to do here.'

He'd considered this, the danger in being idle, here of all places, the emptiness of afternoons without the promise of seeing his wife and daughter later. Of clipped exchanges with his mother as they steered clear of the contrails of the past.

'I thought I could help out around the house, do any odd jobs need doing.'

A flicker of annoyance passed across his mother's face, as if his offer was absurd, insulting even. She'd managed well enough for the past twenty-six years on her own; what jobs did he think beyond her?

How old was she now? Sixty-four, sixty-five? He felt some small guilt at not knowing which. On the cusp of becoming old, then. And was she resigned now to a life on her own? Of her twilight years unfurling in a withering loneliness, broken only by fleeting family visits and a sympathetic friend? Her penance, she no doubt believed. Repaying the gods, or whoever, with monastic sobriety.

When she'd moved into the cottage, he was starting his A levels at the other end of the country. The preceding year had seen her endure several spells in a psychiatric ward, between which she would catch the train down to her brother's to see Stephen. They thought she would return indefinitely on her final discharge, but a phone call to his uncle revealed that she was looking at houses to rent in the town. They presumed it a phase, some aspect of the grief that needed to play out, hoping she would move away in time. But the months became years, and a sanctuary of sorts was created in the heart of purgatory. Stephen came to stay soon after she moved in, the only time he had been back, a difficult few days for them both, the awkwardness following them to the cemetery, where his mother placed fresh flowers on the grave, as she still did every week as far as he knew. There was still some stone-throwing in those days, a group of kids from the other side of town, Stephen's mother shrinking into her chair a little more as each one struck the cottage, both of them waiting for a window to go. On the second evening, on hearing the sporadic patter against the door and roof, he went out, half scared, half seething with anger, to confront them, the dog following him out, sitting by his side.

'Leave us alone,' he'd said, and they'd laughed.

What did he think he could do, other than goad them further, give them the confrontation they craved? The few he recognised had the decency to look vaguely embarrassed, but it was the tall, skinny one at the front whose defiance showed Stephen what his mother would endure when she made the decision to stay. The boy launched the stone he held low and flat into Stephen's cheek, the blood taking several seconds to appear. Despite the injury looking worse than it was, his mother and uncle agreed that he shouldn't visit again, not while feelings were so strong. It would be more than twenty years before he returned.

He rolled a cigarette and went out to the garden. It was almost dark now, and the rain had thinned to nothing. Where the cloud had broken, the first stars shimmered. He could hear the river babbling beyond the end cottage, little more than a whisper. The garden was faintly lit by the neighbours' windows, so he stood close to the back door, tucked into the storm porch, watching his smoke billow into the night. He wondered how much contact his mother had with those around her, whether Peter lived nearby, how much he knew. Initially, according to his uncle, those in the other cottages hardly acknowledged her. Doors would close as she walked by, conversations cease. But when a stone came through her kitchen window, one neighbour, a young woman from the adjacent row, helped her clear up the glass, the others regarding her more sympathetically thereafter. Her landlord, too, seemed beyond such judgements, assuring Stephen's uncle that he would let him know if any repeat of the broken window occurred.

Once able, his mother had returned to work at the nursing home for a few months, the manager sympathetic and supportive to a degree, allowing her to come back on reduced hours. Stephen wondered how her colleagues treated her, whether she was shunned. By this time the papers had shifted the tone of their coverage from guarded sympathy to thinly veiled condemnation. Either way, she left the nursing home by mutual agreement before the end of the year, some small payoff allowing her employer to deflect further attention. She hadn't worked again, not in any sustained sense. The convenience store in the centre of town took her on when they first stayed open late, but it hadn't worked out. And she'd helped at the bakery for several months, coming and going before most of the town had risen. Again, for reasons Stephen was unaware of, she left after the trial period ended.

He wasn't entirely sure how she'd managed financially, assuming that there was some sort of pension, that perhaps her brother helped out initially. There certainly weren't any savings left, living as they had in the end with menacing debt. Perhaps the bailiffs had been stood down after the inquest, what was owed written off or recovered from some lump sum. He knew his parents had put everything into Highfield; that it came with great risk, this seismic new venture, that the stakes for the family were significant. If he could find the words, he would offer his mother something during his stay, though the gesture would almost certainly be declined. He imagined leaving some cash in the room, only for it to be left unspent, or, worse, posted back to him.

He looked around the garden, which was bedding down for winter. In the far corner, by the small pond, the cherry tree rose from the spot where they'd laid Shane's ashes. It surprised him how long the animal had lived, and he suspected that his mother had resented its presence on some level. When Stephen came to stay that time, he'd expected her to have given the dog away, but perhaps it remained an unlikely source of company for her.

The bird table, Stephen saw, was cloyed with food: seed mixes, peanuts, fatballs. It had always been his father, when he was home, who'd fed the birds, but since living here his mother topped up the feeders daily and could spend half the morning watching coal tits and house sparrows plunder the offerings. A lone robin had remained faithful over the years, she said, allowing her to stand just a few feet away as it ate, brazen and unhurried. It was what they spoke of on the phone, the difficult silences filled with an enumeration of species to visit the garden that month. She'd become quite expert, able to distinguish a mistle thrush from a song thrush, a dunnock from a tree sparrow, species he often confused. (Like his father, it was the raptors, the falcons and hawks, that roused him most.) His mother knew their songs as well, her ears attuned to individual notes within the chorus. She seemed to cherish their apparent loyalty, how the simple act of placing food out ensured their daily return. Initially she'd worried that the cats might target them, but it seemed that both had been adopted beyond their hunting prime, preferring instead to watch the steady convergence from a window, as if it were for their amusement.

After Amy's birth, Stephen's mother had come to visit them in Cornwall. They'd sat in the garden at dusk one summer's evening, the four of them, watching pipistrelle bats circle and flit, feeding on throngs of midges, the air heady with pollen. At that moment he'd held real hope that his mother could be convinced to move down, to finally leave the town and settle near them.

Inside, she was tending the fire once more. Again he decided against asking about the tests, what they were for. He would talk to Peter if possible, find out more. Find out more about this man in his mother's life. Tomorrow he would get up early, make them some breakfast. He would call Zoe, talk to Amy before she went to school, and then head out across town, up to the house on the hill they had once all lived in.

Four

The road out of town was quiet. Once over the humpbacked bridge, he parked in a gateway that looked unused. Setting off up the hill, he wished he had a dog or a briefcase, something that gave the impression of purpose. The lane up to the house was narrower than he remembered, little more than a car's width, with one or two passing places cut into the hedge. Hurrying past the gate to the only other house up there, he kept his head down, putting in some big strides, his heart lurching in his chest, but there seemed to be no one about.

The air was still beneath its slate-grey canopy, the dense corrugations of cloud low and cloying. To his right, in the tall beeches, the serrated cry of a rook punctured the silence. As he neared the top of the hill, his thighs burned and a cough reminded him of his promise to Zoe, to Amy, to quit smoking this year.

He'd woken late, almost nine – too late to phone home – the absence of work rendering him more inert each morning, the parallels with his father not lost on him, splintering the sense of himself. Once downstairs, he'd realised the cottage was empty, a cup with a tea bag in it left for him. After making some toast, he'd sat by the window, watching birds bicker as they fed, while a neighbour attended to a raised bed. An hour later his mother returned carrying a handled stick with some sort of grappling implement at its end. In her other hand was a small bin sack, which he saw was full of litter as she transferred it to the main bin out the back. He asked her about it but she avoided his question, instead enquiring what he wanted for dinner that night.

The roof of the house could be seen up ahead now. He had no idea what to expect, who would be living there, what sort of reception he'd get. He'd rehearsed possible reasons for calling, none of which sounded plausible this morning: selling something (what?), asking for directions (to where?), or just that he was lost. Anything that would afford him a glimpse of the place. In the end he opted for honesty: he'd say he used to live here and was just passing. There'd be an awkward pause, his presence not unreasonable but still unsettling. He would see straight away in their faces whether they knew the house's history, as they stiffened slightly, filling the doorway like unfriendly bouncers. He'd feel their stares on his back as he walked away, sensing their fear that he was some doom-laden harbinger. Or perhaps they'd invite him in, wary but not unfriendly as they chaperoned him from room to room as small children looked on bemused.

He had come back here once previously, before being sent away for good, to collect some clothes and schoolwork a week or so after that day, when there was still the sense that none of it had happened. That it was some crazy dream he was still caught in, one that fooled you with its clarity and continuity. He remembered thinking that any minute the dream's colour and sound would fade, images blending into each other, characters switching, absurd and surreal, reality finally resuming. Like his mother, he'd been given something to take at night, just for the first few days, to help him sleep, and was told to expect some drowsiness the next day. This had contributed to the hazing of the actual world, its edges softened and blurred, his actions and thoughts seemingly happening independently of him, as if he was being directed. His uncle had driven him up here, trying but failing to fill the silence in the car. There was a woman waiting for them, he remembered now, who had a kind voice. Once they'd parked, she came across the yard and opened his door, asking if he was sure about the visit, saying that he could come back another time or just tell her what he needed from the house. He recalled how she smelt of summer, of the flowers up in the woods, her smile heartfelt yet tinged with pity. He'd kept expecting Shane to come bounding out, barking at first, then jumping up and slobbering all over his face, his tail submissive, but the dog, he learned later, had been removed by then.

There were a couple of people that day, a man and a woman, walking around inside the house, examining and removing things, placing them in bags. Each time he passed one of them they smiled as if they knew him, the man even saying his name.

Inside, he'd expected everything to have changed, some vast shift from the familiar and comforting to a place of terror. But in a sense it was like coming home any other time: their coats lined up in the hall above the rack of shoes and boots; in the kitchen, food on the surfaces awaiting preparation, dishes from breakfast piled to be washed up, and beneath the table, his sister's school shoes, foolishly left where she'd kicked them off. There was a smell he couldn't place, acrid and smarting, that had laid claim to the house. He went from room to room, the woman behind him, her hand on his shoulder, gently squeezing it every now and then. When he went to go in the front room, the woman ushered him towards the stairs.

'Come on,' she said, 'let's get your stuff.'

His uncle chose to wait outside, but the woman hardly left his side. Despite the time of year, upstairs had been cooler, a breeze from an open window blowing across the landing. The woman seemed to know which was Stephen's room, and they went in together. Again everything was as he'd left it that morning: bed unmade, a few clothes splayed on the floor, a cassette tape of songs that Suzanne had made him on his desk. The woman asked if he had a bag that he used to go away with, and he pointed to the wardrobe. As she looked for it, he stood there in the middle of the room, unable to move, thinking that he might be sick, or that his legs would buckle beneath him. In the end, the woman suggested he sit on the bed while she opened each drawer, held up an item of clothing and he nodded or shook his head. The entire time they were there he didn't utter a word.

He packed some schoolwork and books, stuff he'd need for revision, plus the cassette tape. When they'd finished, he went over to the window. His uncle was sitting against the Cortina's bonnet, looking out towards the town, smoking hard and fast, running a hand through his thinning hair. The man and woman continued to make trips back and forth from their van in silence. Stephen looked at the garden his mother had cleared and created when they'd first moved in, the vegetable plot glistening in the morning dew, the tree swing Jenny loved to sit on swaying slightly in the breeze. An old football, unkicked for months and near-deflated, sat in front of the barn, a few of Shane's chewed-up toys dotted around it. The same question kept repeating in his head: what would happen now?

His uncle dropped the cigarette to the ground and swivelled his shoe on it before lighting another. Exhaling, he turned and looked up at the window, an expression Stephen couldn't fathom on his face.

The woman asked if he was OK in the bedroom for a moment while she got some clothes for his mother. Back on the landing, she offered to carry his holdall downstairs, but he put it on his shoulder, for some reason keen to show that he was coping. The carrier bag of schoolwork was heavy, the handles threatening to break, so he held it from beneath. Pausing at the top of the stairs, he looked along to Jenny's door, the draught coming from it carrying the garden's scent. Again the hand on his shoulder, the woman's soft voice urging him to come on, that they had what they'd come for. And yet he just stood there, unable to move, to speak.

He thought of his mother, her pills apparently stronger than his, rendering her a zombie for most of the day, able only to lie or sit, staring numbly ahead. She wasn't to be left alone, he'd overheard someone say, not even for a few minutes. She didn't eat for the first few days, and only did so later when his uncle or aunt took the spoon or fork of food to her mouth, when she'd chew mechanically, her eyes glazed, unmoving. Stephen didn't feel much like eating either, but managed a little of every meal made. The nights were worst, the unfamiliar house dark and deathly quiet, until, without warning, a low wail would start up, building for several minutes until it drew out, crescendoing into a vast howl, and he would hear someone go into his mother's room, perhaps giving her another pill, the noise slowly dying to nothing. With first light he'd lie there and listen to a blackbird's dawn chorus, feeling some slight relief, sensing that his mother was asleep, the house free of grief for a couple of hours.

Looking hard at Jenny's door that day, some force had pulled him towards her room, daring him to enter.

'Come on,' the woman had said, 'let's get you back.'

At the bottom of the stairs, the phone rang and they'd both jumped a little. He half expected his mother or father to emerge from a room to answer it. Instead, he and the woman looked hard at it until it stopped.

Outside, the man and woman were drinking from a flask by the van. They issued weak smiles as they passed them. As they reached his uncle, he took a last gulp of his cigarette before taking Stephen's bags and placing them in the boot. He asked if they had everything they needed. The woman put his mother's things in her own car, saying she would return if anything had been forgotten, that things could be sent on. Then she asked them to wait in the car while she spoke to the others.

They sat in silence, the sun warming the car, his uncle's

fingers tapping the top of the steering wheel. Stephen could hear the others talking but could make out none of the words. Finally the woman came to say goodbye and they drove slowly away.

Rounding the last bend now, he could see the house. Up here the sides of the lane were strewn with dead leaves, and he remembered how Jenny would trudge through them, kicking them up into fleeting eddies, squealing at the easy pleasure of it all. As he neared the gate, a gustless breeze threaded through the gap between the buildings as if the house were breathing, whispering to him.

Any thoughts of running into the new owners soon vanished as he realised it was unoccupied. The entrance was largely overgrown, trails of ivy gripping the old gate so that he had to force it open, remembering that it needed lifting to clear the ground. Fixed to one of its cross-beams a rusted notice warned of danger, to keep out. Above, the carved lettering on the wooden sign could still be read: *Highfield*.

The house itself rose from a mass of latticed brambles, the grey pebble-dash stained green with trails of mildew. He saw that the front door and the ground-floor windows had been crudely boarded up, some of the boards splintered where they'd been hacked at, others adorned with fading graffiti. On the first floor his parents' and Jenny's windows had almost no glass left in the panels, and he pictured stone-throwing kids cheering each other as another pane was breached. Paint from the rotten window frames had blistered and flaked. Beyond his sister's window he could make out a curtain, faded, weatherworn, barely clinging on as it rippled in the breeze. Above, clumps of grass grew out of the guttering, as if the house had a neglected roof garden. Whether from decay or sabotage, a significant part of the roof had collapsed next to the chimney, the rafters exposed like ribs, several slates hanging precariously over the edge. The chimney itself, listing close to tipping point, had a few token strands of fluorescent tape attached to it, beyond which the television aerial hung down from its remaining bracket.

In the yard, he turned full circle, taking in the ruined barns, the garden that had grown back to the wilderness it had been when they moved in, the skeletal greenhouse. The swing still hung from the old maple, its rope perhaps a large child's weight away from failing. A further danger sign had been fixed to one of the barn doors, this message more compassionate than prohibitive, appealing to trespassers' sense of preservation. He looked inside the barn his father had planned to turn into a workshop, where he was going to strip the Morris's engine, teach Stephen its mechanics as they restored it.

He and Brendan had almost set fire to themselves in there, playing when everyone was out. They were trying to heat a metal rod, to fashion a tripod for fishing, but the small fire they lit kept going out. Brendan had found a petrol can, pouring a little on the flame, which shot back up, setting the top of the can alight. He'd thrown it across the floor, leaving patches of burning stonework. Without thought, Stephen had run to it, cupped the opening with the palm of his hand, denying it oxygen, until it went out. He almost hid the burn mark successfully, until his mother saw it one evening. The collusion, the conspiracy that separated them from his father, was already well established, so he never found out they'd nearly blown up the barn and themselves with it.

All that was left in there now were some upturned crates, arranged as seating, and the brackets from shelves his father put up. Remnants of a campfire lay in the middle of the floor, empty beer cans and cigarette butts strewn around it. More graffiti adorned the walls, some relatively fresh-looking.

He headed round the side of the house, where the oil tank was shrouded by head-high nettles. Behind it was the old Morris, one of so many abandoned projects. They'd been supposed to witness its rebirth, taking it to the coast for family picnics, feeling the wind in their hair as the roof was furled back. Its shell was badly rusted, the seats inside blackened from attempts to burn it, and yet he still recognised it, pictured himself manoeuvring the gearstick, mimicking the engine's sound in adolescent thrill.

Around the back of the house the basketball hoop hung on the wall, its net absent. Below it was the spot where his sister had played endless games of hopscotch, bounding between boxes drawn in chalk, singing a rhyme that kept pace with her movements.

Pushing through the brambles, he tried to peer behind one of the kitchen's boarded windows, but it was too secure. Beside the potting shed the back door was also boarded up, but was loose where it had been forced before. He fetched an iron pole he'd seen behind the oil tank and levered the door open enough to squeeze through.

The first thing to hit him was the smell. Nothing over-powering, more a general dankness that was at odds with his teenage years here. In the hall, wallpaper hung from the walls as if someone had begun to decorate before giving up. Mould spread along the ceiling throughout. Little remained of the kitchen except a few of the fixed cupboards, their doors clinging on or removed entirely; a gaping wound sat where the old stove once was. He pictured his mother baking in here on Sundays, Jenny helping to roll pastry, getting it in her hair, flour on her nose. Other memories gathered. A radio playing. Laughter. His father sick but not yet fully descended into the darkness.

In the lounge, the fireplace had been removed, crudely chiselled out, rubble spewing out from behind it. Again the smell, this time rancid. Moving further into the room, he saw a constellation of small holes that adorned the back wall in irregular clusters. What little remained of the carpet was stained and sodden.

Something moved in the corner of his eye, startling him a little, and he watched as a rat scuttled along the skirting in the far corner, unperturbed by his presence, pausing sporadically, nose twitching, sniffing the air. Above him the ceiling had bowed and a steady drip of water fell from its peak on to the saturated floor below. More graffiti rose on the walls.

Back in the hall, he pictured the day they'd moved in. Bursting through the front door, exploring the rooms, racing Jenny to be the first upstairs. Choosing their bedrooms. Letting her have the larger one at the front – another source of regret – because the other was L-shaped, which he liked. Their parents unpacking the van with a friend, while they ran up into the woods behind the house,

Jenny falling and cutting her knee, returning in tears while he explored his new playground.

He climbed the stairs now, treading carefully where the wood was rotten. Occasionally one creaked, a sound he remembered, echoing through the decades. The noises and smells of Christmases, the couple they'd had here, returned. Of family visiting, the house warm and contented with its abundance of guests. It snowed heavily one winter and the lane was impenetrable: no one could get up or down by vehicle, and so he'd walked with his father through a blizzard to fetch food, cut off as they were for a while. The problems with money had begun then, but they lived like kings and queens for those few days, sealed in their wintry palace.

On the landing, he paused, half expecting someone to emerge from one of the rooms, telling him he shouldn't be there. A series of lines, barely visible, marked the wall beside the bathroom door, and he remembered their mother pencilling their heights one weekend, their ages in years and months, the writing now illegible. Evidence of a fire – a week ago, a year ago, he couldn't tell – scarred some of the walls.

Great whorls of mildew crept down the bathroom walls, the silicone between bath and tiles like an elongated slug. He turned on one of the taps on the sink, perhaps expecting a dry splutter, but it produced nothing.

The door to his old room was stuck, the frame warped, and he had to shove hard with his shoulder to shift it. Memories returned now like a series of images projected across his mind, disjointed, unbidden, and doubts rose at his ability to cope with it all. The room was largely empty, unrecognisable from the two years he'd spent in it. The window had most of its panes intact, probably due to its proximity to the hillside, allowing little room to get a good throw in. His Led Zeppelin poster, yellow and faded, still hung from the cupboard door. The only other piece of furniture in the room was his old iron bed frame, the metal discoloured. He pictured again packing clothes in the numbness of that day, the kind woman he never saw again. In the far corner he noticed the loose board he used to prise up to hide the secret paraphernalia of adolescence: tobacco, a dirty magazine Brendan had given him. Placing his car key between the wood, he managed to lift the half-plank enough to get his fingers beneath it. For a moment he was a teenager again, some synaptic impulse firing a memory, a taste in the back of his throat that was somehow then. The hollow was empty save a lattice of cobwebs, and he replaced the board. Closing his eyes, he strained to hear the voices of his parents, of Jenny. Instead it was someone else who spoke, though laughter rather than words. Suzanne had sat on his bed, playing with her hair, their shyness diminishing. She wasn't supposed to be there, he remembered, their initial liaisons furtive, treacherous. They kissed on the bed and she told him it was over with Brendan, a month-long relationship she regretted. It was Stephen she wanted to be with, him she thought about all the time.

Once he realised that nobody lived here, that the house's legacy was too much to bear, he thought that more signs of their life here would be apparent, some pristine detail preserved. But together the elements and successive generations of the town's teenagers had reduced it to a husk.

A slowly perishing relic that bore down on the town in judgement.

His parents' room was the same as the others, though the graffiti was more profuse. This time he brought himself to enter his sister's room. The remaining curtain fluttered in the wind, the room colder and damper than the others. Shards of glass lay scattered beneath the window. Every wall was blackened by mould to some extent. He'd forgotten about her wallpaper, an elaborate jungle scene that rose into a background of sky. Their father had spent an entire weekend putting it up, carefully cutting around the animals and plants so that, halfway up the wall, they seemed to come alive in relief. High up in one of the corners was the mulch of an abandoned swallows' nest; below it, perhaps two or three feet, there was a mark on the wall, circular, unremarkable. He walked over, seeing that it was the same as those downstairs. Standing on tiptoe he could just reach it, its circumference big enough to accommodate his index finger.

He crossed to the window, the glass crunching underfoot, and looked out. The town could be seen over the roof of the barn, the sky above it leaden, shafts of an unseen sun attending to the hills beyond. Below, the yard looked desolate. Rain had begun to spatter, darkening the ground. He listened hard, for the sound of them playing, or of Shane barking. And then he imagined the noise of that day. Of Jenny standing here behind a curtain, his beautiful sister, still grateful she wasn't at school. Watching the madness develop.

Five

He cut down to the river and headed out of town. The copper-coloured sky of an hour ago had darkened so that the water resembled tar slipping by, although there was still enough light to walk by, dusk not yet fully deepened. From the tall trees across the water he heard an exodus of rooks, their wings clattering upwards in applause. So many hours of adolescence had been spent along this path, watching floats in case they bobbed, or moving upriver hoping for a change in fortune. He wondered if there was any other pursuit with quite such a poor ratio of return for the time invested. Yet Brendan never wavered in his garrulous optimism of what would be caught on the next trip – always the next trip – his enthusiasm infectious enough to drag Stephen from a warm bed at all hours. And in time Stephen learnt that his friend's passion came not from the success or otherwise of their trips, but in the small rituals they performed, the days of planning and preparing and gathering, the anticipation, which was somehow as important.

It felt strange to experience some small nostalgia for this place, recalling the innocence that had up to now remained inaccessible, sheathed as it was by circumstance or his reluctance to look at it. He'd forgotten how, before the horror of that day, there existed a joyful, ordinary childhood in which for the most part he delighted. Pausing, he strained to hear the sounds of this particular aspect of his youth: the purr of their reels once cast, the sonorous slop of weights striking water, and then the metrical click-click as they wound in the slack. Comfortable in the silence, they only spoke to suggest some tea or a cigarette, or a change of position, the hours sliding by in heightened meditation.

The air was sharp now, the trees thinning as the path banked north. Another half a mile and he would emerge on to the road where the pub was. Returning from Highfield, he'd spent the rest of the day in quiet reflection, broken only by brief exchanges with his mother.

'Where did you go?' she had asked.

'For a walk, up in the hills, not far. Places we used to hang out after school.'

He felt she could sense the absence of something in his answer, but they'd prepared dinner together without further reference to it. And although she hadn't expressed any surprise when he spoke of walking to the Woodman's Arms, he saw that the idea unnerved her.

As he'd wandered through the decaying rooms of Highfield, scenes from their time there had played out with such clarity; parts of his life he'd worked so hard to banish, to eradicate not just from his own mind but somehow from history itself. It amazed him how far this could be done, the pious occupation of the present, a refusal to acknowledge what had passed, to allow it oxygen, for in what real sense did it actually exist? And yet its influence still held dominion over him, whether in a darkened corner of his mind or some impervious chamber of his heart, he wasn't sure. Like the faint cosmic static still heard from the Big Bang, the noise never entirely dulled.

What he hadn't expected from visiting the house was the profusion of memories of the days following his father's return from war. They knew to give him space each time he came home, a day or two to adjust back into family life. Whenever Stephen and his sister fought or were making excessive noise, their mother would intervene, pack them off to another part of the house or the garden, reminding them that their father needed some quiet time. There was also the adjustment in hierarchy. Whereas for weeks or even months their mother had been solely responsible for parenting duties and discipline, suddenly there was a new adult telling them what they could or could not do. A familiar but part-time parent, whose presence was resented, like that of a strict teacher returning after illness, relieving their more lenient replacement. The smells and sounds of the house changed too in these times: their father's scent, his heavier tread on the stairs, Shane's animation – all ushering in the transition. Friends weren't allowed to visit for the first few days, and only then on the promise that they play outside.

But this time, when his father had been away for real, to the other side of the world, it was as if he didn't emerge from those soundless few days of convalescence.

Usually, on his father's return, Stephen would hear familiar and frantic noises from his parents' room for the first few nights, a sound he'd come to understand in adolescence. But even that ceased this time, the house silent save for wind booming in the rafters.

The only one whose attention remained undiminished was Shane, his father rarely seen without him. Two long walks each day – they were never told they couldn't go too, as they often would with their mother at weekends, but their father would just leave without a word and they'd not see him for two or three hours.

So it was a surprise when his father woke him that morning. It was still dark in his room, the merest blush of daybreak behind the curtains. He could just make out someone's silhouette above him as his dream faded to nothing and his father told him to wake up. He instructed him to get dressed quietly, not to wake his mother or Jenny, and as Stephen wiped the sleep from his eyes, he finally remembered what they were doing.

Downstairs, his father stood in the gloom of the kitchen, swigging tea, a pair of binoculars around his neck, Shane at his feet, alert and loyal.

'Want some breakfast?' his father asked.

Stephen shook his head, the excitement and fear, the early hour, suppressing any appetite he might have had.

'You can eat when we get back,' his father said. 'Get some layers on.'

When they'd first moved in, before his father went away, he'd begun walking Shane at first light, sometimes taking one of the guns from the cabinet. He'd checked with the farmer, who'd said he could shoot as many rabbits as he liked, as long as he took a few up to the farmhouse every now and then. Stephen knew his mother didn't like it, but it was free food, and so it fitted in with the plan to be more self-sufficient, even before things began getting tight with money. His father showed her how to gut and skin them, and they were soon having them in stews once a week, although Jenny cried when they told her what it was, refusing to eat it initially.

A few days after he got back from the Falklands, he asked if Stephen wanted to go with him next time. They'd done nothing, just the two of them, since he'd returned, his father's presence spectral. His mother looked troubled at the prospect, but in the end Stephen said yes, mostly so his father wasn't disappointed. Later that evening, when he turned his music off, he heard his parents arguing about it.

A few nights afterwards, over dinner, his father mentioned it again.

'So, you coming hunting tomorrow?'

His mother glared across the table, while Jenny asked if they would catch any wolves, like the hunters in her book.

Stephen had put his warm coat on that morning, the one with the hood that he wore for fishing, despite it being summer. His father told him to get his fingerless gloves and went into the back room, where Stephen heard him unlock the gun cabinet. As they left the house, dawn bled over the hills across the valley, the garden glistening with dew, the world somehow both still and aquiver.

They took the path at the top of the garden that wound up into the woods, his father leading the way, their pace neither fast nor slow. When they hit the treeline, Shane was let off the lead, his father keeping the dog close with a series of whistles. Every now and then Stephen stumbled on a root, losing his footing, and his father would turn and glare at him, the need for silence blazed across his face.

It was then that Stephen got the first sense of what would become an obsession for his father, how rabbits were incidental to their pursuit. Whenever the trees thinned into pasture, they would stop and his father would scan the hills through the binoculars, looking hard into the sky above their steep slopes. Stephen followed his glare but could see nothing. A few days later, his father told him about the pair of peregrines that wintered in the valley. He spoke of them with reverence and exhilaration, glimpses of his former self returning momentarily. Stephen had never known him to be interested in birds; through childhood it had always been his mother who pointed out and identified wildlife for them. But when his father talked about the falcons, how privileged they were to have them nearby, his face was luminous with an intensity none of them had seen before. He would even walk a third time some days, without Shane, saying that it improved his chances of sighting one of the peregrines. At dinner, when he still ate with them, they could tell if he'd been successful in his quest, his mood lifting a little. And when the mobile library next came through the town, he asked Stephen's mother to find him a book on them.

Deeper into the woods that day, they paused, sitting down on a fallen tree, and his father began, in a whisper, to tell him about the gun. It was one of three he kept in the locked cabinet in the utility room off the kitchen. Stephen had looked at them in fascination when they were first brought home, showing them off to Brendan, pretending he was allowed to take them out. It was only this one – the gun that had always been around, the one that hadn't required a cabinet – that Stephen was ever allowed to handle, and then only at times like this, when supervised.

His father held the weapon out for him to take. 'Go on.'

It was smaller than the others, but still heavier than he'd have thought. He held it awkwardly, as if having no contemplation of what it was. As he swung round, his father snatched it from him.

'Never point it towards someone. Even when you're sure it's not loaded.'

'Is it loaded?'

'You tell me.'

'I don't know.'

'You need to always know.' He handed it back to him. 'It's an air rifle. Do you know what that is?'

Stephen nodded his head. His father took the gun from him again.

'You break the barrel here,' he said, snapping the gun almost in half. 'Then you pull it down and towards you, to give it its power. Go on, try.'

He handed it back. Stephen tried, but it was too stiff, the tips of his fingers too cold. Teeth gritted, he tried again. His father gave a little laugh. 'Put the butt into your stomach and use two hands.'

Still he couldn't do it.

'Here.' His father took the rifle and bent the barrel back on itself until a loud click was heard. 'That's the spring-piston compressing down and locking.'

After passing the gun back to him, his father took a round tin from his jacket pocket and opened it. 'Do you know what these are?'

'Bullets?'

'Pellets.'

He gave him one, showed him where to put it.

'Other way round,' he said. 'Now close it up.'

This was easier, the mechanism offering little resistance.

'Good,' he said. 'Come on.'

He called Shane to heel with a click of his fingers and put his lead back on. Stephen went to hand back the gun but his father had already set off.

They walked more slowly now, half crouching, every small noise their feet made amplified, echoing off the trees. Finally they broke the cover of the woods and his father squatted low, motioning him to do the same, the dog alert, primed next to them. Gradually they edged around the field, stalking nothing in particular, the silence occasionally broken by the unearthly cry of a crow. At one point Stephen stumbled in a furrow made by a tractor, falling in a heap, something between a scowl and a smile conveyed in his father's face. It was light now, and they could see across to the far side of the field, where a low mist sat, furring the edge of the coppice. They crept along like this for a while, stopping every now and then when his father raised a hand. He would then take the rifle from Stephen and bring it up to his shoulder, peering through the sight, scanning the far hedgerow. Sensing the theatre of the moment, the dog could barely contain itself, a thin whine emanating from its throat, its eyes large and animated.

As they rounded a bend, his father put his hand up again and they crouched down low. Ahead, about thirty yards away and a few paces from the treeline, a rabbit munched on the grass, its breath misting upwards in bursts. Alert, it paused every now and then, but didn't notice them. His father beckoned Stephen to his side, gesturing to take aim. Stephen moved forward but was reluctant to raise the gun.

'Go on,' whispered his father. 'Find your shot.'

Slowly he lifted the weapon and pointed it in the direction of the rabbit. His father eased the butt back into Stephen's shoulder, its hard surface pressing into the bone, despite the layers he wore.

'Now, close one eye and try to find it in the sight.'

He could see the trees and the far hedge, but nothing else. His father put his head next to Stephen's, looking along the gun, adjusting it downwards and to the left.

'You got it?'

Stephen nodded. His father loosened Stephen's bottom hand, which had been squeezing the barrel tightly, so that the gun just rested on his palm.

'Now, breathe in and out slowly.'

He could see the rabbit's glassy eyes, its nose twitching as if it were about to sneeze.

'Next time you breathe out,' his father said, 'hold it halfway and squeeze the trigger gently.'

His left hand shook – the fear, the weight of the gun, he wasn't sure – the tremor making it hard to keep the animal in sight for more than a couple of seconds at a time. He soon forgot about the breathing, whether he was supposed to pull the trigger when breathing in or out.

'When you've got it,' his father said, barely audibly, 'take your shot.'

Again the rabbit stopped eating, its eye fixed on them, sensing their presence. Stephen could feel his father's impatience, the dog's whimpering threatening to give them away. A tear pooled in his open eye, blurring his vision. He thought about fishing, tried to tell himself it was the same thing, that Brendan would have fired by now.

Finally he lowered the gun and wiped his face on his sleeve. His father gave out a huff, took the weapon from him and slowly, deliberately took aim, the action smooth, natural, his body entirely still.

A moment later there was a pop, the sound softer than Stephen had expected, and the rabbit leapt an inch or two in the air, flipping on to its side. Shane gave out a yelp, and as they stood, his father let him off the lead. The dog tore on ahead of them and was beside the rabbit in seconds. After sniffing it for a moment or two, he ran between them and the creature until they caught up.

The entry wound was barely visible, just a small mark on the rabbit's side, the fur around it damp and ruffled. Its eyes, black and dead, were still open, and Stephen wondered if the animal might suddenly get to its feet and scurry into the undergrowth, but when his father nudged it with his boot, he could see it was lifeless.

The blooding over, they headed home, his father taking the rabbit into the barn to hang it up, while Stephen went up to his room.

* * *

He could see the pub now, set back from the road into town, woodsmoke from its chimney stack swooping down to him on the wind. Several cars were parked along the stone wall, and for a moment he considered turning back, fearing that his appearance perhaps hadn't changed sufficiently from adolescence. His boots were heavy with clods of mud from the path, which he started to remove on the tussocky bank until the road behind him was lit with headlights. Ignoring the anxiety that grew, he opened the door of the Woodman's.

He thought that his father had used this pub often, while on leave, at least before they'd moved to Highfield. There had been a welcome home reception held for him here, a banner over the door, bunting festooned throughout, free drinks for the returning soldier. They'd been allowed – he and Jenny – to go for the first couple of hours, a stack of coins, a Coke and some crisps each to keep them quiet. He remembered the cigarette smoke hanging thickly in the rooms, the jukebox up loud, the same songs over and over. His father sitting at a table in the corner, pint after pint placed in front of him, their mother sipping halves of cider, forcing awkward smiles at all the attention. There was a reporter from the local paper, a weaselly-looking man who seemed to be everywhere at once, lingering on the edge of people's conversations, asking them about his father. A picture was taken, to accompany the piece, he and Jenny allowed in the other bar for it. The man taking it kept repeating the same thing, telling their father that he was a hero and to smile, before finally accepting he wasn't going to.

Looking around it now, he could see that the lounge was

still divided into two sections. Several people stood against the bar, chatting amiably, the occasional laugh issued. The log fire burned steadily on the far wall, a few drinkers looking up to see who'd come in, soon returning to their exchanges. A couple of older men stared longer, scrutinising a face they perhaps thought familiar, not *the* face, but one with enough similarity to propel them to that other time. While they informed the others, Stephen entered the quieter room, where a young couple sat deep in conversation. Without the fire it was cooler this side, a little darker. The pool table had been replaced by more seating, the games machine also gone. As he sat at the bar, the couple eyed him in turn, but again with indifference. Removing his jacket, he heard a woman call through, saying she would be with him in a moment. It was only once she appeared that something registered in him, a flicker of recall, the slow calibration of the face in front of him with a bank of submerged memories. Her own reaction was slower still, as she asked routinely what he'd like, before stiffening, staring indiscreetly as the men next door had. He remembered how she didn't give up her smile easily, even as a girl, and if it had started to form now, she quickly discouraged it.

He pointed to one of the pumps. 'A pint of that, please, Suzanne.' Hearing himself say her name had a hint of comfort to it. After a few seconds in which she hadn't moved, he spoke again: 'Or something else, if that's not on?'

Composing herself, she reached slowly for a handled glass, filling it with a few pulls on the pump handle, then placing it on the bar. He held out a note, and for a moment he thought she was just going to stand there, silent and inert, until finally she turned to the till. Placing his change in front of him, she spoke, her voice uneven and fragile, as if it was about to break.

'Hello, Stephen,' she said.

Six

The man unloaded the logs he'd brought from a wheelbarrow into the shed, pausing every now and then, the palm of his hand easing the small of his back. He was older than Stephen had expected, his voice on the phone belying the decade or so he had on Stephen's mother. Introducing himself with that same voice – soft and fluid, like water – he shook Stephen's hand, smiling warmly, his eyes almost hiding the flicker of awkward condolence. Stephen's mother was upstairs, silently attending to something, so Stephen put the kettle on while Peter made several trips back and forth to his car, politely declining the offer of help.

'Should do her till spring, this lot,' he said.

Stephen put the man's tea down and helped to stack the last load. 'It's very kind of you.'

'She should probably get the chimney swept again soon, especially burning wood. Creosote builds up, and before you know it you've got a fire where you don't want one.'

The two of them stood back to admire the pile before sitting on the bench beneath the kitchen window, the morning sun for once barely dimmed by flecks of cirrus. What little traffic the road accommodated had diminished, the only sound above the noise of the river an occasional throaty *airk* from the rookery beyond it.

Stephen had stumbled back from the pub last night, shortly before closing time, the path along the river dark but for the gloam of the moon. There had been a missed call from Zoe, a message that she was off to bed and not to ring now. The air of admonishment in her voice was tempered with concern, that she hoped he was OK, that Amy missed him. They both missed him. He would phone before dinner tonight.

He thought there'd been the beginnings of a tear in Suzanne's eye last night, as she recognised him, though she recovered quickly. Their conversation, broken every few minutes by demand from the bar behind her, began tentatively.

'How are you?' he said, before thinking he had no right to ask this. She was still too taken aback to speak, so he filled the silence for her. 'How long . . .'

'Twenty-nine years.' There was perhaps nothing barbed in the speed of her reply, it being a simple calculation.

'You look well.'

'You think? Must be the gloom.'

'It's so good to see you.'

She offered a half-nod at this, nothing more, her hands attending to some unnecessary cleaning of the bar. Was it outlandish, naïve, to term her his first love, curtailed as it was in its infancy? They'd walked in the woods a lot, held hands, kissed languorously, his world shifting into some glorious new realm he didn't fully understand. He strained to evoke the sensation, recall how it felt to be a teenager lost to life's first raptures, but it ebbed from his grasp. Not love as he knew it now, but something approaching it. Something fierce.

Pretty in a homely way, she'd been in several of his classes through the final two years of school, her plainness – though he didn't regard her so – keeping her below the radar of other boys. Both he and Brendan had been drawn to her, their own shyness with girls mirrored in her demure manner, a factor that should have prevented either of them progressing beyond watching her from afar.

He remembered first learning that Brendan was seeing her, if that was the term then. There'd been a party, someone's parents out of town. Such gatherings grew in frequency during their final year of school, a typical night yielding little more than loud music, some stolen alcohol and an argument that culminated in a fight of sorts, the police often called. They were invited, he and Brendan, to these spontaneous congregations through a mutual friend who somehow bridged the gap between the studious and the unruly among them. They would sit in the corner, drinking cheap lager, envious of those who were lost in the music or who disappeared in pairs upstairs, not to be seen again that evening. But it was enough just to attend, the promise, as with the fishing, of some spectacular and triumphant outcome next time sustaining their enthusiasm.

It was the first time they'd seen Suzanne at a party. Like them, she occupied its fringes, observing the more raucous behaviour of her friends with weary tolerance, embarrassed but aware of the dangers in spurning such occasions. Whether Brendan had drunk more than him, or whether he was just done with the fruitless surveillance of other people's fun, Stephen never knew. But some epiphany or new-found courage drove his friend to approach the girl sitting alone in the far corner. And from this came something akin to a date, and then another, which in turn led to Stephen meeting her.

In the Woodman's last night, several drinks in, Suzanne and he had reminisced a little – about school, certain teachers – careful to keep the conversation away from that last summer here. When the tense silences rose, she would go to the other bar, where news of his arrival was no doubt proliferating, perhaps making it harder still for her to talk to him. Watching her serve others, he thought how well she'd aged, blossoming into an exacting beauty, one who likely stood out in a small town.

Pointing at his ring, she'd asked about his wife. Stephen kept the answers brief, playing down what would look like an idyllic life.

'How about you?' he said.

'I married a guy in the year above us, only found out he was an idiot after the birth of our daughter. We're divorced now.'

'I'm sorry.'

'Why? It's not your fault.'

She said she'd wanted to go to university but had put it off until it was too late. The bar work was temporary, she added a little defensively, the result of a recent redundancy. As she served someone, Stephen tried to recall the precise sequence of events that had led to her affections shifting from Brendan to himself, the sneaking around for a week or so, then their confession to him. Stephen had managed to avoid him for a few days, skipping the one class they shared. When they eventually passed each other in a corridor, he thought Brendan might be about to cry.

'Give him time,' Suzanne had said. 'He'll come round.'

Whatever his friend thought of him, whatever showdown they were building towards, it was so engulfed by what came next, it hardly mattered.

He hadn't even said goodbye to Suzanne back then; there had been no real chance to before moving to his uncle's. And the subsequent visit to his mother had been as clandestine as possible, the thought of seeing people from the town, especially those he'd known, overwhelming.

Peter was asking him about work, again that soothing voice suggesting that all was right with the world. Or that what was not could be forgotten amid the splendour of the morning. Stephen's mother was in the kitchen now, a pipe clanking as she turned a tap on. He wanted to ask Peter about the litter-picking, about the tests, but the single-glazed windows suggested the exchange would not be private. Instead he spoke of his career, sensing for the first time since the suspension how much he cherished it, how important it was, this vocational domain he'd fashioned, providing ballast to a life that might have been overrun by circumstance. It wasn't merely a job that allowed little time or scope for his mind to wander, to sabotage itself, but so often it saw him surrounded by marvels of nature, oceanic worlds that rendered this one inconsequential. Perhaps that was its appeal, the escape to an underwater realm where who he was, who his family were, meant nothing at all. He appeared to need the proximity of moving water, where waves – relentless, reliable – surged inwards in an endless cycle. If possible, he would always live by the coast now, in sight of the sea, near the currents and tides that bestowed on him a sense of freedom, the faraway horizon the converse of this cloying, landlocked town.

His mother opened the window above them, asking if more tea was needed. Peter stood to go inside, waiting for Stephen to follow.

'Tell her I'm heading along the river,' Stephen said. 'I'll be back for lunch.'

The climb out of the valley took longer than he remembered, its steep pastures finally levelling out into the larch grove. He looked back at the town; the sun glinted off its windows, trails of smoke rising from a few of the houses. Beyond it, on the other side of the valley, he could just make out the roof of Highfield, its listing chimney appearing perpendicular from this vantage point. Following the curve of the hillside with the binoculars, he saw the farm that his father had once taken rabbits to, its buildings also abandoned, derelict.

High above him a bird drifted idly on the thermals. He trained the binoculars upwards, but it was only a gull, buoyant in its long arcs, slowly heading out to the coast. His father's obsession with the pair of peregrines had been at its most pronounced leading up to that summer. Whole days would pass when he was either out looking for them or shut in his room reading about their world. In his occasional lucid periods he would share with Stephen his new-found knowledge, explaining their habitats, how they hunted. How some of the eyries were hundreds of years old, with subsequent generations returning to their ancestors' nests again and again. And whereas the summer months saw the birds remain in the uplands of the north and west, autumn provoked a relocation to the lowland marshes and grasslands to the east, where prey was plentiful. Kills were invariably made from above, often with the sun behind them, the falcon stooping from anything up to a thousand feet, at more than a hundred and fifty miles an hour, its wings tucked in, corkscrewing into its airborne target with a sickening blow. (Whether his father had witnessed such kills or merely read about them, Stephen was unsure.) This impact was often enough to render the wood pigeon or gull or partridge dead before it fell to earth. Otherwise the job would be finished on the ground with talons and beak, swift and efficient. The prey's feathers were then plucked, its bones picked clean with expert butchery, or the carcass returned to in the days that followed. Peregrines liked to bathe daily, his father told him, preferably in running water, ridding themselves of lice acquired from kills. As the falcon scanned its hunting territory, crows would rise to mob it, unleashing their fury amid the safety of numbers. Unperturbed, the peregrine would perform mock attacks, practising as if honing its skills, before climbing steeply, preparing for another kill. First to die were generally those birds out of place: the sick, the old, the lost – the unlucky. Often a wood pigeon would divert from the panic the peregrine had caused, inadvertently flying towards danger instead of away from it.

He made a long sweep with the binoculars, taking in the

copse to the north, the hazel coppice on the hills behind Highfield. He'd not knowingly seen a peregrine in the wild; several times he'd been unable to identify a distant raptor, the distinctive crossbow silhouette of its body and wings just as likely to be a hobby. A pair nested on a church tower twenty miles or so from home, but he'd wanted the sighting to be a solitary affair, away from any urban drone. The peregrines here in the valley had taken on mythical status for his father, each pursuit of them a pilgrimage, their sighting causing in him a jubilance that briefly lit up the darkness of his mind. Often it was just the search itself, the stalking of these glorious birds, that saw him come to life again, as if some spiritual bond formed, hardening every time, regardless of whether he glimpsed them or not. Out walking one weekend, perhaps shortly after the shooting of the rabbit, he told Stephen how the hunter must become the thing it hunted.

Stephen headed into the wood, the trees filtering some of the sun's glare. His mother had chosen this as his father's resting place, far enough out of town for her own peace of mind.

It had been late spring the last time Stephen had been up here, the tree canopy dense, brimming with life, with birdsong; finding the spot had been easy then, but the trunks now around him had little to distinguish them from each other in the barrenness of early winter. His mother had been advised not to mark the place in any way, that to do so would draw attention, invite those for whom the anger still seethed to converge here, to decimate what they found. And a permanent grave in the town would have been subject to habitual desecration, so she'd walked up here, Shane skulking behind her, and chosen a tree, dusting its base with the remnants of her husband.

After a few minutes Stephen, too, chose a tree at random – for what did it matter now, when countless winds had long since dispersed the vestiges of his father? – and issued a silent acknowledgement to the man who'd known death long before it had visited him. Once he'd decided to come here, to the town, to this spot, Stephen had expected a surge of emotion to overcome him, perhaps even to weep. Instead a wordless anger rose, churning away at all that had been lost. At the havoc still wreaked.

Despite the shame that had followed his rage and his suspension from work, he'd felt, for the rest of that day, exultant. Looking back, there had been other moments of fury, moments he'd managed to control. Last month he'd driven Amy to school on his way to a meeting. Late and flustered, he'd taken a series of short cuts through the town's back streets, only to be held up several times. When he had finally reached the road the school was on, a man in an Audi had lurched in front of him, causing him to brake hard. A simple apology would have sufficed to placate him, but the driver didn't even acknowledge his mistake, and instead sped onwards. When Stephen caught up with him at the next traffic lights, he flashed his main beam a few times, only to be given the finger. Again nothing registered consciously, and a few seconds later he found himself standing by the driver's door, blood pulsing hard in his neck and chest, his eyes – he could see in the window – wild and intense. It was only the sound of a car horn somewhere that made him glance back to see his daughter's frightened face, defusing the situation.

Walking back to the cottage, Stephen checked the skies each time something flitted at the edge of his vision. The winter sun was as high as it would get for the day, the sides of the valley burnished in its watery glow. A distant crack sent up a dozen fieldfares from a pasture beyond the gully he was tracking. He hoped Peter would be gone, not because the man's company left him feeling uncomfortable, or because he desired time alone with his mother, but the weight of all that was unsaid, all that was unacknowledged, could choke you at times.

Back on the river path, he found himself heading instead to the Woodman's.

Seven

Her house was an end-of-terrace new-build, similar to the ones he'd passed driving into town a couple of days ago. She'd made the most of the limited space, kept it simple and uncluttered, the furniture often serving more than one purpose. A Picasso print dominated the far wall of the lounge, while a large mirror over the gas fire gave the illusion of depth. Wiping his feet, he offered to remove his shoes.

'If you like.'

The laminate wood flooring caused their voices to echo around one another, the room magnifying their now-timorous exchange. She apologised for the slight mess – clothes he assumed were her daughter's strewn on the sofa – before heading to the kitchen. He shouldn't drink any more; there had been a couple at lunchtime, several tonight. It was his rule, increasingly spurned of late, to stop before he passed beyond the happy numbness of a few drinks. Life lived through a three-pint haze: why was there no way of sustaining it instead of sliding on into inebriation or falling back to a cold soberness?

His father liked to drink when home – presumably it came with the territory when he was away too, the drug of choice to unwind after a hard day's soldiering. The weak lager when he was on leave, though, progressed to whisky when the leave became permanent, his breath forever acrid and loamy. Initially the man had been a loud drunk – boisterous almost, ebullient right up to the second he fell asleep in the armchair and their mother had to haul him upstairs with Stephen's help. If he was too drunk, too heavy, she'd leave him there with a blanket placed over him, Shane furled at his feet. Then, everything he did while drunk was done noisily, as if the drink amplified him. But later his intoxication became a private, soundless affair, the consumption itself a furtive act, occurring steadily throughout the day until by teatime his eyes had narrowed, the pupils glazed, his movements deliberate and stealthy, always without noise. Once he stopped frequenting the town's pubs, he made sure there was a ready supply, though nobody was witness to its procurement. Stephen assumed his parents argued about this, especially when money became an issue, though he couldn't remember such clashes. What tension there was between them seemed to linger wordlessly for days and weeks, the pressure building as if the whole house might detonate at any moment, triggered by some small noise or remark. But then suddenly the gloom would recede and they'd have him back briefly.

As he was looking at the framed photographs on the bookcase, Suzanne returned with a half-drunk bottle of red and two glasses.

'She'll break some hearts one day,' she said.

'Does she see her father?'

'She's with him now. He does the nights I work late.'

'It must be tough.'

She looked at him, perhaps irritated at what could be taken as condescension, and he tried to think of some swift repair, but it all sounded trite in his head.

'We all have our cross,' she said.

As he rolled a cigarette, Suzanne opened the lounge window before pouring the wine. She placed his glass near him and sat down.

'I remember you smoked at school,' she said.

'Everyone did, didn't they? I gave up for a while.'

'You should again. For your daughter.'

The drizzle they'd walked back in fell lightly on his face as he exhaled smoke up into the night. A pool of orange light from a street lamp stained the pavement below, the rain threading through its beam in a thousand prisms. The road was empty in both directions, the town inert, slumberous. The people in the other bar had recognised him almost immediately this time – he had his father's aquiline nose, his sunken eyes – but hadn't approached him, though he assumed his presence would be ubiquitously known by morning.

'Does it always rain so much here?' Stephen said.

'Pretty much. Something to do with the hills.'

'It didn't when we were growing up.'

'We probably just remember it differently.'

In the field across the road an outline of something, perhaps a barn owl, ghosted low across the furrows of ploughed land, silencing its prey.

'You never wanted to move away?' he said, turning round.

'No, I love it here.'

There was more than just sarcasm in her tone. A trace of bitterness, perhaps. He offered an empathetic half-smile but she was looking away, and so he let the silence gather as he tried to think of something benign to say, the act of small talk intangible now. Their exchanges in the pub had flowed more towards the end and he'd relaxed a little for the first time in weeks. But the mood had shifted on their return here, as if the bar had served as a barrier, preventing their proximity becoming awkward.

She'd been the one to suggest coffee. He'd joked about sneaking into his mother's house quietly, as they'd done at Highfield all that time ago, tiptoeing up to his room, stifling giggles when a stair creaked, but she hadn't indulged his nostalgia, regarding it as either inappropriate or irrelevant, he couldn't tell. The landlord had encouraged her to go after time was called and so they'd left together, Stephen sensing her unease at being seen with him. It was just coffee, he told himself. A chance to prolong what had become a distraction from recent events, to have a friend in what felt like hostile territory.

She emptied the bottle into their glasses, the wine overly fruity, a harsh aftertaste encouraging small and infrequent sips. He closed the window and moved to the sofa. Suzanne was looking through her CDs now, annoyed at not being able to find something. He would stay to finish his drink and then go.

'So you couldn't stay away any longer?' she said.

'My mother's not well. I want to get her to move nearer to us.'

Some music started up – bluesy, inoffensive – and she joined him on the sofa.

'She won't leave, not now.'

'Why do you say that?'

'No reason. When I see her walking about – stooped, picking up litter like some crazy person – I feel sorry for her, how she's on her own, with no friends or family—'

'She has family.'

'I meant around her, popping in every day.'

'It's difficult to get up here. It makes sense for her to come and live where we are.'

'It wasn't meant as criticism. I just think she's part of the town these days, like the rest of us. If she was going to leave, she'd have gone by now.'

'She's not crazy.'

He knew nothing of the line concerning such matters and where it was drawn. Perhaps quiet eccentricity and withdrawal was as indicative of madness as gibbering mania, the line crossed once aspects of reality were denied, regardless of the manifestation. He saw his mother so infrequently, their contact by phone rigidly formulaic, a checklist of small talk, conversations that resembled a couple of monologues. How *would* he know? It was feasible that grief could mutate over the years, slowly eroding the layers of the mind that calibrated reality. A defence, perhaps, the mind protecting itself through distortion and misrepresentation once it sensed that no more could be borne. This would tie in with Peter's remarks on her cognitive deterioration, his hunch that something was amiss.

'What do people think of her?' Stephen said.

'Same as me, I guess. They see a woman older than her time, gripped by anguish and guilt. Some of them would like to help, perhaps, but can't bring themselves to.'

'Even now?'

'She reminds them. I mean, not like at the start. Everyone just wished she'd leave then – why would you stay? But there's an acceptance now, a tolerance. They're not rude or anything. They just choose to have nothing to do with her.'

'What about people who've moved here since?'

'They see an eccentric old woman who keeps herself to herself. And once they've heard, well, you'd be inclined to leave her alone, wouldn't you? I always think I'll ask how she is, whether she remembers me, but I only ever see her in the distance.'

'It wasn't her fault. They must see that.'

'It's been carried down to the next generation, forgiven but not forgotten, I guess. I don't think it'll ever go away, but nobody talks about it.'

'How about you?'

'How about me what?'

'Forgiveness.'

He'd not known her uncle, a twice-married painter and decorator who lived across town, only realising the connection at the inquest. Suzanne exhaled in exaggerated fashion. 'Is that what you're here for, to ask on behalf of others?'

'Would it help?'

'Probably not. Look, everyone's moved on as best they could.'

'Is that your way of telling me I shouldn't be here?'

'I don't have a problem with it.'

He ran a finger around the rim of his glass, wishing he was either less or more drunk. The music was louder now and Suzanne crossed the room, turning it down. As she bent down, he studied the contours of her neck, tousles of hair tucked behind an ear as if to invite this. What would have been their fate had their lives not been ruptured so emphatically? Theirs was a young affection, one unconsummated by anything more than the first fumblings of desire. But it was an age when you were susceptible to intense feelings and gestures, and he remembered thinking it was the start of something vast and glorious, the world opening up to a litany of romantic experiences. He had kissed one or two girls before her, enjoying the mechanics of the sensation without any yearning to prolong the interaction. But with Suzanne, between the intimacy, they'd talked about music and films, about escaping the town's clutches, exploring the world after college. Within weeks she'd become his first female friend, their conversations somehow richer than any he'd had with Brendan.

On that final day, Stephen had thought they might make love. For weeks they'd kissed heavily, frustration emerging at the limitations of a fully clothed lust, their hands hungry for the pursuit of unexplored regions. It was unspoken, but the intensity was mutually felt, the appreciation that something would soon give. He'd not wanted it to happen at Highfield for some reason; perhaps the fear of his sister walking in, or the presence of his father in the next room rendering it more awkward than it would already be. Suzanne's parents maintained an almost pious vigilance over their daughter's chastity, not least because both Stephen and Suzanne were still several months from their sixteenth birthdays. And so he'd reasoned, given the mild spring they were having, that the act would occur up in the woods somewhere. They'd already spent hours after school walking deep into its heart, Stephen rolling cigarettes, Suzanne hiding behind trees, jumping out on him, their laughter echoing around them, oblivious to the rest of the world. He'd planned to siphon off some of the vodka at home, pack a blanket and suggest they head to the clearing they'd found a week or so ago. In the glorious image his mind had drawn, it was dusk, the gloam of the moon burnishing them as they undressed each other. Recalling it now, he couldn't remember if he'd considered contraception, or whether Suzanne would regard the woods a suitable place for virginities to be lost. In those last moments of innocence that day, their eyes had met on the bus, a sparkle at the promise of what might occur later, hopeful that Brendan sensed none of it.

'Tell me about your wife,' Suzanne said as she sat next to him.

Her words brought the situation back into relief, as if he'd been walking blindly into some small betrayal, and again he vowed to leave shortly.

'She's a lecturer where I work, marine biology. We met on a field trip to Sweden.'

'An academic. Is she beautiful as well? I'm sorry. It sounds like you got yourself a nice life down there. I'm happy for you.'

This was said without resentment, and for a moment he thought he might talk about the trouble at work, as if his connection to Suzanne – and theirs to that day – would elicit empathy. Her life appeared blemished by misfortune, but perhaps it was simplistic to attribute it all to the turbulence of that time.

'It's a nice corner of the world,' he said. 'I like it there.'

'And far enough from here.'

He nodded, though he suspected that no distance was great enough.

They spoke about their daughters, swapping anecdotes with barely veiled boasts, revelling in the unceasing delight children had brought them.

'She deserves a better father than me,' he said.

'Will you have more?'

'Possibly. You?'

'I hope to. I don't want her to be an only child. Just need to find someone who'll put up with all the, you know. It must be worse for you. How does Zoe . . . sorry, it's none of my business.'

She went to the kitchen, brought back another bottle and opened it, ignoring him when he declined a top-up. After listening with closed eyes to the music for several minutes, Suzanne spoke again.

'Do you remember that tape I made you?'

He pretended not to, happy to risk causing offence, while hearing the songs in his head, remembering playing it endlessly in his room, attempting to discern any meaning she'd intended in the choice of music. She dismissed his poor memory, pursuing her train of thought anyway.

'Funny to think of cassettes now, song after song layered over each other, trying to unravel the ribbon when the stereo chewed it. You must remember it.'

'Sorry.'

'How about Brendan?'

'What do you mean?'

'You remember him?'

'Of course I do.'

'Have you seen him since you've been back?'

'No. Does he still . . .'

'Live here? Yeah. He's a landscape gardener. I see him about; he comes in the pub sometimes. His mother moved away, met someone, but he came back – see, it's impossible to stay away. I think he's married. Has a son, a daughter too.'

It was strange to think of Brendan as a father, Stephen's image of him as a teenage boy frozen in time. He'd prefer that they didn't talk about his friend, yet beside the trauma of remembering, there was something pleasing in the shard of nostalgia he felt, as if Suzanne had given him some small but precious permission to contemplate the adult Brendan. How had he fared in the aftermath? Did he ever think about Stephen?

'It would be good to see him.'

'Don't bank on him feeling the same.'

The album played out to a finish, Stephen emptying his glass and standing. 'I should probably get going.'

'If you want.'

She followed him to the door.

'Do you know if peregrines still nest here in winter?' he said.

'What?'

'In the valley or up in the woods. It doesn't matter.'

He opened the door, but she placed her hand across it, keeping it ajar.

'Will I see you again before you go?' she said.

He shrugged his shoulders. 'I don't know. Maybe I'll come by the pub.'

She leant forward and kissed his cheek, a lingering kiss that would have been easy to lose himself in, to pursue. She seemed to smell of that other time, some combination of skin and hair and clothes that evoked it. As teenagers, they'd kissed so greedily, as if each one might be the last, though at the time it felt they had an eternity to explore each other. It was an exceptional termination, he supposed. No one had lost interest or gone off with someone else. They hadn't grown weary with familiarity over the years.

He pulled away, hugged her instead. 'Of course I remember the tape.'

'Say hello to your mum for me,' Suzanne said as he set off in the rain.

The night was moonless; he headed back through the town instead of along the river. There was something surreal in walking home to his mother's house in the early hours, as if he were a teenager again, discovering the hedonistic pleasures of the world, the future vast and unknown. Just as then, he would let himself in with the spare key, stumble about, yet this time knowing she was awake.

Had he forgotten that Suzanne had also lost someone that day? Not forgotten, but not remembered either, it being entombed in the hinterland of his memory. If she was right, if it was forgiveness he sought, had her kiss held any?

He could hear a group of young men now, a hundred yards or so behind him, probably beneficiaries of a lock-in at the Woodman's, their voices boisterous but absent of malevolence. He imagined turning the corner to find Brendan there, the convergence of two drunks, once rivals in love. They used to ride this way on their bikes, Stephen's an old Chopper, his friend's one of the early BMXs, playing cards fixed to the forks so that they clattered in the circling spokes. Stephen would sometimes give his sister a ride on the back, tearing down the slopes next to Highfield, hearing her scream as he pretended the brakes had failed, the cards clacking furiously. As they skidded to a halt at the bottom she'd be close to tears, yet still wanting to go again.

'Once more, Even, please,' she'd say, the nickname coming from a time when she couldn't pronounce the start of his name. He said it now, out loud, enjoying the shape it made with his mouth. Even. Not odd. Even, like level. And then at home their mother would come into the lounge, asking crossly who'd drunk straight from the milk bottle, and with a white crescent over her grinning top lip his sister would say, 'Even did, Mum. It was Even.'

The streets were empty now, slick with rain. Few shops were the same, yet it all resonated, as if the buildings themselves had waited for his return. The bookshop they'd had an account with was now an Oxfam, and he stood staring at the mannequin posing in its window, imagining it bursting into a rakish dance for his pleasure alone. The barber's shop his father used to take him to when he was on leave still stood there, and for a second, the heady concoction of cologne, talc and sandalwood was remembered by some corner of his mind, receding the moment he tried to indulge it.

He listened to a message Zoe had left on his phone, her voice soothing, the urge to be held by her overwhelming. In the background, Amy asked her mother something. As the message ended, he said his name into the phone, his real name, the one before he'd started using his uncle's. The one Zoe knew nothing of, taking as she did one that carried no shame. Briggs. Stephen Briggs.

Walking on, he could see the church on the corner, the graveyard in which he and Brendan had once sat smoking before being chased away by the churchwarden. He stopped and looked up at the spire, rain threading down into the amber street light. He spoke a few words, too drunk to tell if he had said them aloud. He remembered someone else uttering them once, originality beyond him, and when he repeated them, he was uncaring whether or not he was heard.

'Where was God that day?' he said, before walking on.

Part Two

Summer 1982

Eight

She checked her hair a last time in the mirror by the front door, thought about changing her top again, or putting on some make-up. In the end she did neither. It was strange to feel nervous at his return, as if an important and infrequent guest were coming to stay, the anticipation a source of contrary emotions. She gave the downstairs rooms a last inspection – tidy but homely the desired effect – before putting Shane in the back of the car. The dog had seemed more subdued than ever in recent days, as if resigned to the shorter walks and minimal fuss she and the children gave him. It was touching, she supposed, this blind loyalty that manifested as something resembling grief. She regarded pets, dogs especially, as opportunists, shifting their affections to whoever controlled feeding, their devotion emanating from their stomachs alone. But Shane's allegiance to her husband appeared to go beyond the conditioning of simple behaviour and reward mechanisms. They'd formed a bond, Richard and the dog, in the short time the family had had it, so that whenever her husband was away, the animal would skulk by the front door, its ears down, waiting for signs that signalled Richard's return. And so for almost four months now, except when it was being fed or walked, the dog had affected a sullen disposition at the back of the hall, its jowls low-slung, big liquid eyes drawn down in melancholy.

They'd got him shortly after moving in, as if the extra space of Highfield demanded another presence. The children had long been promised a pet, though Mary had had something less onerous in mind. Jenny had wanted a kitten or a rabbit, but Stephen, spurred on by his father, made the persistent case for a dog.

'All that garden, the fields and woods behind,' Richard had said. 'We should get something that would appreciate it. This is the sort of house that has a dog.'

Mary wouldn't allow talk of a puppy; there were enough strays at the rescue shelter in need of a home, and she suspected the children's fascination with a young dog would soon wane, leaving her with the bulk of the duties. And so the next time Richard was on leave, they'd driven to the shelter a few miles out of town on a wet Sunday afternoon in November to choose one.

They'd stood in front of the caged sections, the four of them, sometimes greeted with an exuberant or fierce bark. Other dogs, morose and wretched, remained impassive. Along the last row a scruffy Border collie shuffled to the front of its space as they approached, tail arced between its back legs, gently wagging in submission. Jenny put her fingers through the bars for the dog to lick, her father shouting a rebuke, snatching her hand back.

It was clear, though, that the animal was nothing but friendly, and five minutes later they were walking it around a field behind the shelter, the children squabbling over who held the lead. A single visit to their house from staff, to check its suitability, and the dog was allowed home with them a few days later. The children wanted to name him something else, but the woman from the shelter said this would be unfair; he'd been Shane for nine years and was used to it.

Within hours of getting back, the dog latched on to Richard, the children too animated for him, Mary largely indifferent. Her husband had grown up with dogs around the house, his parents never having fewer than two at any one time, and perhaps animals sensed this, judging their most likely source of companionship.

A week later, the novelty of feeding and walking the dog on their own had worn off for the children. That the latter had to happen whatever the weather hadn't occurred to them, and talk soon returned to other pets. Richard, though, when home, would never fail to rise first thing and could be gone half the morning up in the woods and fields behind the house, the dog, more used to the sedentary regime of the shelter, returning exhausted but content.

The car eventually starting, she eased the choke in. At breakfast, Jenny had asked to stay off school in order to come to the station.

'No one will care, Mum.'

'It's been four months,' Mary told her. 'A few more hours won't make any difference. He'll be here when you get home.'

Their daughter was due to begin secondary school later this year, where her appearance would once again become an issue. The birthmark that covered most of her left cheek and half her forehead was, despite best intentions, the first thing you saw, drawing your eye like a flare in the night sky or a bloodstain in snow. Walking Jenny into primary school for the first time, Mary had noticed that even the teacher failed to hide her stare at the florid discoloration of skin, resembling a wine stain, a pulsing beacon. They'd been told it wasn't hereditary, but caused by a faulty nerve supply to the blood vessels, which remained dilated, as if in a permanent blush. Other than her appearance, it would cause no medical problems, and in time classmates and friends became used to it, as they had as parents. But with the prospect of a new, bigger school, Mary had spoken to the woman in the town's chemist, enquiring about possible make-up or creams to camouflage it. The options were scant. What little they had relied on such a precise match in colour that the effect was often equally flagrant. And if they did achieve a good match, it diminished a few hours later, the attention merely postponed.

Mary eased the car around the lanes out of town until she joined the main road. She checked her watch: Richard's train arrived in forty minutes, enough time to park and meet him on the platform.

Stephen had seemed cooler on the matter of his father's return, though he'd clearly missed him on some level. Something of the war had permeated his resistance to matters outside the cocooned territory of adolescence, and several times Mary had found him watching the coverage with concern etched across his face. If ever she remarked upon his disquiet, asked whether he wanted to talk about any aspect of it, he quickly retreated to the safety of apparent disregard.

Richard had been away for almost as long previously – spells in Ireland and Germany, training in the jungles of

Central America – but she'd learned to settle into a routine, to keep busy. It had been difficult once the children started school, the loneliness intolerable at first, and she would count down the hours until their return home. Her husband would write occasionally, though she knew he struggled to express emotion this way, his letters a litany of the physical hardships the men endured, or merely the prosaic cataloguing of the duller aspects of army life. In the early years, a careful reading of his words might have revealed something of his own experience of bullying, a time Mary had hoped would prompt his departure from the forces. Once this ceased with promotion, there was just a general sense of his unhappiness, again hardly articulated, just felt, a lowering of mood in the days before his return to base, of a career hastily chosen in the confusion of youth. And now that he was finally getting out, world events had conspired to ensure they had just a little more of him.

The date they'd set for their new life to begin had been snatched away by the invasion of some small island group in the South Atlantic. Richard had bought himself out, given his year's notice, and had only a few days left to serve before his premature voluntary release, as it was termed. They'd purchased the house, put everything they owned plus a lot they didn't into it. As his release date approached, he applied for several engineering jobs, the only interview missed with the outbreak of war. Last week, anticipating the need for recuperation on his part, Mary had spoken to the manager at the nursing home, requesting more hours until her husband found some work.

And now he was home. Unscathed as far as she could tell

from his phone call yesterday. She'd followed the war on television initially, incredulous for the first few days that it was happening, seeing hordes of well-wishers at the docks, the long journey south at sea and their eventual arrival. It was like watching a documentary at first, none of it quite real. She knew Richard was there in a literal sense, but the physical distance between the two realities acted as mist, blurring the coverage of its sharpness. But then the first casualties were announced and the television became a source of ambivalence as she was both drawn and repelled by it each day. In the end, she opted for the radio.

As she pulled into the station car park, the dog sat up on the back seat to inspect their whereabouts. How would her husband react to the gathering that had been planned for this evening, a homecoming party at the Woodman's? She'd had no part in it, other than being told to keep it a secret, to just get Richard there under the pretence of a quiet drink. If he wouldn't come, she was to tell him something small had been arranged.

In recent days she'd watched on television as the first servicemen returned, stepping off the plane to a military band and a small crowd of families and journalists, the SS *Canberra* docking in Southampton amid a flotilla of boats, the sky filled with balloons and bursts of 'Land of Hope and Glory' as the country basked in its victory.

In his phone call, Richard had told her not to travel to the barracks to collect him, that he would get the train down today. He sounded calm, as if he'd merely been on a week-long exercise, his voice somehow compressed as though the call was across continents. She'd felt some small guilt at the relief that he had come home, wondering how others explained to children that the absence would be permanent. Stephen and Jenny were used to his being away, their resilience born from knowing no different, but they too must have sensed her near-permanent dread in recent months. At ten, their daughter was too young to understand the true implications of war, that until now their father had merely gone away to practise. The few years her brother had on her, though, meant he was appreciative if not of the politics, then at least of the fact that his father might not return.

Thinking back to that day in spring, her husband on the phone confirming what the news people were saying, she recalled a real sense that it would be called off before it began: how important could this colonial outpost nobody had heard of be? That beneath the jingoism were level-headed diplomats charged with resolving the dispute. After all, wars were something that occurred in the past or between other countries.

She put Shane on the lead and walked through the small station building and on to the platform, where a few people stood in glum anticipation. After tidying the house this morning, she'd gone into town and bought some steaks for tonight, the occasion justifying the extra cost. And there was some expensive-looking wine they'd been given several years ago.

She wouldn't mention the bills, not for a few days. Or how the roof leaked in several more places in the spare room, that empty ice-cream containers were needed to catch the rain in there. The urgent tasks aside, the disrepair at Highfield would have to wait, the large projects that would see the old barns converted into accommodation put off at least until next year. It was never going to be easy, she reminded herself, this self-sufficient life, one they controlled, where they didn't work tirelessly for others. It would take time: the steady transformation of the house and its outbuildings into holiday lets; the garden rescued from its tangle of scrub and bramble, cultivated for the production of food. They'd talked about buying some goats this year, perhaps a couple of pigs and some hens. An apiary the year after. In time, the car would go, replaced by bikes and public transport. If Richard ever got round to making the Morris roadworthy, they'd tax it for the summer months alone, using it for trips to the coast, to visit parents. They'd hunker down in the winter, cooking whatever summer and autumn had yielded, enjoy having the place to themselves. If the business took off, she could reduce her hours at the nursing home, perhaps not working at all for part of the year, other than attending to the needs of guests. They could run courses on self-sufficiency – Richard had teased her that it would become a commune, with throngs of hippies ensconcing themselves everywhere, a lure for anyone with a guitar and a beard. The image had some small appeal, she had to admit, were it possible without the petty politics and inevitable infighting. A community of shared values, rejecting the more obscene excesses with which people were filling their lives these days. A return to the sort of life her parents had lived, where you accepted what you had, lived within your means, consumed only what was necessary. Perhaps being at war would remind people of such times, despite its spectacle occurring so far away.

She walked to the end of the platform, allowing the dog to relieve itself on the grass. On the opposite side, across the track, swallows flitted low under the eaves of the old station house, their cream bellies swooping close to the ground, the birds' presence summer's true harbinger. Beyond the hills, the sky brimmed with high cloud. Behind her Mary noticed that a Union Jack had been draped over one of the noticeboards, its hem crimping the puddle below in the breeze. Presumably other soldiers had alighted here in recent days, tearful reunions before departing to provincial towns and villages, returning to lives that had been on hold.

She wondered whether they would make love tonight or in the coming days, as they generally did on Richard's return. She'd missed their intimacy a little this time, the circumstances of her husband's absence perhaps intensifying it. Waking in the night, often emerging from appalling dreams, she would forget he was away, reaching across the bed to find a vacant expanse, cold and hollow. It was his physical presence she missed most, a warmth and permanence next to her; the frenetic passion that marked his return was, these days, something she could take or leave. If she were lucky, alcohol would render his efforts scant and he'd fall asleep, whereupon she'd cuddle into his side, content at not being alone. And yet there existed a selfish streak in her now, a part that relished the time he was away, the house, with the children at school, hers alone. In the evenings she would come in from work, light some candles, listen to music her husband loathed. At weekends, long, languorous baths were taken following an afternoon's gardening; then she would help the children with homework before settling in front of the fire with some wine and a book. Sometimes, weeks into her husband's return home, she'd find herself guiltily reflecting on the date he was to leave again, as if the loneliness in the long hours of the night had been sated enough for it to be tolerated again. She wondered if this desire for solitude would pass once he'd left the army, whether the intensity of his coming and going would play out another way.

For a moment she forgot that he'd not merely been away this time. She could hardly guess at the horrors he might have witnessed, friends who'd fallen, action he'd been compelled to take. That he was not really built for army life would presumably have loomed large when all the rehearsal was exchanged for the real thing. When he was home, he often spoke of men who blazed with the desire to fight, to test their skills in the arena of battle, their lives ultimately devoid of meaning until this time. She tried to understand it, evoking analogous pursuits you trained all your life to perform, yet never did.

She could hear the train now, a thin chatter from the next valley. An announcement was made on the tannoy, to stand back from the track, causing Shane's ears to twitch in anticipation of some new episode in the day. The front few carriages were now visible beyond the hedgerow, the train making its long, banking curve towards them. She tightened the dog's lead and strained to see the faces of those aboard.

Nine

She watched as he cut the last bit of his steak in two and fed the pieces one at a time to a salivating Shane. The dog, as if knowing there would be no more, lay down in the corner of the room, eyes fixed lovingly on Richard. She'd told the children they were allowed to come for an hour or so, a little longer if it wasn't too smoky, suspecting that nobody would object to them being there tonight.

'Can I have some beer?' Stephen asked.

'We'll see,' Mary said. 'Perhaps a shandy.'

Her son gave a little cheer as he went upstairs to change out of his school clothes.

'Can I have a shandy?' Jenny asked.

'Of course not, darling. Go and get changed too.'

She had told her husband about this evening in the car on the way home as the dog nuzzled him from the back seat, the conversation predominantly one-way.

'A few people from the pub, that's all. I don't even know who organised it. I said you'd want some time at home first, a few days, but they wouldn't hear of it. I think it's more an excuse to stay open late.'

It wasn't as if they'd kept up any social links with the town since moving to Highfield, and she regretted mentioning at work her husband's imminent return. For most of the journey home from the station he had stared out of the window, into the passing fields or swivelling his head to look up into the sky. She'd hardly recognised him when he stepped off the train, his face significantly thinner, gaunt almost, despite being hidden beneath a copious beard. It had taken all her strength to keep Shane from tearing across the platform, the animal beside itself on seeing him. Richard met them both simultaneously, a three-way embrace of sorts as people shuffled around them, one or two offering her husband a congratulatory word or two.

They walked across the field, the four of them, down into the town, Jenny skipping on ahead, stopping to pick buttercups, which she held one at a time beneath her chin before placing them in the pocket of her dress to press later. The late-afternoon drizzle had thinned, the evening sun edging beneath low cloud, casting a mellow light across the line of elms up ahead. Shane flanked them in wide arcs, returning every now and then to the path to round them up with exultant barks, delirious to have them all together again. As the slope levelled out, Richard paused to observe a bird in the distance as it soared high on the breeze, his face for a moment like a child's.

'Come on,' Mary said, smiling. 'You'll be late for your party.'

As they reached the stile at the edge of the field, Richard whistled, a single, strident note that saw Shane bolt towards them. The evening sun had emerged fully now, warming their faces a little before they entered the copse. Inside the wood the rain had fashioned an earthy smell that fused with the honeysuckle to produce a sweet, loamy scent. Mary felt good in her cotton dress, the sense of making an effort to go somewhere almost forgotten. She'd put on some make-up for the first time in months, finishing with a mist of the perfume Richard had bought her years ago.

Emerging from the wood, they could see the pub up ahead. Some token bunting had been strewn above the windows and a Union Jack hung limply below the sign. Several people idled outside, men Mary recognised from the town, men whose stares would linger longer were she alone. One of them had come up to the house a week or so after her husband had left. The children were at school and she hadn't heard the knock, Shane's bark finally alerting her. When she'd opened the front door, the man had had his back to her, as if he was taking in the view of the town, curious at the novel vantage point. As he turned round, his eyes scanned her up and down, a careless grin breaking out on his face.

She greeted him, holding the door ajar to stop Shane from emerging.

'Looks good,' he said.

'I'm sorry?'

'What you've done to the place.'

'Oh, thank you. It's just a start. There's so much to do.' After a moment's silence, she spoke again. 'Can I . . . ?'

'I was just passing. Wondered if you wanted any help, what with your old man being on the other side of the world.'

She felt flustered, knowing he wasn't a neighbour, the

offer inappropriate. As she fumbled for words, he looked beyond her, into the house, and she wished Shane's growl sounded more menacing. Again he grinned, conveying someone who wasn't embarrassed to try his luck, to see where it led.

Declining his offer politely, she thanked him, suggesting that they were managing fine. After a final scan of the house, the man turned and headed back towards the gate.

As they neared the pub, a couple of cheers went up, though nobody approached them. The men greeted Richard in turn, the man who'd come to the house nodding at Mary. She ushered Jenny along, her daughter stopping to stroke a small dog lying beneath one of the tables.

Inside, the low murmur of conversation fringed the noise from the jukebox. Someone recognised them and called out, and within seconds, people were lining up to shake Richard's hand, while others patted his back, her husband unresponsive to the gestures. After telling the children to go into the lounge bar, Mary ordered some drinks, the landlord ignoring her when she went to pay.

Following the initial exuberance, people filtered away, back to their game of darts or to attend the fruit machine, the far side of the room almost lost to the fog of cigarette smoke. When they'd lived in the town itself, they'd come in here a few times, it being the better of the two pubs on offer, but it wasn't somewhere she liked to be. A woman was expected to conform more than usual in here, her presence an adornment of the men, whose conversation often revolted her. She had smiled, laughed in the right places, but the move to

Highfield, in her mind, had signalled an end to putting up with such unpleasant occasions. After tonight, Richard would have to come here on his own.

They sat in a corner, by the door to the kitchen, Shane settling down at her husband's feet. Every now and then she checked on the children through the gap of the bar, seeing Jenny watching Stephen and a friend play pool, her daughter looking increasingly bored, the promised party not as she'd imagined.

'You should pretend to be a little grateful,' Mary whispered to her husband.

'We have no ties to these people. It's just a charade.'

As others arrived, they would approach their table, offer some clumsy acknowledgement of Richard's return, insist he was bought a drink, or that one was put in for him. Occasionally someone sat with them until the awkwardness of small talk became burdensome, her husband's monosyllabic answers condemning the exchange to a premature end. In truth, she hardly knew anyone there: a few faces that were familiar, perhaps termed acquaintances, characters glimpsed in the fabric of small-town life. It saddened her, this absence of friends, and she vowed to correct it, to extend their lives beyond the concerns of Highfield. To become part of a community, despite living in a large house that overlooked the town. It felt important not to isolate themselves in their search for a more sustainable life.

The evening trudged on, becoming a little more raucous. The group of men they'd passed coming in were now assembled at the bar, Mary sensing the man who'd come to the house, his stares less and less subtle. Perhaps they could leave soon without it seeming rude, an exhausted soldier, grateful for the gesture but in need of his bed. He'd hardly be missed. She looked at her husband, but he was lost to thought or fatigue. A moment later, one of the men, perhaps the youngest, approached them, placing more drinks on the table before Mary could decline. Buoyed by his advance, he began asking Richard questions about his time away, what part he might have played, her husband refusing to be drawn, dismissing them with an almost shy modesty.

Finally one of the others called over: 'Did you kill anyone?' The words cut the air, the chatter around them fading for a moment. Still the men received nothing in return, and she sensed resentment rising among them, that Richard was neglecting his role of the soldier returning with glorious accounts of victory, denying them their vicarious warfare. As the chat became more jingoistic, she went to check on the children. The pool table had been covered up now and a man was setting up to play music in the far corner. Stephen and his friend were playing on the games machine, tapping its buttons furiously, while Jenny asked the man about his guitar. Mary observed her daughter for a moment, the ease with which she spoke to newly met adults contrasting with her self-consciousness around children she didn't know, most adults being able to disguise their reaction to her face. Mary sat down, telling Jenny that the man was busy, to stop bothering him.

'It's fine,' he said. 'She's no bother.'

His Irish accent had a soothing lilt to it, distinct from the barbed voices next door, and she found herself hoping he'd speak again.

'What does that do?' her daughter asked, pointing to the amplifier at the man's feet.

'It's so they can hear me through there,' he said.

'I'm not sure that'll be big enough tonight,' said Mary.

Stephen's friend came over, asked the man for some coins, and she realised he was Brendan's father. The boys had known each other for a year or so now, fishing together down at the river, staying at each other's houses on occasion. She remembered Brendan mentioning that his father was a musician, how he was away from home a lot, going to festivals or performing gigs. Perhaps they would become friends with Brendan's parents now, invite them round, though Richard would probably regard their lifestyle as too alternative.

She watched the man tuning his guitar, concentrating hard on a small device that informed him of each string's pitch as he adjusted it. Seeing her interest, he explained to her how it worked, how it could only be done by ear until recently. Satisfied that the instrument was in key, he played a few riffs, his fingers dancing expertly across its neck, while those on his other hand gently plucked the strings. They watched him perform a few more sound checks, before moving to a table near the far wall. As they were the only ones in there, Mary decided to stay for a while, the thought of the man having only children for an audience causing a heaviness in her heart. She got Jenny another drink, checking through the bar on Richard, who was now being asked by some sinewy man to pose for a photograph. Her husband looked over and she smiled, but his eyes remained glazed, empty.

The music started up. She supposed it was somewhere

between folk and blues, the man's voice higher than she'd have thought, the song alternating between melancholic and sanguine. It didn't sound like a cover and she wondered if he wrote his own stuff. It had been years since she'd listened to live music, perhaps before the children were born, and she'd forgotten its unique spectacle, how it could lift you above petty concerns as you lost yourself in the theatre of it. A few people, on hearing the music, had come in, the room rivalling the other for headcount now. The second song she recognised as a Dylan cover, the man lending its chorus a witty twist that went over the heads of the others, Mary giving the faintest smile to let him know his repartee wasn't entirely wasted.

Several verses into the cover, she noticed a couple of the men who'd been around Richard remonstrating from the other bar, their tone indignant, angry even. When the song finished, she realised it was Brendan's father they were unhappy with. As more voices of dissent joined in, someone shouted across a request, that he play something more patriotic, something that fitted the occasion better. A man behind them shouted his disapproval that *some Irish fucker* had been booked at a time like this. The landlord, after making the case that the man played there regularly, looked across, hopeful that the song request might be met, but Brendan's father ignored them, continuing his set with one of the few Donovan songs she knew.

As the tension between the bars rose, Mary told the children it was time to go home, that it would be dark soon, Jenny protesting that there was no school tomorrow. Through a gap in the crowd of men, she could see her husband, staring absently at nothing, somehow both drunk and sober. Again the landlord attempted to placate the men, but they had spurred each other on, wound themselves up, perhaps to impress Richard, perhaps just to have a fight of their own. As she took the children back through, an ashtray was thrown across the bar, hitting the wall to the left of Brendan's father, but still he played on. Reaching her husband's table, Mary saw he had three full pints lined up in front of him, the man with the camera, a reporter from the local paper, sitting opposite. Despite the agitation at the bar, the man corralled them all together, a family shot essential apparently, after which Mary told Stephen to walk his sister home, that they'd follow them in an hour or so.

The stand-off concluded with the landlord pulling the plug on the music, a boisterous cheer coming from the men as they congratulated each other. He then took some money from the till and gave it to Brendan's father, who looked defiant but resigned as he packed up his stuff. More nationalistic slurs followed him as he left.

The anger churned in her as she watched the men revel in self-satisfaction, as if their victory were a continuation of what had occurred on the other side of the Atlantic. For years she'd vowed to take a stance in the face of such bigotry, perhaps spurred on by treatment her husband had succumbed to over the years, her daughter's bullying. Fantasies had formed where she intervened, challenging prejudice regardless of the hazard to herself. All her life she had let the fury broil and fester, before retreating into silent self-loathing. The next time she would find the courage to speak out. Always the next time.

With Brendan's father gone, the atmosphere returned to its earlier ebullience. A burst of 'Rule, Britannia!' filled the room, the men at the bar encouraging but failing to get Richard to join in. One of them stood on Shane's tail, laughing as the dog snarled, her husband pulling the lead tight, as animated as he'd been all night. She thought of her son and daughter at home, wishing she was with them. Or still in the next room listening to the Irishman's songs.

The house was quiet when they returned. She'd expected the walk home through the field to be a struggle, given how much Richard had drunk, but he seemed unaffected, throwing a stick for Shane in the vestige of moonlight. They'd left a little after midnight, slipping out unnoticed, the bustle of the pub continuing behind them. The air had been heavy with the scent of summer, a hint of warmth still radiating up from the ground. She talked most of the way home, to fill the silence, telling her husband about Jenny's friend who'd stayed but hadn't slept for fear she had heard a ghost. Of how Stephen rarely did as he was told, his petulance wearing her down at times. How they'd all missed him. He'd responded with quiet efficiency, as if the effort of speaking burdened him.

She offered to make some tea, but he poured himself a large whisky and sat at the kitchen table, smoking hard. More than earlier, she saw how thin his face had become. Beneath his eyes, semicircles the colour of plums emanated a rich lustre. She wanted to talk about the men in the pub, their treatment of Brendan's father, but judged it a potential source of conflict. Instead she spoke about the plans for the house she'd made in his absence, how this was the start of their new life. As she looked at her husband, this battle-weary, taciturn man, she tried to work out what the overwhelming emotion in her was – be it joy, relief or something else.

She took her tea upstairs, touching Richard's shoulder as she passed, telling him to come up soon.

Ten

As she sat in the kitchen window looking out across the garden, it felt to her that the house had renewed itself in Richard's presence. Already its disposition had shifted, as if he had laid claim to the fabric of the place, the rooms themselves thick with the suggestion of him.

A parchment of cloud had yet to burn away beneath the morning sun, the sky inert and colourless. Beyond the town a pall of mist lay low in the valley, its vaporous mass migrating imperceptibly. She remembered summer mornings as a child, her mother also sitting in the window seat of their home, watching the day unfurl, as if each new one was to be marvelled at.

She thought for the first time of the man who'd lived here before them. They knew little about him, except that he'd lost his wife some years ago, Highfield's upkeep beyond the means of one person. His children had visited frequently to begin with, but when this tapered off, his health declining, he had been forced to sell up. Given the house's condition, there had been little interest, and the estate agent encouraged them to put in a low offer. They did so, Mary embarrassed at its brazenness, and the man accepted it later that day. She pictured him sitting here in the window, straining to hear the sounds of a house that had once brimmed with life, mourning his inability to maintain the garden without help.

It would feel too vast, this house, with only memories to follow you from room to room, the ambient murmur of others receded for ever. And yet there was something to cherish in these moments before her family were awake, the experience of each new season here hers first. She loved how dawn graced the tips of the distant hills before it swept through the valley. How, in their first winter here, the elements had pummelled the house as they sat around the fire, windows rattling in their frames, beams and joists groaning above them. Snow had drifted hard one January night, a three-foot-high perfect white curtain greeting her when she opened the door. One morning, a few weeks before Richard had returned, a vixen had cautiously traversed the garden, sniffing the air before slinking through the far hedge, and Mary had pictured its cubs, hopeful of observing them later in the year as they tumbled and cartwheeled over each other on the lawn. There was a badger run nearby, too, a trail established through the hedgerow, its sett up in the woods.

She looked at the small section of ground she'd planted since moving here. What could loosely be termed a garden had been choked with weeds and brambles, decades-old debris strewn within it. It had taken her several days last autumn to clear an area big enough to grow a reasonable crop this first year. At the start of spring she'd broken up the soil, drawing out four sections of furrowed rows with an old hoe she'd found in one of the barns. She would assess what worked well this year and develop more beds the following spring, rotating crops over the years to add nutrients to the soil. Eventually they would be able to grow all their own vegetables, selling any excess produce to local shops. The work was tough on top of her job and without help from Richard, and as their income dwindled, there would be real pressure to make a success of it.

In March, she'd cleared out the lean-to at the back of the house to use as a potting shed, the hours spent in there deeply pleasurable, almost meditative. Beyond the stone wall there was a dilapidated greenhouse she'd repaired enough so it retained most of its heat, and already the sweet, earthy fragrance of tomato vines cloyed the air inside, while peppers and aubergines glistened from their watering.

It was a start. In time, she would learn to make use of the profusion of food that nature offered, foraging in the hedgerows and woods this autumn. There were blackberries, sloes, rosehips and bilberries nearby; two types of mushroom up in the top field that she suspected were edible. For soups, there was watercress growing down by the river, as well as sprigs of wild thyme snaking through the grass that fringed it. Salads from the produce of the greenhouse could be enhanced with yarrow and wood sorrel, and there had been redcurrants in spring, wild strawberries early in summer.

She'd found an orchard a mile or so along the valley and would approach the owner to ask what fruit might be surplus or whether she could exchange something for it. Eventually she would get to know every wild plant that could be harvested, herbs and shrubs that were both food and medicine, taking care not to uproot any, keeping the supply abundant. And while she doubted Richard would ever be sympathetic to this extent of alternative living, it felt an important part of what they were trying to achieve at Highfield. To use less. To be responsible for what they did utilise. For their relationship with nature not to be an occasional pilgrimage, something acknowledged from time to time, but one where they became part of its great unswerving cycles, where they gave as much as they took, immersed in the rhythms and order of the seasons.

She'd surprised herself with how much she'd achieved in Richard's absence. In addition to the garden, she'd cleared out the smaller of the two barns, junk and rubble the previous owner had been unable to tackle. This, too, had left him impotent during the sale, their offer allowing for the fact that they would take care of it. After moving in, Mary asked Stephen to help her one weekend, but despite a reluctant commitment to do so, he made plans with Brendan, apologising as he hurried out before she could protest.

The small barn, despite being damp, was the safer of the two, its roof almost intact, the stone walls largely unblemished. They would convert this one first, the project, if her husband was to be believed, conceivable without too much outside help. Once the building work was under way, Richard could connect a water supply from the mains. They'd need help with electricity, but the plan was to do the rest themselves, have it habitable for the start of the holiday season next year. More than this, though, she wanted the restoration to be sympathetic, for them to be curators of the house and its land, responsible for its rescue, its evolution. It mattered to her the materials they used, that the spirit and character of the place wasn't lost, its history preserved, the memories held in its centuries-old beams regarded. Highfield would be a place people loved again, where they felt welcome and safe, a home the children returned to with relish once they'd moved out.

Sorting through the old man's rubbish in the barn, seeing if anything could be salvaged, she'd found an old oil painting, a bucolic scene, perhaps local, its tones sombre and brooding yet not without appeal. She rang the estate agent but they reiterated that the man hadn't wanted anything that had been left, so she'd found a place for it in the lounge.

Jenny's floorboards groaned above her now and Mary smiled at the prospect of company. Their daughter was waking earlier these days, perhaps anxious at what September would bring.

'Stephen will be there if you need him,' Mary had said, to little effect.

She decided to let Richard sleep his hangover off before taking him up some breakfast. Shane, usually wanting to be let out once someone was up, remained curled on the floor by her husband's side of the bed.

Mary had woken around six, confused by the sense of another presence, the bed for so long hers alone. A trapezoid of light slanted through the window, illuminating her husband's back, and she watched the gentle rises and falls of his torso. He'd lost a couple of stone, she estimated, his spine trailing down his back in painful relief. She realised, as the evening had passed, that they wouldn't make love, that there was something different in the nature of this homecoming.

Undressing, she'd been nervous, the evening's tension at the pub heightening the awkwardness of bodies that had forgotten each other. They'd kissed good night once the light was out, a perfunctory gesture as Richard turned over. She'd reached out to touch him, to curl into this stranger, but pulled back at the last minute, sensing that her touch would be unwelcome. The snoring she'd expected to start up almost immediately didn't come, and they'd both lain there listening to the silence.

The first time she woke, Mary thought the noise had been a dream, an animal-like cry emanating from her husband as he tossed about in a fitful sleep. This time she did put an arm around him, realising that his body was slick with sweat, the sheet sodden around him. She held him until the cry became a whimper, finally fading to nothing. Waking an hour or so later, she felt a dull pain, its source initially unfathomable in her half-sleep. Pursuing the sensation, she realised that Richard was gripping her arm, firmly enough that she was unable to release it, his fingers deep into her muscles. She said his name, wriggled a little, but this merely caused him to tighten his grasp. Finally she used her other hand to peel back his fingers one at a time, before shimmying to the far side of the bed.

She heard her daughter's footfall on the stairs. Nothing had been planned for the weekend; she would wait and see how her husband felt, a quiet couple of days together as a family, shut away from the world, his preference, she suspected.

Their first summer here was already waning; autumn's golden membrane would soon appear as the yard became burnished with leaves from the copper beech and sycamore. A surge of russet and ochre would furnish the slopes of the valley, the woods behind them. She thought how such edifying beauty was quickly acknowledged in the natural world, yet the gratuitous colour in her daughter's face was cause only for bemusement or discomfort in others, the stain a thing to mistrust, as if indicative of some malevolent force. Despite the medical wisdom, Mary had blamed herself for years, recalling times of upheaval during the pregnancy, arguments with Richard, as if her anger and frustration had manifested as a birthmark. A book on folklore she'd found in the town revealed more elaborate precursors, such as the wound from a battle in a previous life, or the pregnant woman touching her belly while looking at a solar eclipse. More prosaically, she'd read that port-wine stains were caused by the mother's insatiable craving for strawberries or jam. But whereas in other cultures such marks were regarded as blessed, lucky if touched, here Jenny was an aberration, a freak. That she was a girl, for whom beauty would be graded all the more, felt crueller still.

She looked at her arm, the beginnings of a bruise rising, the skin an iridescent violet where each of Richard's fingers had held her. Jenny stumbled in, wiping the sleep from her eyes, and Mary smiled at her as together they set the table for breakfast.

Eleven

From the garden she watched the man struggle with the gate, finally calling out to him to lift it before he pushed. She hadn't heard a car, but people often parked at the bottom of the lane, unsure that it led anywhere or that they'd be able to turn around. The noise brought Shane into the yard, the dog settling into a low growl as it held its ground a few feet from the front door. Something in her husband's return had brought out an excessively protective streak in the animal, to the point where she felt unsafe herself whenever she had to discipline it. A line would be crossed if it bit either of the children, she'd told Richard, whereupon it would be returned to the shelter. For now she ushered the dog into the utility room and headed back outside, where the man stood in the middle of the yard.

'Mrs Briggs?' he asked.

Mary nodded, thinking that perhaps she recognised him, though not from the town.

'I'm Philip Taylor. Richard's sergeant.'

She could see now that he was one of the men in a photograph her husband had once shown her, a group of six or seven soldiers posing for the camera in front of an army vehicle, some bare-chested, some with rifles, one or two smoking. He'd named them, the men in his unit, and had spoken kindly of Sergeant Taylor, a man, she felt, her husband looked up to, who'd helped him through a difficult time. He was younger than she would have imagined – younger perhaps even than Richard by a few years – but there was an air of self-assurance about him, of someone who coped with anything thrown his way. He was well groomed, and his features had a leanness to them, his face a series of sharp angles, as if sculpted, and she supposed some would regard him as dashing. By contrast, her husband had not shaved since coming home, the beard he'd returned with seemingly a thing of permanence.

The man offered her his hand to shake, dismissing her apologies at having soil on her own. His grip was neither firm nor limp, though she could sense the power of him. Looking beyond her, he asked if Richard was home, saying that he'd tried to call first but, unlike their address, their telephone number hadn't been updated on the records. When she said that her husband wasn't up yet, the man looked bemused, before giving a half-laugh.

'Life good to him now, is it? Don't let him get too used to it.'

She could think of nothing to say, her smile an effort to summon.

Sergeant Taylor explained that he had family down this way and apologised for not visiting sooner, saying that he was keen to see how Richard was doing on civvy street. Mary looked at him for a moment, desperate for some small and immediate insight, a sign that this man was here to deliver hope, perhaps the announcement of some support or an explanation, but she realised he would know nothing of what was playing out here.

'Do you want to come in?' she said.

She washed her hands in the sink while the kettle boiled. With the children back at school, she'd settled into a routine of clearing up indoors before spending a few hours in the garden and potting shed. Her current shift at the nursing home began after lunch, meaning that she had to prepare dinner for them all, something simple that could be reheated or that required minimal cooking. Stephen seemed to like the extra responsibility, the sense that he was still in charge until his mother returned later in the evening. In almost every sense it was the same as when Richard was away, the order and rhythms of the day unchanged, his presence more felt than observed, as if the pipes and wires of the house carried some essence of him. Their behaviour became increasingly modified so as not to disturb or annoy him, his need for solitude and silence heightened a little more each day. She tried to reassure the children that it was a phase, that he just needed more time than usual to adapt to being home again.

The staying in bed until she'd gone to work had begun a month or so ago, a couple of weeks after he'd returned. At first it had seemed reasonable for him to ease back into things; a week or so, she'd presumed, to acclimatise, to adjust to the absence of a life he'd lived since leaving school. He had, after all, returned from a war, albeit one that lasted barely a couple of months. But as the days passed, instead of emerging from this doleful stasis, he slid deeper into its grip, withdrawing from them a little more each day.

The fact that his daughter had started secondary school this week, his son beginning his final year, did nothing to rouse him. Mary encouraged the children to seek their father out each day when they got home, to try to engage him, but by this time, according to Stephen, he would be out walking the dog.

As she placed the teapot on the table, Sergeant Taylor asked what her husband was doing with himself now, joking that there was always room for him to return, in case he missed it all. He gave his words more emphasis now, as if once his voice carried upstairs, Richard would join them.

'He's not found work yet,' she said.

She'd pointed out jobs in the local paper, but he'd got no further than tearing them out, staring at the words as if they'd been written in another language. Initially, she'd thought his prolonged presence at home at least meant that some of the larger projects would be tackled, yet on the rare occasion he did start something, she'd get up the following morning to find a semblance of work undertaken, perhaps an hour or so, the job then abandoned, seemingly forgotten. When she tried to discuss it, he claimed the absence of some tool or material, saying he'd acquire them when next in town, despite the fact that he now only left the house to walk Shane. After almost a month of his being home, Highfield looked the same, only with another half a dozen tasks in need of completing.

According to her son, his father often missed dinner,

instead coming home as the light faded, a look of confusion or just emptiness on his face, taking his plate of food upstairs, where Mary would find it later, half eaten beside the bed. By the time she arrived home from work, he'd be back in bed, or in the spare room, sketching in a notebook, or just sitting there, the dog at his feet.

Last week, when for once he'd come to bed after her, she'd smelt whisky on his breath, though when she checked the bottle the next day, its level appeared undiminished. Searching the house and barns, she'd found nothing.

For now, all she could do was try to maintain some degree of normality, to ride it out. Their debt was becoming more of an issue, the extra hours she was doing helpful but ultimately insufficient, and Richard's army pay had ceased now. His pension would be moderate due to the early release, and the last of their savings had gone. As each day passed, her vision for Highfield seemed to retreat further. She tackled the jobs her strength and knowledge allowed, finally getting Stephen to help her shift some of the heavier debris in the larger barn, but she knew nothing of masonry, of how a roof was made waterproof. She'd spoken to her mother a few days ago, concealing her concern, hoping that her father's arthritis had improved enough for him to help. She found herself lying, describing a leg injury Richard had picked up when away, how everything would be fine soon. Her parents had always been unenthusiastic about the move, seeing the risk as unnecessary: what was wrong with the life they had? Why take on such a dilapidated house? Despite the opportunity to feel vindicated, her mother managed to hide any hint of self-righteousness, but no, her father's health meant he couldn't really help. They could visit next month, if Mary wanted, although the journey was difficult.

For the first time in her adult life, she found herself missing her parents. An ache had formed, born of the realisation that they wouldn't always be there, that time now spent with them was the creation of memories to hold on to once they had gone.

She poured the tea, offered Sergeant Taylor a biscuit. He was perhaps a little self-conscious with the situation now, a series of glances towards the stairs suggesting a desire to climb them and find Richard for himself.

'I can tell him you're here,' Mary said. 'But he probably won't come down.'

'He's not well?'

'It's been tough for him.'

'Has he any plans? He spoke of engineering or something.'

She looked at Taylor, scrutinising his face for some recognition that he understood, that his visit would cast light on the gathering gloom. But if something terrible had happened to her husband down there, this man knew nothing of it, or at least nothing of its legacy. He was merely visiting an old friend, someone he'd served with. Or perhaps his kind chose not to acknowledge weakness, in case it proved contagious.

She ignored his question, instead asking him about his own family, his children, how they coped with him being away. As he spoke, she saw a man at ease with himself, someone who'd found his calling in life, who could no doubt both lead men and be respected by them. She imagined his war as a glorious affair involving decoration, imminent promotion. As if sensing her thoughts, he spoke of a victory parade next month, in London, to salute the task force.

'Richard should be there,' he said. 'See all the lads again.'

Mary pictured her husband, how last week she'd asked him whether he was getting up that day, and his response had been 'What for?' It was already difficult to imagine him in uniform again, clean-shaven, a soldier's demeanour about him. For most of the night now he lay curled up tightly in a ball, holding himself as a frightened child might, or as if gripped by cold. She'd observed their bodies drifting further apart in the ocean of their bed, as if they were land masses on different tectonic plates, the contours of where they'd once fitted together still visible. His sleep was fractured, easily disturbed by whatever nightmare had caused him to cry out, names and words that became familiar to her. She hoped the children slept through it, or were able to dismiss it as a dream of their own and not their father's torment. Some nights she would wake to find Richard scrambling about the room, crying out that his arms were on fire, beating them furiously with his palms until she turned the lamp on, the realisation of where he was dawning on his face. Or he'd just be standing naked at the window in silence, staring out at the night.

'Come back to bed,' she would say, tenderly at first, becoming more weary with each occasion.

There had been a few repeats of waking to a dull pain, her arm or waist clutched firmly, Richard's hand or arm in need of prising open. She hid the bruising as best she could, grateful that the arms of her uniform came down far enough.

Last weekend she'd come in from the garden to hear a curious whimpering. Initially she'd thought the dog had injured itself. Following the sound upstairs, into the spare room, she found her husband huddled in a corner, sobbing uncontrollably, and for once he allowed her to comfort him.

'You need some help,' she said. '*We* need some help.'

He'd agreed to see a doctor, next week, in the town. She made a morning appointment, so she could drive him there, ensure that he went in.

'They'll be able to give you something to help you sleep,' she said, hopeful that the intervention would not stop at this.

Selfless devotion to the care of others, to those incapable of looking after themselves, had been part of her life for as long as she could remember, in both a vocational and domestic sense. A virtuous calling, to subvert one's wilder impulses and desires for the good of others, be they strangers or kin.

She'd entered nursing at a time when it was becoming more academic, the top teaching hospitals requiring A levels, which she'd taken, her grades competent if not spectacular. She'd lost her nerve for university life, so the mix of vocational and academic pursuits was an appealing one. They learnt on the job, completing twelve-week ward assignments, which were assessed and graded at the end by the ward sister, something she found terrifying. Further courses followed, in children's and adult nursing, before more general training, after which she became a staff nurse.

And the role of dutiful carer continued into parenthood, the maternal instinct flourishing bright from the moment of

Stephen's birth. But recently, as mid life approached, she'd found this altruistic proclivity waning, replaced by an examination of her own life, or of the life she hadn't led. She dwelt on missed opportunities, on frustrations that had been suppressed. Nurse, wife, mother: all of these things she cherished, yet they were no longer in themselves enough, defined as they were by their connection to others. It was as if a dilution had occurred somewhere along the way, a watering-down of the woman who'd hoped to go to university, to travel, to make a small impact on the world. She thought of the Lennon quote, of life being what happened to you while you were busy making other plans, and it made her cross, this acceptance that despite your best intentions, the world buffeted you according to its own arbitrary blueprint, one that was generally more prosaic. Or perhaps this interpretation was a cynical one, that it instead alluded to the infinite potential of life, its chaotic splendour that refused to be dictated to. Either way, she'd given her time to motherhood, to supporting her husband's career at the expense of her own aspirations. The pull of a new life – since Richard had given the army notice, the children growing up fast – had felt irresistible. The chance to escape the dreary formula they had succumbed to, a sequence of unvarying chapters, safe and unremarkable.

And yet here she was, burdened with a new, unfathomable strain, her husband returning from the far side of the world, a debilitating affliction visited upon him like some exotic disease, her place as full-time carer more entrenched than ever.

She wanted to ask the man at her kitchen table how the

army allowed someone who obviously wasn't suited to such a regime to serve for so long. How there wasn't a filter to catch him. And then, finally, when he did get out, how he was just left to get on with it, no after-care.

'What happened to him?' she said finally.

'What do you mean?'

'Down there. On those islands.'

Taylor again looked at the stairs, perhaps concerned that a trust might be breached, his composure momentarily slipping.

'He won't hear you, don't worry,' she continued. 'Nothing gets through. We tiptoed around when he first got back, but nothing stirs him now.'

'Look, I . . . It was tougher for some than others. You know, some of the things people had to see. Stuff they can't train you for. He probably just needs some more time. Get it out his system. Perhaps a holiday would help.'

They drank their tea in silence. When Mary spoke again, she fought the tremor that was forming in her voice.

'Do you know what he does, when he finally gets out of bed? He goes for a walk, up in the woods somewhere, I don't know. Takes the dog, gone until dusk, sometimes later, looking for birds in the sky, he says. And at night, when he's not thrashing about or crying out in his sleep, he sits in the spare room, in his pants, drawing these birds from pictures in a book. What little he eats, he does alone. That's his life now.'

A look of bemusement passed across Sergeant Taylor's face, whether from surprise at this artistic inclination or at her frank account of Richard's behaviour in general she was unsure.

'I can't remember the last time he touched me.' She hadn't wanted to say this, the words articulated before she could restrain them.

As the silence deepened again, they heard an upstairs door close. A few moments later, the toilet flushed, followed by the sound of another door. When they resumed their conversation, it was in a conspiratorial hush.

'I should at least say hello,' Taylor said. 'Perhaps it will help, seeing me.'

Mary shook her head. 'It might make him worse. Remind him.'

'I could tell him about the parade.'

'I'd rather you didn't.'

She thought to ask him what he'd meant by the things people had seen, both wanting and not wanting elaboration. Richard had still not uttered a word about his time there and she'd known not to ask; it had been sufficient to have him home when others had not returned. She knew enough of his role to understand what he would have been doing, the nature of his combat, but something in Sergeant Taylor's face had hinted at the unspeakable, of something he himself had managed to seal away in a box deep in his mind.

Finally he stood, thanking her for the tea.

'If you give me the number,' he said, 'I'll phone him next week, talk about the plans for the parade.'

Mary did as he asked, then saw him to the door, where, turning to say goodbye, he stood still, looking over her shoulder.

'Briggs,' he said.

She followed the sergeant's gaze up to the landing, where

her husband sat on the top stair in just his socks and pants, the dog now by his side.

'Hey, buddy, you coming down?' Richard looked through them, impassive, as if they weren't there. 'What's up?' Taylor continued. 'You getting too used to the cosy life? Come and say hello. Your missus tells me you're being a right pain in the arse. I offered to come up and sort you out, but she wouldn't have it. How about that pint some time?'

Without responding, her husband turned his attention to the door frame opposite the banister; reaching his arm out, he started picking furiously at the paint, flaking it off with his nail, the white flecks falling down into his hair like dandruff. Taylor gestured to her, asking whether he should go up, though it was clear now that he too doubted the wisdom of this course of action, bewilderment playing out on his face at Richard's appearance, his weight loss, his beard and hair.

'No, I think just go.'

After a further plea, he allowed himself to be ushered into the yard, where he placed his hand on the side of her arm. 'I'm sure he'll be fine,' he said, before heading to the gate.

As she got ready for work, Mary listened for signs of life above her. She'd sensed her husband listening at the top of the stairs, at least for some of the time Sergeant Taylor had been here. Perhaps she'd been wrong not to allow the man upstairs, his confronting Richard the prelude to some small recovery, a familiar and friendly face to snap him out of it, someone who'd shared whatever abomination had occurred. But it had felt incendiary, like sending up an embodiment of all her husband's terror. Better to seek some professional help, a psychiatrist or someone; she'd ask for advice at work.

After putting some food in the dog bowl, she left a note for the children. She called up that she was leaving, and listened to the silence for a moment before setting off across the field.

Twelve

The surgery's waiting room was sparsely furnished, its few rows of seating assembled as an L shape in front of a rectangular hatch in the wall. Without lifting her gaze, the receptionist marked a sheet in front of her and told them to take a seat, that they were running twenty minutes or so late. Mary led the way to some chairs in the far corner, Richard shuffling behind her. She'd thought they might walk here, to save petrol, but despite giving her husband an hour's notice, he was still undressed when it was time to leave and had to be corralled to the car, his movements often sluggish now, as if part of him was shutting down. In between this inertia were woven periods of agitation that verged on paranoia, bouts that left him exhausted to the point of collapse. Sudden noise – a door slamming, the first ring of the telephone – caused him to flinch, though it was becoming rarer for him to be downstairs for any length of time. Still he disappeared into the woods each day, binoculars slung round his neck, Shane at his heel, the pilgrimage bestowing on him a routine of sorts. Other, more visible changes had emerged in the past couple of weeks. Where once his eyes had brimmed with mischievous intensity or a vulnerable lustre, they were now increasingly devoid of animation, as if the organs were mere orbs of pith sitting in their hollows – functional and expressionless. Despite the endless hours spent outdoors, his complexion had become sallow, his skin bloodless. Sergeant Taylor had told her it was to be expected that they lost weight, given the size of their combat rations, the calories expended each day. But whereas the man who had visited their home had blazed with renewed vitality and a fullness of physique, her husband's indifference towards food had kept his build as frail as that day at the station. His voice, too, had thinned from even-toned and resonant to a sound that was almost muted, the words perishing immediately upon utterance.

Mary had spoken to her mother-in-law last week, a dutiful woman who lived in the shadow of her husband, but it was clear that Richard's parents regarded such difficulties as private matters, to be resolved from within, discreetly, without fuss. The fact that nobody was prepared to discuss what *such difficulties* even were only furthered the sense of isolation. She knew that his father was bitterly disappointed at Richard's premature departure from the forces, that he regarded his son as a failure even before this, his relatively lowly rank a source of embarrassment. She felt angry that they'd not even visited him since his return. And now they had cause not to, suggesting that it would be better to wait until their 'domestic troubles' had returned to normal. Had the conversation gone well, she might have broached the subject of money, especially as their son was the one with a reduced income, the one not pulling his weight at Highfield. In the end, she'd terminated

the call with a brusque retreat, ignoring enquiries about
the children.

She browsed the pile of magazines to the side of them,
settling on the least tatty of the gardening ones. Every
now and then she looked up, sensing a few stares, issuing a
defiant look to those who made eye contact. They would
be curious at this stranger among them, bedraggled and
bearded, accompanied by the woman from the house on
the hill.

He's the one who went to war.

He's in the army?

No, he left.

What's he doing now?

Nobody knows.

What about her?

A nurse, over at Parkwood. They used to live in the town.
Bought the Russell house.

What, the old ruin up there?

She tried to dismiss it, the border where a sense of
community and concern crossed into whispers and suspicion.
It was the sort of place, in the absence of a rooted generation
or two, where you never quite belonged. Perhaps this was
a feature of all small towns: you were an outsider, on
probation until further notice. But the alternative was to live
in the sprawl and tumult of a city or to isolate themselves
further.

She offered the magazine to Richard before returning it to
the table. To their right, a small boy was building something
with toy bricks, the tower toppling over around her husband's

feet. The boy looked sheepishly to his mother, wondering if it was OK to retrieve them. Mary was about to intervene when Richard slowly gathered them up, handing them almost in fascination to the boy one at a time.

Finally her husband was called through, Mary looking hard at him, as if to say, *remember why we're here, that you need some help. This cannot go on.* Those sitting around them looked on as he walked through to the doctors' rooms, and for a moment, she considered accompanying him, to ensure that the case was well made, its severity emphasised. Instead she thought to walk along the road, perhaps settle up the account at the bookshop, but the idea receded with the prospect of Richard emerging before she returned, perhaps wandering off somewhere. She would wait for him here.

She recognised the man as he scanned the room for somewhere to sit and she nodded at the chair next to her. He smiled, picking his way around the labyrinth of seats and outstretched legs, stepping carefully over the boy's latest construction. Bohemian was how she supposed he'd be regarded, someone who stood out, especially here: the tight jeans and cowboy boots, the same colourful waistcoat from the pub. A tattoo, ornate and detailed, adorned most of his right forearm. He apologised for not remembering her name, though she didn't recall saying it that night, and he told her his – Aiden. He'd had his hair cut since she last saw him, though it still sat just above his shoulders in auburn whorls. As he sat down, she noticed that his left ear was pierced, a thick silver ring tight to the lobe.

He made a joke about the place being full of sick people,

and how those who weren't would be by the time they left. His clothes smelled faintly of something musty, though not unpleasant, perhaps stale woodsmoke.

'So, our boys play together?' he said, which made them sound younger than they were.

'I think they go fishing a lot.'

'Perhaps one day they'll even catch a fish.'

They both laughed a little, and when those around them stared, Aiden gave a mock shush, which made her laugh some more.

'So you've got old man Russell's house, up on the hill?'

'You know it?'

'I did some work for him once, a bit of rewiring. Not that he paid me for it all.'

'So you don't . . . the music?'

'It brings in a few quid, nothing more.'

She wanted to make some compliment about his voice, but the words sounded mawkish in her head. In the end, she asked how long he'd been playing to audiences.

'I started in Dublin in the late sixties. Small clubs and pubs, traditional stuff mostly. I was never going to be any good, not so I'd make a living of it.'

'How did you end up here?'

'Just sort of happened, I guess. Drifting around, found some work. And then I met my wife. It's not a bad town for kids to grow up. I'm still a foreigner here, mind.'

'I've always wanted to go. To Ireland.'

He gave a little laugh.

'What?' she said.

'Everyone says that. It's only a few hours on the boat.'

She wanted to say that she knew this, that it wasn't the distance, or lack of, that had prevented her. That she'd been to other places, the Channel Islands, Germany when Richard was stationed there at the start of their marriage.

'My husband's been there,' she said, a little defensively. 'To the north, that is.'

'I've family thereabouts.'

In the pause that followed, she recalled the scene in the pub, the mindless discrimination, and was keen to point out that she was no part of it.

'That night, at the Woodman's,' she said. 'Does that happen often?'

'What, getting hassled? A bit. More since the Falklands. They think we're all in the IRA. Mostly it stops when I start playing.'

'I'm sorry Brendan had to see it.'

'You know what they're like; he probably didn't even notice. It'll all be forgotten the time I next play there.'

'You'll go back?'

'It's hard to get gigs these days; you can't be choosy.'

'I knew some of the songs, but not all of them.'

'I try to write my own, slip a couple in when no one's listening.'

He told her about musicians who'd inspired him, some of whom she'd heard of, and how he was happiest immersed in a song, seeing the joy on others' faces as they sang along or were touched by the words. His voice was starting to go now, he explained, the higher notes beyond reach. Modern music appalled him for the most part, the sixties and seventies seemingly being replaced by a decade that looked set to value synthesised noise and sentimental pap, the acoustic guitar an endangered species.

'Where are all the songwriters?' he said. 'What are they singing about?'

Mary shook her head, unsure how to respond but feeling engrossed all the same.

One of the doors opened at the far end of the corridor, an elderly woman emerging, examining her prescription. Richard had been in a while now, which was a good thing, she told herself. It was hard to imagine him articulating this thing, capturing in words the wretchedness he'd succumbed to. But perhaps it would be easier to talk to a stranger, one whose judgement manifested as clinical rather than emotional. Since Sergeant Taylor's visit, she'd thought more about how inadequate Richard's post-war treatment was. That he'd left the army hardly seemed relevant, given how much of his life he'd given them. Weren't there specialists for such situations, for the ones whose anguish didn't subside? He'd done what was asked of him – served his country, risked being killed, perhaps killed others – only to be abandoned. If Sergeant Taylor did ring, she'd make her case more forcefully, demand some assistance.

Aiden was talking again now and she welcomed the distraction.

'You doing up the house, then?' he said.

'Highfield? It's a work in progress.'

'A lot of damp, I remember.'

'We didn't realise how bad the roof was.'

'Russell let it go, I think. Once his wife died. Didn't you have a survey?'

'We only got a valuation, to save money.'

'Not so clever.' He said this with sympathy, she felt, rather than as a rebuke.

'We want to convert the barns into accommodation, and to run courses. By next summer, the plan was.'

'But not now?'

She lowered her gaze, surprised at her urge to tell this man everything.

'It's been tough since my husband got back. He was going to do most of the work himself. I've made a start, but . . .'

'Well, I know a good electrician. He talks a lot, but I can vouch for him. He can turn his hand to most things, actually.'

She smiled, hopeful that her face didn't imply lack of interest at the offer. In truth, there were no funds for such work, nor were there likely to be.

'I'll keep it in mind,' she said with a smile. 'Thank you.'

Again they lapsed into silence. She wondered whether to ask him about her old violin. A reward from her father following A levels, it had languished in the corner of rooms in various homes, untouched, barely removed from its case. She'd got as far as tuning the instrument once, filling the bow hair with rosin, but when her efforts to produce a sound of any kind – let alone something vaguely tuneful – failed, her enthusiasm waned. And in the absence of a tutor, it became something else she would get round to one day, once the clouds of life's tumult parted for a moment.

She watched Aiden's fingers tap out a rhythm on the side of his thigh, imagining some composition occurring, an artistic breakthrough to be stored in his head until he was home. Was this how the part-time artist worked? Moments snatched from the daily grind, mined for their lyrical potential? Perhaps the music was always playing within him, his songs an undercurrent to all else, eddying in the background as they formed. Again it encouraged analysis of her own life and the absence of any artistic pursuit. She supposed the vegetable plot showed an element of creativity, as did the plans for Highfield itself, though focus on these was now a source of disquiet. There was pleasure to be found in gardening, in the aesthetic betterment of the space around them. And yet none of this quite nourished the creative part of her, which had remained fallow for as long as she could remember.

The boy to the side of them had given up on the bricks now and was smashing a plastic fire engine into his mother's chair leg.

'So, do you always come to the doctor's with your husband?' Aiden said, leaning towards her.

His overfamiliarity, the attempt at humour, could easily have been offensive or irritating, yet it was delivered with enough charm to be neither.

'I was coming to town anyway.'

'It's OK, I'm just kidding.'

She went to speak again, but the receptionist called out his name. He wished her well with the house, said goodbye. The other women in the waiting room looked across as he stood, their gawking barely hidden.

Something in their haughtiness, perhaps together with the scene at the pub, gave her parting words an emphasis. 'Will you be playing again soon, somewhere nearby?'

Thirteen

She took his tea out to the barn. The balminess of autumn gone now, winter's hand held the town, dusk arriving a little earlier each day. She was more prepared this year, knowing how best to heat the house, which rooms retained the day's warmth. They had enough wood to last into January, the farmer giving her a good deal again. It was best left for the following winter, he'd said, to dry out some, but nothing remained of last year's supply. Being damp, it would at least burn more slowly. She'd taken delivery of a half-tank of oil last week, hoping the invoice would arrive after her next payday. This too would see them into the start of the following year, but not much further.

She had collected her husband's prescription on the way home from the surgery, somehow both relieved and disappointed to learn that he'd been given tranquillisers. Her probing into the nature of the consultation was largely resisted.

'At least tell me it was useful,' she'd said, parking the car, taking Richard's hand in hers. His gaze turned outwards, scanning the banking cloud above the valley, looking for a distant fleck that soared beneath the expanse of sky.

Later, she'd made a list of what else could be cut back on. Non-essentials had all but gone now. She'd cancelled the paper, plus the cream and orange juice that were delivered once a week with the milk. She would cut her own and her daughter's hair from now on – Stephen said he'd just grow his rather than risk enduring some terrible spectacle on his head. (Her son's appearance had become of increasing importance to him in recent weeks, since mentioning a girl he liked at school.) Where possible, clothes could be repaired rather than replaced, again Stephen the only one to protest. When they required new garments, the town's jumble sale was a good source, especially if she arrived early. She would use her mother's old sewing machine to make curtains and cushion covers, buying the fabric from the remnant factory shop out on the estate. When there was more time, in the depths of winter, she would learn to knit.

She had already begun using the children's bathwater after them, stopping short at asking them to share it with each other. Richard maintained the barest personal hygiene. Recently his flannel and toothbrush remained dry for days at a time, his clothes, unless she removed them from the bedroom and washed them, worn day after day. Dirt had begun to encrust under his fingernails in swarthy crescents and his untended toenails often scratched her during the night. One morning his sweating had been so pronounced it had soaked across to her side of the bed; on changing the sheets after work, she realised he'd wet himself.

It became increasingly tempting to sleep in the spare room, despite the leaking roof, but for now she was keen to maintain as much normality for the children as possible.

The vegetable garden had continued to provide into autumn and beyond, and she'd learned how to store food for longer, even pickling produce from the greenhouse. But soon all their food would have to be bought again. She remembered Aiden's joke about the boys one day actually catching a fish, half hoping that a meal or two might emerge from this unlikely source.

In many ways she relished the challenge of fashioning free entertainment for them as a family, pastimes harnessed from what was around them, from their imaginations rather than the electronic games that some of the children's friends were rumoured to have. At weekends, Jenny helped her bake, her daughter's face a picture of concentration as she measured out flour and butter and sugar with unnecessary precision, the pastry clagging in her fingers and hair. They made sweets and toffee, jams and jellies. On Saturday afternoons in autumn, the two of them had embarked on epic foraging trips, gathering berries and fungi, collecting feathers and fir cones, exploring deeper and deeper into the woods and hinterland around them. And Stephen, although increasingly reluctant to spend time together as a family, seemed to sense its worth as his father's remoteness intensified, her son accompanying them more and more. They would even run into Richard on occasion, or at least Shane, the dog confused as to which way to go as it ran between them, attempting to corral them together. In one of the top fields there was a horse they'd got to know. Past its prime, underfed, it had a sullen air as it stood solemn and unmoving in the centre of the field. Seeing them, the animal would sometimes make its way over, allowing them to pat it as it scoured its neck against the gatepost. Jenny asked if they could take it home, and they'd hatched mock plans to sneak up in the night and rescue the wretched creature. Instead they took it apples, feeding it at the start of their circuitous walks, until one day it was no longer there.

On a walk back in March, they'd penetrated an overgrown forest of laurel, emerging from its clutches into a snowdrop wood that bordered the river. It had been like stepping into some enchanted ancient place, with fronds of fern specked among the thousands of pendulous white flowers, and she watched the wonder on Jenny's face.

These were the times Mary treasured most, immersed with her daughter, sometimes Stephen too, in their modest wilderness, embarking on great outings, before returning to Highfield to light the fire, gathering around the flagstoned hearth, its glow mollifying. Yet all the while, great forces seemed at work, prising the family apart, isolating them not only from the town but from each other.

Glancing back at the house, she entered the barn, handing Aiden the mug. He cupped his fingers about it and surveyed the stonework around him. She'd got his number from Stephen, who'd asked Brendan for it at school. Once he'd agreed to come and have a look, Mary had made two requests, hiding her embarrassment while telling him it would be understandable if he changed his mind. Firstly, she wondered if he might work on the promise of payment being made the following summer, when some National Savings matured. They could discuss this, he said, but it was possible; the work would go well into next year anyway, and as long as there was money for materials . . . She didn't tell him the savings were her daughter's, an investment both children had been given by Richard's father almost five years ago. Her husband away, Mary had opened the accounts, which Stephen and Jenny were allowed to withdraw from when they reached sixteen. For Stephen this was just a matter of months now, but she would have years to replace her daughter's lump sum. Nothing about it felt good, and yet it was absurd that the money would just sit there in meagre accumulation while their problems worsened. She would repay it all once the business was up and running, nobody any the wiser.

Secondly, she'd whispered into the phone, her husband was unwell but that didn't mean he'd lost all sense of pride. She feared he might be against asking someone to carry out tasks he'd planned to do himself, that it might affect any recovery, his impotence brought into relief. Again she'd expected Aiden to decline, but after a pause he'd agreed to at least come along and have a look. They'd settled on a time, Mary asking him to park in the gateway halfway up the lane and walk the last bit. She would make sure Shane was shut in the house.

He sipped his tea, circling the barn, inspecting its walls, tutting each time something displeased him.

'There's a lot to do. Not just the walls, but the roof and the floor. And you say you want electricity in here? And water?'

She nodded.

'We'll need to dig down, put some drainage in. And the lintels need replacing – I'm surprised that wall's still there. Have you a room plan?'

'I thought I'd wait until you saw it, ask your advice.'

He smiled. If her lack of foresight frustrated him, he managed to hide it. Again he surveyed the barn's interior.

'He'll hear me working. I'd rather he knew what was happening.'

'His pills knock him out at night. He never wakes before midday. You could start early, finish before then.' She saw now that this was the wrong strategy, that she was losing him. 'No, you're right. I'll tell him before you start. He'll be fine, I'm sure.'

Another walk around the barn, more scrutiny. She could see the doubt continue to leaven in him. Trying to keep the desperation from her voice, she said, 'Please, Mr Doherty, I don't know any other way.'

Finally he spoke. 'I wouldn't be able to come often.'

'I was thinking one morning a week. Perhaps you could show me things I could get on with when you're not here.'

His smile was sympathetic rather than patronising. They agreed on an hourly rate, Aiden promising to let her know where this stood every few weeks. She would pay him for materials at the end of each month. Mary held out her hand to shake; after a final glance around the barn, he took it.

She pulled her daughter closer, looking around the kitchen, thinking that it had been months since the four of them had been in the same room together.

'It'll be OK, I promise,' she said.

By now Jenny's sobbing had shifted into tremulous wheezes, Mary's jumper soaked with snot and tears.

'How will it be OK?' said Stephen.

She had no idea, beyond hoping it was a phase to be

passed through, that the dynamics of the thing would right themselves. What else could she do other than speak to the school, demand action be taken? She parted her daughter's matting curls, kissed her forehead, kissed the source of her tormentors' attentions.

'Do you want to tell us what happened?' Jenny shook her head. 'Perhaps later, then.'

Mary continued to dab her daughter's bloodied elbow with cotton wool, her uniform, if not ruined, then in need of much repair. It would be easy to keep her at home for a few days, something she suspected would only amplify the situation. As would driving Jenny to school, although according to Stephen, whatever had occurred didn't take place on the bus.

The graze clean, Mary fixed a plaster to Jenny's arm, promising her she could choose what they ate for dinner tonight. Richard watched from the far side of the room, if not fully engaged with them, then still affected by the scene playing out before him, his daughter's trauma keenly felt on some level.

Fourteen

Winter slipped slowly by, the town sepulchral in its wake. Lives were lived quietly at this time of year, as if in torpor, people's energy conserved where possible. For once the Woodman's had some appeal, and she imagined regulars converging around its fire, sharing tales of the hardship and inconvenience the snow had brought.

Much of the valley lay untouched by the sun in the shortened days, its slopes casting shadows that bled over the land. As with last year, they burned more wood than anticipated, the temptation for one last log each evening always too great, as outside wind breathed frost on to Highfield. Despite the harshness of the landscape, its palette deficient at this time of year, there was still beauty to be found: crisp, glassy afternoons walking out of the valley to the fields that steamed in the low sun, the air knife-sharp; or seeing a lone oak, serene and skeletal mid field, its branch tips like spiny fingers reaching into the dusk sky; or listening to carrion crows squabble among themselves, their voices reverberating across the pastures as if it was the only sound in the world.

To her surprise, the occasional wild food had still offered

itself into December: velvet shank and oyster mushrooms, honey fungus and chickweed. She'd finally succumbed to shopping at the large store once a week now, telling herself she'd support the smaller shops in the town when they could afford to again, although it had angered her that none of them was prepared to give her credit on account.

They would grow more of their own food this year. She would learn about cultivation and storage, the combinations that worked best. The vegetable garden would be expanded in spring, new crops trialled. Meanwhile, the wind that barely ceased up here had given her the idea of somehow producing energy from its squalls, a miniature windmill perhaps, connected to some sort of battery. She would ask Aiden about this.

Their arrangement had worked well so far, with only the coldest weeks making it impossible to work in the barn. The thaw had come as a relief, as much for having his company once a week as seeing progress resume.

'Your husband's OK with this?' he'd said that first morning, and she'd hoped the lie didn't show on her face.

Having dwelt for months on all that bore down on her, she tried now to focus on what had been achieved, what had not yet been lost. Simple delights that endured. The crunch of her boots in the snow as the sound echoed from tree to tree. Or sitting around the fire with her daughter.

But it was as if the stasis of the season had permeated Richard too, his condition neither improving nor worsening, the pills sustaining a steady lethargy in him as he existed among them like an elderly relative might. There'd been a return to the doctor, an increase of his medication, but nothing else as far as she could tell. Still there had been no contact from the army enquiring as to his welfare. Sergeant Taylor had phoned before the parade, hopeful that Richard would be attending. Thinking the event might prove a catalyst to recovery, she had pleaded with him to go.

'Don't you want to see everyone again?'

'Why would I?'

In the end she'd raised her voice. 'You have to try something, for God's sake.'

But she had given up any form of confrontation now, as if part of him, the man she'd known before the war, had receded beyond reach. Attempts to argue, to provoke a reaction, got no further than a monologue; she was unsure he even heard her words at times. The nightmares, at least, seemed to have tapered off, the chemical dulling of his emotions allowing her some sleep too.

Several times in January the water pipes had frozen overnight and she'd spent an hour with Stephen in the biting wind, armed with jugs of boiling water, trying to locate the blockage, hopeful that nothing had burst. Where the pipes were most exposed they'd insulated them with old towels and a plastic sheet she cut up. Realising some of their heat was escaping up the unused fireplace in the back room, she wedged several pillows up the chimney. In the bedrooms, ice had formed on the inside of the windows, breath from their dreams appearing on the glass in the morning as filigree whorls. Stephen and Jenny rarely complained, the struggle against the cold regarded in terms of its challenge, to be defeated by cunning and the judicious placement of hot-water bottles and extra blankets. Yet watching them contend with the adversity of the last six months, their father unravelling before them, made her heart ache.

She grew stronger as a result of the work, the chopping of logs, helping Aiden on Wednesday mornings. To her relief, he parked the other side of the barn for convenience.

Progress had been slow in the early stages – the accommodation unlikely to be ready this summer – but she'd begun to enjoy his company as they worked together, chatting about music they liked, the vast changes that were occurring in the world. She caught herself laughing at his often cruel humour, jokes at the expense of the town's characters or just anecdotes from his time growing up in Dublin. Later she found some batteries for her old radio and took it out to him, but he preferred to hum his own tunes.

Once the children had left for school, she would take him his tea, watching as he prepared the lime mortar, making good where the stonework was weak. The roof secured, he'd excavated the floor before filling it with hardcore, followed by some insulation and a layer of concrete. When she helped, he never patronised her, regardless of what she could or couldn't do, often taking time to explain the detail behind his work, tricks of the trade his father had taught him as an apprentice in the business back home.

He spoke of his family, how he'd worried about bringing Brendan up over here, but the boy had soon settled in, endearing himself with some of his father's charm perhaps. She thought about this as a tactic, how Aiden had tried to deflect the anger at the Woodman's by playing on, entertaining the hostile crowd, as if his kind could be only terrorist or jester, tolerated as long as he assimilated. She wondered what his views were on nationalism, whether his devotion to music was the whole story, or if the indifference to the politics of his land merely made for an easier life here. She tried to ignore her fear that Richard and Aiden might meet, the foolishness in gambling on her husband's inertia preventing this. Not that Richard had ever expressed the same mindless prejudice as those in the pub. But he was, had been, a soldier in the British Army, one who'd fought in a war, perhaps witnessed friends die, friends who'd lost fellow soldiers across the Irish Sea, albeit in the north.

She thought of other shifts occurring within her as their new life took shape beneath the constant threat of failure. Half a lifetime of conformity, of supporting someone who defended the status quo, who was part of the establishment, had now lost its cogency. And not merely in how they themselves lived; a sense had grown in her of all the violence in the world, how it repeated, went barely challenged. For as long as she could remember they'd lived with the insidious threat of nuclear war, this quiet menace that, although not dwelt upon unduly, lurked at the edges of her generation's mind. Should tensions between superpowers escalate, they were reliant on a mutual fear of annihilation preventing someone from initiating the sequence to destruction. All of history, all of what was to come, removed in a moment's insanity by men whose own ego and pride ensnared them. Perhaps there was false security in being so far from the major cities, with proximity preferable, your demise instant rather than protracted.

She'd read about a group of women who'd set up a peace camp at an RAF base in the south of England, in protest at the American cruise missiles sited there. There were thousands of them, forming a human chain around its perimeter fence, their number growing by the day, returning each time they were evicted. Mary was surprised how much the report had affected her, for the first time in her life feeling the sense of collective outrage and triumph despite not being part of it. She'd told no one, for who was there to share it with beyond her children? Or perhaps Aiden? It was her secret, a rebellious part of her that allowed her to remain sane, the wife of a soldier who wanted to protest for peace. She imagined the disgust of those in the town, of Richard's parents. Yet wasn't her case a more poignant one given what her husband had become? War had an even greater absurdity to it now that it wasn't some abstract concept, now that it had touched her own life. Men (although it had been a woman this time) sending other men to die, for land, for empire. Why shouldn't she join the women at the camp if they remained there?

But it was her job too that had prompted a yearning for something else. Caring for those who couldn't look after themselves – who navigated their final years with dignity and often grace, but also with an acceptance that their time here was nearing an end – had finally stirred into life some unrealised part of her.

Fifteen

Wiping away the condensation from the bathroom mirror, she studied the detail of her face, wondering if beyond its lassitude others saw a residual beauty. It had been a lifetime since she'd last dwelt in any sustained way on her appearance, given care to the adornment this precisely. She had shown Jenny how to apply foundation when they were looking at concealers last term, but otherwise, perhaps with the exception of her husband returning for leave, she hardly glanced at herself from one day to the next. Faint lines ran like tributaries out from the corners of her eyes, her cheeks now defined by creases rather than the smooth curvature of the face's structure. Her lips, once full and pliant, had become thinner, taut as if pursed, and depending on the light, the semblance of a moustache could sometimes be seen, a dozen or so tiny hairs that had turned sable over the years. She wondered whether people noticed them, whether, unlike her mother, she might finally do something to remove them. Certainly the past year or two, since they'd lived here, since Richard had returned, had plundered any last youth from her, and yet today her eyes gave off a forgotten vitality.

She tied her hair back, leaving a few strands to fall across her cheeks, before allowing a hint of perfume to settle on her neck. In the bedroom, she put on the old clothes that had become her uniform on such mornings, the milder days with the onset of spring allowing for fewer layers. She wondered whether he was here yet, picturing him high on the ladder or attending to the door frame they'd started last week. It was a curious contrast, the force his hands applied to the more arduous aspects of the work, and the delicacy with which his fingers had traversed the neck of the guitar that evening. At no time did he seem concerned that an injury might be sustained, one that would curtail his playing. Or perhaps there was little choice, his living earned in this way. She thought she might ask today if he knew anyone who could give her violin lessons, indicating that she might take it up at last. It felt like a risk, that it might be seen through, but the momentum of the thing seemed beyond her now, her behaviour no longer compelled by something she recognised. They'd touched a few times, the skin of his hand brushing hers as she passed him some tool or material. And when he took his tea, their fingers sometimes made contact, though she conceded that this was likely accidental, that she was overplaying it. Last week she'd caught herself staring at the back of him as he fitted a support bracket under one of the beams. At any moment he could have turned round, asked for something, seen her standing there entranced, lost to ridiculous thoughts. She never asked about his marriage, though he would often speak of it, especially on his return from the Christmas break, during which they'd apparently rowed the whole time and he'd slept several nights in the spare room.

Christmas at Highfield had been less difficult than Mary

had imagined, Richard joining them for the opening of a few small presents before lingering silently on the fringes of the day. He'd even helped prepare some of the dinner, the kitchen filled with the sound of an old cassette of carols she'd found, glimpses of Christmases gone by playing out. During the week before, she and Jenny had made decorations, to go with the few they already had – painting fir cones silver, assembling paper chains – while Stephen helped her put up the huge tree the farmer had given them. They collected holly from the woods, tied ribbon around clusters of cinnamon sticks. For a few days it seemed she might be witnessing the healing of her husband's ailment, a gradual exorcism of whatever gripped him. But by the second week of January he'd sunk further into the gloaming of his mind, so that even the sight of him became a rarity. Often the only way they were aware of his presence was the creak of a floorboard above them as he scuttled between rooms, or the back door closing in his wake. The medication, while still rendering him soporific in the mornings, was failing to curb the more eccentric performances that had become commonplace. Although he never answered the phone, she could sense him at the top of the stairs listening to the conversations she or the children had. His mother rang once a week, happy to exchange small talk with Mary, any reference to her son's disintegration resisted like a child with its fingers in its ears, refusing to acknowledge the words, replying with a banal non sequitur. Meanwhile her own parents simply failed to appreciate the severity of the situation, managing only unconvincing reassurances that things would improve.

Richard was spending more and more time in the spare room now, taking what meals he ate in there, reading the same bird book over and over. She sometimes stood by the door, listening hard, the only sound the rhythmic dripping of rain into containers. If she knocked, asked him whether the dog needed letting out, the silence remained unbroken, or on occasion the door would open enough for Shane to be shoved out and then closed again, the animal snarling at her when she tried to walk it.

Parting the curtains a little, Mary looked out across the yard, trying to see if there were any signs of life in the barn yet. She checked her hair again, hoping that the few filaments of grey were indiscernible. Beside her, the covers of the bed rippled as her husband turned over, Shane's head lifting at the prospect of activity before lowering again.

Outside, the day shimmered with the manifestation of spring, Highfield blushed in the morning sun, the swelling chorus of a blackbird announcing the shift in season. In the coming days blackthorn would begin to blossom, stitchwort and red campion colouring the hedgerows. Celandine would burst through in the meadow down by the river, the first cuckoo heard on a walk if she was lucky. The garden demanded more of her now, and she was happy to spend long hours in the vegetable plots and potting shed before getting ready for work.

Last night she had cleaned the violin. She told herself it should be sold, that it served no purpose to keep things with little sentimental or practical value in such times. There was a shop in town Aiden had told her about who would give her a fair price, especially if she mentioned his name. It had been a way to raise the subject with him, that she possessed such a thing and had once harboured musical ambition. She had hoped he might ask her to elaborate, perhaps even encourage the instrument's resurrection, but he'd merely gone along with her strategy for its disposal. Removing the violin from its leather case, she had placed it beneath her chin, drawing the bow slowly across its strings in a discordant gesture. More than ever, even than when she'd been given it as a teenager, she longed to produce a series of notes, rich and soothing, a melody that filled the space around her with an edifying flourish. She thought about tuning it, though even how to do this much had been forgotten. Wiping the instrument down with a cloth, she had replaced it in the case, returning it to the cupboard beneath the stairs.

The children's breakfast things cleared, she thought about her daughter, hoping that Jenny was thwarting the worst of the bullying. Friends from primary school had apparently rallied around her, but the transition to the comprehensive several miles away had gone badly. Mary could still recall the cruelty of children from her own school days, how momentum could build against the weak, those who differed, until the bullying became ingrained, part of each day. Jenny had been stoical in the first few weeks, the name-calling attributed to one or two unpleasant children, Mary assuring her they would soon tire of it. Teachers acknowledged that she had come in for her fair share of teasing, but assumed it would settle down as new friendships formed, her appearance eventually regarded as unexceptional. It was also clear, in the absence of specific complaints against another pupil, that they were powerless to tackle it, fearful that vague intervention would only make things worse for Jenny. Although there'd been no repeat of her coming home bleeding, Mary had noticed small shifts in her daughter's behaviour and mood. Her posture was of some crestfallen creature, her shoulders slumped, her head bowed much of the time. Her voice had thinned to an apologetic whisper and she'd taken to following Mary around in the evenings, wrapping herself around her mother as she had done as a toddler. Nothing of substance could be extracted from her, other than that a gang had homed in on her, deciding to make her life miserable for now. Mary spoke with little optimism to Richard about it, and despite his silence on the matter, some aspect of their daughter's turmoil permeated him, his eyes emerging briefly from indifference into quiet rage. Next week she would make another appointment, this time with the headmaster, insisting that more was done.

As she made some tea to take out to the barn, Mary noticed her daughter's school shoes beneath the kitchen table, likely kicked off at dinner last night. She wondered what Jenny had worn instead, whether she'd get into trouble.

Sunlight slanted across the interior of the barn in vaporous shafts, dust eddying through them. Aiden was planing one of the uprights for the door frame, whistling a familiar tune as he scrutinised the wood. She put their tea down, watched as peels of pine spiralled to the floor around him, his forearms shifting back and forth like calibrated pistons. Hair curled out from under his woollen hat, the golden tones muted until sunlight picked them out, bringing them to life. There was a simplicity found here, a realm untouched by the onerous reality beyond these walls. The day would begin with a plan of what he hoped to achieve, what she could do around him. Sometimes she'd head into town to pick up materials he'd forgotten or had not anticipated needing, resentful of the time away. In recent weeks she'd taken to baking a cake on Tuesday mornings, slices of which accompanied their second cup of tea. They'd work side by side, sometimes chatting, other times in a comfortable silence. Around midday, they'd survey the progress or lack of it, before he'd pack up the tools and she'd get ready for work, counting down the days until the following week.

He took some sandpaper and began to smooth the timber. Blowing away the sawdust, he felt along the edge of the wood with his fingers, satisfied with its shape and texture. She gave a little cough to announce herself and he looked at his watch before giving a mock tut.

'I was going to dock your wages if you were any later,' he said.

She smiled and walked over to inspect the frame. She wanted to make a joke in return, something about him cutting the wood the wrong size or how there had been a change in the room plan, that he would have to start all over again, but the words wouldn't form in time.

Again the smell of him found her, some combination of sweat, woodsmoke and aftershave, subtle yet intoxicating. Last night she'd imagined being in here, laying her face against his chest and breathing in his scent, getting lost in its glorious bouquet. In this scene, his fingers, the ones she'd watched dancing on the guitar, had combed her hair before navigating to the small of her back, where he'd lifted her dress, placing his palm against her skin, pulling her in. Moving her head back, he'd kissed her greedily, sunlight warming their bodies as they undressed.

It both shocked and thrilled her, this new-found capacity for fantasy that had waited until her late thirties to emerge. When she'd met her husband at the end of her teens, there was as much fear as anything else when they first made love, a panic that she would do the wrong thing or not be good enough. Pleasure was found not in her own bodily delight, but in the performance she'd given, knowing that were she desirable, he would likely remain keen. In that time a crush manifested entirely in her head, still as obsessive thoughts, but ones with little corporeal relevance. Now her body pulsed with a new longing, and at night, when she was certain that her husband's pills were deep in his veins, she would touch herself to some version of the scene in the barn.

There had been guilt initially, the thoughts unsolicited, but this faded with each day her husband looked at her with empty or contemptuous eyes, his inertia mitigation for an imagined infidelity, if nothing else. Resentment, too, played a part. She was now not only the main breadwinner, but responsible for all the family's needs, be they physical or emotional. Stephen had his O levels fast approaching, a career to think about. Her daughter's problems at school were hers alone to tackle. And hanging above all this, the threatening debt, the life she'd imagined for them more preposterous by the day.

All this burden needed an outlet, the playing-out of a

fantastical encounter at least enough for now. There was no serious consideration of a life apart from her husband, not in any real sense, for how would such a thing occur, the man as good as an invalid in her care?

They worked side by side for the next couple of hours, Aiden making small adjustments to the door frame, while she passed him tools, held the wood in place as he fixed it to the stone. There was no sense that he harboured similar thoughts, the jocular behaviour she'd seen as flirtatious probably reserved for everyone. And yet what could you really know of the thoughts that passed behind a person's eyes?

He was talking about Dublin again. Of its medieval streets, narrow and cobbled, of writing songs as a teenager on the banks of the Liffey, lights shimmering beneath the arches. Of the smoky bars he'd sat in with friends. She wondered how else this could be prolonged, once the work was finished; whether the larger barn might be tackled if their finances improved. She had considered going to see him play once he'd spoken of an upcoming venue, but she would look ridiculous sitting there on her own like some ageing groupie. And if she sought him out afterwards, hung around as he packed up his gear, gossip would rise like sap until it reached the whole town.

She thought about his wife, wondering what she looked like, how old she was. She pictured a plain woman, a little frumpy perhaps, her formerly desirable figure plundered. She'd asked Stephen about her once, careful to sound indifferent, but her son was at an age where all adults blended into one, their appearance of little consequence to him. It pleased her that he'd started a romantic involvement of his own, a girl at school he'd brought to Highfield a couple of times, Stephen briefly introducing her as they scuttled up to his room.

A little after noon, they finished for the day. She helped him clear his tools away, hopeful that some small sign of reciprocation would occur if their eyes met. Again the banter, the teasing, and she laughed more than she meant to, as a girl nervous on a first date might. She picked up the spirit level and performed a few mock stabs into his belly, insisting he surrender.

For a moment she thought the smile falling from his face was emblematic of a gathering feeling on his part, the intensity a culmination of the months spent in here together, his own feelings finally beyond denial. She looked hard at him, eventually following his stare to the door in the far wall, where Richard stood watching them, the dog by his side.

Part Three

Summer 1982

Sixteen

He could see the dog now, sitting obediently by her side on the platform. Something in the animal's ignorance – both of his return and of all he'd seen – lifted his spirits for the first time in ages, and he longed for its undemanding company. He had phoned Mary from the barracks last night, their exchange, to his relief, absent of emotion. Did he want her to drive up and collect him? There was no need, he'd said, the station was fine. It was agreed that Jenny and Stephen should go to school, leaving Highfield quiet for a few hours on his return. They would break up for the summer holidays soon, she reminded him, a chance to spend some time together as a family, perhaps a trip to the coast.

'Are you all right?' she'd said finally.

There would be much for him to do to the house over the summer. He tried to picture its rooms, this place that became their home last year, the images grainy, as if he'd been away longer than a few months. There was the main gate that had to be lifted to open it, the front door that became stuck in winter, the large hallway that had smelled so richly of shoe polish and pipe tobacco when they moved in. But beyond this, much of the detail inside took effort to recall, his mind somehow confusing it with their old home in the town. He remembered the steep path that led up into the woods behind the house, how last winter they'd negotiated it in the snow, laughing as each of them slid into one another, their arms linked like tethered mountaineers. And at the top, how his daughter had thrown snowballs at Shane, the animal confused as they powdered to nothing in its mouth. It felt important to heighten these scenes, to etch them deeply enough into the strata of his memory so that time could not overlay them. And yet already the mechanism allowing this seemed defective, the procedure beyond him.

The train eased to a standstill, the squeal of its brakes seeming more strident each time since leaving the barracks. He let the family opposite get up first, the boy who'd stared at him for much of the journey unable to resist a final gawp and, on reaching the doors, a quick protrusion of his tongue. The carriage empty, he realised that Mary was standing beyond the window, her face fixed between curiosity and apprehension as she peered in, perhaps thinking he wasn't on board. Leaning forward to reveal himself, he caught his reflection in the dirt-encrusted glass, his beard more profuse than he'd thought, and for a moment his face appeared as if it resided on his wife's head, the image both faintly comic and grotesque. Adjusting slightly so that they could see each other clearly, he looked at her as someone might a stranger, observing a smile of sorts forming on her face. Then he reached for his luggage and made his way along the aisle, civvy street a few steps away.

* * *

They should only have had him for another few days. The end of an unremarkable career, his heart never really in the job, built as he probably was for something else. And yet this new life that beckoned, that he could almost touch, had been postponed – by a few days, a few months, no one knew. As they loaded up buses for the long journey to the ports of the south, he'd consoled himself with the knowledge that giving his notice in a week earlier would have made no difference. They'd still have called him back, as they had those on leave, the rules changing in such times. It was in the small print: they owned you.

When they'd amassed their equipment, much of it proved to be faulty and had to be replaced, but still it had taken less than two days to prepare the entire battery, something they'd trained for without ever thinking it would be necessary. There had been time for a quick call home, a queue of men delivering unwelcome news to loved ones, the mood with a volition of its own. Answering the phone, his wife had sounded distant, quietly anxious, the radio already carrying news of the events that were unfolding. He thought she might point out that he'd done his final year, make some plea for him to refuse to go – to take whatever punishment this resulted in – but she'd sounded resigned to the matter. He told her it would likely come to nothing, that some small posturing would see it called off, a climbdown, diplomacy triumphant.

She had called the children to the phone. Stephen was rushing out to meet a friend down by the river, his frustration at being held up barely hidden. It was always hard to know what to say to his son these days, the passage through adolescence making their conversations tentative. There'd been a time when the two of them spent whole days together, before the move to Highfield, assembling models of the great ships at weekends, building a miniature steam engine in the garage, his return on leave still a source of jubilation. In those days Stephen tried his best to remain aloof with him for an hour or two, at both the start and end of Richard's time at home, as if withholding some aspect of himself, perhaps a mixture of distress and resentment that he was unable to express in any other way. It was as if his son had to forgive him each time for the betrayal of leaving them all. But it quickly dispersed, a contrived sulk breaking into reluctant laughter as they play-fought, Richard tickling the boy until his resolve fell away. In a couple of years he hoped to teach his son to drive in the Morris.

By contrast, his daughter still erupted with joy when he arrived home, her tearful episodes as he packed to leave upsetting. For all the attachments he and his wife had with their children based on shared gender, a deep bond had emerged between himself and Jenny. Away on exercise, he'd missed Stephen's birth, and so his daughter's arrival had drawn from him an emotional intensity the like of which he'd not known. From the moment the midwife handed Jenny to him, her bloodied head resting on his chest, through those first few days with her at home, he would watch for hours this miraculous and delicate thing Mary had given them, terrified that her breathing might cease, her heart stop. As if to confirm her exception, the side of his daughter's face was adorned with a brilliant maroon smudge.

Jenny had snivelled on the phone as he told her he

wasn't going to be home this weekend after all, that work, the people who told him what to do, meant he had to stay away for longer.

'When *will* you be home?' she'd asked, her voice fracturing.

'I don't know, darling. Soon.'

Then Mary had come back on the phone and told him not to take any risks, that she loved him.

'Look after Shane,' he'd said.

As the bus had pulled out of the barracks, heading for the docks in Plymouth, the thing that struck him most was how nobody had heard of the place. A group of islands on the other side of the world that apparently were British – some far-flung colonial outpost, he assumed – had been invaded and it was their task to take them back. All the training, the preparation: few had believed it would be needed beyond the streets of Belfast.

Their role was one of air defence, his unit of the Royal Artillery charged with protecting the task force from enemy attacks from the sky. Rapier missiles were fired from a static surface-to-air launcher that they took turns manning. Once there, the unit would be airlifted to land, where they'd dig in and set up, camouflaging themselves as best they could. A potential target would be picked up on the system's radar, the tracker head and missiles swivelling automatically. Once it was close enough, they would locate it in the optical sights, keeping it in the cross hairs. When the target was in range and had been confirmed by the system as belonging to the enemy, the order to fire would come. The missile, once in the air, could then be steered towards the plane using a joystick, although the absence of a proximity fuse meant it had to hit its target in order to destroy it. It was a complex, temperamental piece of equipment, prone to developing faults, but its manoeuvrability and fast reaction time had given it a formidable reputation.

There were seven of them to a system, each unit containing a sergeant, a bombardier, a lance-bombardier such as himself, and four gunners. Known as long-range snipers, in theory they would see little in the way of hand-to-hand combat, though they were trained for this if attacked. Their sergeant, Taylor, was a fair man, a soldier's soldier, who had earned most people's respect. He knew of Richard's difficulties, his reasons for transferring to the RA, and had taken him to one side during his first week with the unit. Assurances were given: that he didn't tolerate bullying, that Richard would be starting again afresh. The others in the unit were cooler with him at first, keeping their distance, getting on with the job, but despite the fact that he was due to leave that week, he felt they regarded him with some fondness.

None of them had had much practice at live-firing the Rapier, the cost of missiles meaning it occurred annually, usually in the Outer Hebrides. A couple of the gunners in his unit were still youngsters, a year or two out of basic training, keen to get stuck in, their enthusiasm thus far undiminished by active service, a stint in Dortmund their only taste of army life. He tried to recall the early part of his own career. Leaving school without the first clue as to who he was, what he might do, despite his father's own military service. Friends had moved on to apprenticeships, one or two to college, or into the family business. But despite loathing his father's insistence that the forces would be the making of him, he found himself enlisting after a visit to the army careers office.

The fact that he'd always had high levels of fitness served him well, and he kept his head down, did as he was told. He enjoyed the physical challenge, exercises that pushed you to your limit, showed that you could do more than you thought. But the endless drills and inspections, the inane menial tasks, the punishment beastings and blind obedience wore him down in those first years. Twice he had to be persuaded by a sympathetic major not to leave; on both occasions it was suggested he give it another twelve months, that everyone found it difficult initially.

Then came marriage, fatherhood early in his twenties. Army life got a little easier, though by then he'd achieved a reputation as something of a loner, a man who did his job but who was unlike the others. He accepted that this was deserved: a preference for his own company in the evenings, the books he read, the interest he took in wildlife and birds on exercises all understandably alienating him.

But whereas in those early days most around him grew to accept his strangeness, perhaps referencing it only in banter, one private took exception to it, never failing to express his antipathy. Initially this took the form of a general coldness towards him, an exclusion during conversations, a contemptuous glare that lingered a second or two. Later, though, while others joked about Richard's unsuitability as a soldier, this man would go beyond the wearisome teasing, always having a final sentence that was both condemning and vitriolic. For him, perceived weakness in any of them reflected badly on the unit, tarnishing it in the eyes of others. There

179

was no place for difference: you pulled in the same direction, held the same beliefs. Assimilation and homogeneity. Mavericks, eccentrics, individuals harmed the cause, which was to think and act as one. The army was a mechanism that operated through its harmony, its cogs in perfect synchronicity. It was true what they said about it: how you were stripped down, broken almost, then rebuilt in its mould. It was the only way such institutions could function successfully.

All of this Richard understood. And he had conformed where possible, trying to fit in, laughing at the same things; there was nothing to be gained from life on the periphery. But the best he could manage was to perform his duties with neither excellence nor incompetence, and withdraw into himself when his time was his own. It was this disinclination to give every part of himself, the social as well as the professional, that particularly affronted some. Diversity was a source of suspicion, the rationale being that you were training to reach a point where you trusted those around you with your life. The decisions you took – if one day they were made in the theatre of war and not on some Welsh hillside – could determine the fate of others. And so men needed to know how you worked, the machinations of your mind and whether it would be both consistent and reliable. Doubt was the enemy. When a soldier behaved not from instinct and instruction, but began harbouring misgivings, thoughts that could lead to hesitation, he became a liability, a threat to the mission. More so than those you were fighting. This, too, Richard accepted. At least in theory, because he could do the job, he could execute the skills taught him. But somehow he remained an outsider, access to the fraternal realms of army life beyond him. And this made him, to one soldier in particular, a source of revulsion.

Alone with this man on exercise, Richard had tried to make conversation, hopeful that the hostility would expend itself eventually, an acceptance making both their lives more tolerable. But it proved to be another misjudgement, the clash that followed seeing Richard's head forced back against the trunk of a tree, the man's face pushed into his own, telling him to fuck off, that this life wasn't for him.

Following the incident, his thoughts had turned again to his daughter and the birthmark that would ensure her own feeling of otherness. With her for life, this purple stain splayed across one quarter of her face would darken with age, finally resembling more the colour of port wine, as the mark was often termed. There was nothing hereditary to it, no rogue gene that had skipped a few generations; she was just unlucky. Friends became used to it, but each time life ushered in a new era for her – starting school, joining a club – they worried how she'd cope with the reactions. He knew it was impossible for people not to stare initially, and over the years Jenny had become used to this, often putting them at ease with some witty acknowledgement, or even getting her retort in first, before any scrutiny occurred. She deflected people's own embarrassment by immediately drawing attention to her face, allowing them to move on. But starting secondary school later this year would probably yield fresh challenges for her, new audiences to overcome, some whose resistance would endure regardless.

As the bus travelled south at the start of April, there had been Union Jacks everywhere, unfurled from windows, draped across road signs. Motorists sounded their horns as they passed. People stopped what they were doing and waved excitedly. A woman lifted her sweater and pressed her breasts against the passenger window, the men in the car cheering. It had felt strange to be regarded as heroic without having done anything. Still, the consensus had been that they would be heading back north in a day or two, his new life only briefly stalled.

They spent that night in a couple of the city's pubs, where locals queued up to buy them drinks, to slap their backs. A young woman staggered from her group of friends and kissed everyone in Richard's unit, a suggestive wink perhaps intended to sustain them. Songs were bellowed out, then chants for the local football team that they were encouraged to join in with. Armchair warriors tagged along, the rhetoric now bellicose, of how they'd love to come too and help annihilate the enemy if only circumstance allowed. There seemed a general confusion as to who this enemy might be, the abuse aimed at South Americans in general.

Later, when he could bear it no longer, he told Taylor he was heading back to the barracks, but instead walked up to the Hoe, where he sat and smoked, watching the lights shimmer in the Sound, the occasional gull gliding by.

Seeing him on the platform, the dog was unsure at first, sensing that the man approaching them was of significance, yet unable to recognise Richard. Finally something shifted in the animal's brain and it lunged forward, Mary barely able to keep hold of the lead, and the three of them met as the train began to pull away. Once Shane had calmed a little, his wife held him properly, the sensation not unwelcome, yet not as he'd imagined it either. He offered to drive back but she ignored him, instead conveying how much they'd all missed him.

As the road narrowed into country lanes, he relaxed a little, Mary's voice soothing him as he focused on its timbre if not her words. He watched a distant bird drift high above them, before losing it to the glare of the midday sun. Finally, as they settled into silence, the perfumes of an English summer filled the car, and for a moment he thought he might fall asleep for the first time in days.

Seventeen

Something about the noise made him want to join the dog beneath the table. It was inconsequential in comparison to the thunder of war, yet the music from the jukebox, laced with the chatter around him, thrummed inside his head like a series of explosions. It had been harder to get drunk lately; the steady line of pints now accumulating in front of him barely registered as he quaffed them in good time, each one sobering him further. Whenever there were more empty glasses than full, another drink was placed down, as if he was the final component in a production line.

He supposed the children were next door, Mary flitting between the rooms, ignoring requests from the men at the bar to dance. Earlier they'd come home from school, Stephen a little wary on seeing him, his sister alternating between elation and tears as she flung her arms around him, telling him he mustn't go away again. After holding back for a moment or two, his son joined them, their three-way embrace ungainly but intense.

He didn't have to attend tonight, his wife had told him, saying that it was nothing to do with her, the gathering organised by some well-meaning busybodies, Richard being the only soldier to honour the town in the recent conflict. She could phone the pub, tell them he wasn't up to it, feign injury or illness. In the end it had seemed less fuss to walk down there for an hour or two, and so, after some steak for dinner, they had set off across the field.

Standing to go to the toilet, he saw Mary and the children in the other bar, his wife talking to someone tuning a guitar. It upset him how she couldn't see men flirting with her, or if she did, how she was able to dismiss it as harmless fun, ignorant of their true agenda. How had she repelled it in the months of his absence, when the temptation to reciprocate was at its greatest?

Watching his piss flow slowly along the base of the urinal, he fought hard to dull the clarity of the images gathering in his mind.

The ship loaded, they had slipped away at dusk, a low-key departure with a handful of dock workers looking on in the murk. There were accounts of other boats leaving with grandiose send-offs, thousands of locals lining the quayside, waving and shouting. The Paras left on the luxury liner the *Canberra*; others, such as the Scots Guards, sailed on the *QE2*. In contrast, Richard's unit were heading to the other side of the world on the civilian-manned *Sir Geraint*, a rusting hulk that resupplied warships at sea or transported army units and their equipment. Conditions were cramped, with more than five hundred men plus all their stores on board and little space for personal items beyond the essentials. What privacy there was could only be achieved by hanging a towel from the top of your bunk, cocooning yourself in a coffin-sized recess. But morale seemed high for the most part, many of the men excited by the prospect of something other than endless drills and exercises, as if they were firefighters en route to their first real blaze.

The tedium of life at sea soon made itself known, a routine that varied little. You queued to wash and shave. You cleaned the mess deck before the captain's inspection. There was some commando-led training on how to cope with the cold, what to do in the event of hypothermia. Briefings were given on the kind of terrain they would have to negotiate. Someone taught Morse code; in return, Richard went through the basics of aircraft recognition. The Rapier system should have made this superfluous, designed as it was to identify potential targets as friendly or otherwise using coded radio signals. But the potential for mistakes still existed, so visual recognition was a necessary back-up.

Within a couple of days he began to feel an intense loneliness, more than the normal feelings of being away from home, the injustice of his presence keenly felt. Others seemed to find a sense of freedom seeing water for mile upon mile in all directions, but he found the vastness, the absence of anything save an occasional seabird in the distance, disorientating. Even then many thought it only a matter of time before the whole thing was called off, the ship turned around. But the further they sailed, the more unlikely this seemed.

He thought of home a lot in those early days, their new life on hold. Picturing Highfield the day they'd first looked at the house, he remembered wandering around it, the four of them, realising the work that was needed, his wife's vision at odds with what stood before them. They'd gone away and worked out the finances, which didn't add up, even if the bank lent them a large amount.

He'd have been happy to stay where they were, their life uncomplicated, without risk. But Mary pushed and pushed, tweaking the numbers until the shortfall appeared manageable, her enthusiasm gaining an air of obsession. She used the children's excitement to win him around, a three-way campaign launched each time he returned home, until finally he yielded. It was easy to feel overwhelmed by it all, the scale of things clearly beyond two people. He hoped Stephen could help out in the school holidays, Jenny too in a few years if necessary. For now, though, according to his wife, they would concentrate on producing as much of their own food as possible. They would throw away less, recycle what could be used again. An adventure, Mary kept calling it.

He wondered what work he might do. There'd been an interview lined up, with an engineering firm based out of town; perhaps they'd keep the job open until he returned. There were other skills, gleaned from almost two decades' service, knowledge gained that somehow didn't lend itself to an obvious career but which surely had its demand. He just knew he could no longer do this, the aggression, the deference. And yet here he was, on a boat, heading to the South Atlantic, to fight for somewhere nobody knew about.

He'd heard of those who left the military, who couldn't cope on the outside; much like prisoners, he supposed, who needed the routine of an institution, their choices made for them. To them the real world loomed like some vast realm with endless possibilities, where rules were complex and ambiguous. Where life had once been predictable, it suddenly brimmed with doubt and uncertainty. Men often signed back up within months of leaving, this world the only one they could endure. Perhaps the order and discipline ensnared you so that deviation eventually became impossible.

Once they hit the Bay of Biscay, the weather worsened. Waves rose in giant swells now, the ship rising and falling in a slow and endless bucking motion, its decks heaving with each lurch. He pictured his father, a proud and obdurate Royal Navy man, laughing at his landlubber son, green with nausea, already homesick. There were injections given for the vomiting, but they had little effect, and it felt as if he would turn himself inside out. Given the choice, he'd have curled up in his bunk, closed his eyes, but they just had to get on with it.

The first real inkling many of them had of it being more than just an extended exercise was when Taylor handed out wills to those who hadn't made them. You could see it in men's eyes, a focusing of the mind, a small sense of what was now happening.

As they neared the equator and the weather turned warmer, the ship had succumbed to the permanent stench of sweat, what fresh water they could carry rationed to allow minimal washing but little else. A few lads were badly sunburnt, their punishment the docking of several days' pay. Those who'd burned their backs were made to leapfrog each other again and again, the spectacle both comic and pitiable.

Evenings were spent mostly in the canteen, drinking their ration of beer, playing cards, smoking. A few of them had radios and kept in touch with news back home, though this was discouraged for fear of homesickness. Others watched the porn that was shown, something Richard was neither drawn to nor repulsed by, his indifference further evidence to them of his estrangement.

'Hey, Briggs, come and watch this. Make you a real man.'

Occasional fights broke out between units, the boredom, the claustrophobia causing tempers to flare from nothing, as they might among dogs cooped up in a kennel. They were told that a couple of drunken commandos had argued with a sergeant major, throwing him overboard. Arrested and charged with mutiny, they'd been flown home to a military jail.

As they headed ever southward, the atmosphere on board shifted. Their training was upped, with endless exercises, running around on deck in the blistering sun, mile after mile, the perpetual stamping of boots an ambient pulse, as if the ship itself were alive. Everywhere he looked, there was nothing but horizon, the sea spilling away over the earth's edge, and he thought how they could be the last people on the planet. At night he would gaze upwards, trying to discern some of the great constellations strewn across the sky, the stars' ancient light seeming to possess some great sorrow.

Weapons skills and first aid were practised, more sessions given on aircraft recognition. They were reminded of the rules of the Geneva Convention, how they should treat prisoners, how they in turn should behave upon capture. Personal items – letters, photos of loved ones, anything that could be used against them – were to be left behind, though most, Richard included, would ignore this. The realisation that war now loomed, that this wasn't some elaborate exercise, could be seen on the faces of the younger ones. Those who'd barely had time for a stint across the Irish Sea. Hints of what lay in their minds, the first signs of doubt, were betrayed by their eyes. Others, the more seasoned or just unhinged, gave nothing away; they were ready for whatever was to come. His own apprehension, now that he too felt this to be real, manifested in its own quiet way, withdrawing as he did even further from those around him. Again he felt resentment that he was here, of what he would be asked to do. And what would his reaction be during that first contact, when the posturing and politics came down to men killing each other? Would his training carry him through it, or would he wither and freeze, his true nature emerging?

Taylor told them they should write letters home if they wanted to, that the words should be chosen carefully, in case they were their last. Richard tried writing to Mary and the children but couldn't find the sentences to match his thoughts. The distance seemed unfathomable, as if they existed in another time. In the end he wrote only to his wife, drily cataloguing the aspects of his days that they were allowed to discuss. He asked her about the garden, what else she'd planted in his absence, whether Shane was all right. He spoke of going away when he returned, of a weekend somewhere, asking her parents to come and stay with the children. He said that he loved them all.

In the days to come, they received two pieces of news, one that bolstered morale, one that saw it ebb. One of their submarines had torpedoed the Argentine flagship *General Belgrano*. Cheers went up, soon muted by the act's confirmation that attempts at diplomacy were now redundant. And then the news that their own ship, HMS *Sheffield*, had been destroyed by an Exocet missile, killing twenty-two sailors.

After weeks at sea, they were finally nearing the islands. Occasionally an iceberg slid by them, sombre and imperious. Flotillas of penguins bobbed comically in the swell. An albatross flanked the ship for a few miles, perhaps in hope of something edible being jettisoned, and Richard recalled the curse of a poem his father used to read to him as a boy.

Later, Taylor called them together below deck to announce the call sign and go through the landing plan. When the ground had been cleared, they were to be taken by helicopter to San Carlos, on the west side of East Falkland. Once ashore, they'd dig in and provide air cover for the ships in the bay, which would be the target of the Argentine Mirages and Skyhawks.

That evening a church service was held, its attendance a matter of personal choice. A few of the men headed to the temporary chapel, a mess room on the far side of the ship; Richard stayed on his bunk, polishing his boots.

They checked their equipment in near silence as the ship was prepared for battle, its hatches sealed, the red emergency lighting faintly luminous. He lay awake the entire night, listening to the sounds of the *Geraint* as it idled into position, waiting for the air attack that would surely come.

At home, the dog followed him upstairs, waiting outside the bathroom. The whisky had been a bad idea on top of so much beer, but at least he might sleep some. Back on the landing, light bled from under Stephen's door, and Richard stood there for a moment, wondering how his son had grown up so quickly, how Jenny too had been an infant barely any time ago. The photographs he had of them, that he'd looked at whenever there'd been a lull in fighting and he was alone, were several years old now, yet it was these images he saw whenever he thought of his children since returning home, his mind choosing to suspend their development.

It was a relief to be back at Highfield, away from the clamour of the Woodman's, where every noise, every fragment of conversation had amplified in his head like some speeded-up sequence in a nightmare. Why had they wanted him there? To celebrate his return, his glorious war? To feel righteous?

Mary was undressing in the quarter-light, the room still heady with the scent of a summer's evening. His eyes followed her silhouette as it shifted towards the bed, and he wondered whether she too felt this awkwardness. He'd thought of this moment for so long, craving it so intensely on those desperate, lonely nights, that it had become almost sacred, the memory of it wielding more power than the reality now he was home. Even in the pub earlier, when they were surrounded by idiots staring at Mary's legs and the urge had risen to push his glass into one of their faces, he'd known he wouldn't be able to hold his wife tonight, let alone make love to her.

Eighteen

He gave his son the gun to hold. Already the trees were shedding their leaves, the early autumn sun weaker as it edged over distant fields. He let the dog run free for now, calling him in every few minutes with a single whistle. Despite Stephen filling out a little in the last year, he was unable to break the air rifle's barrel, and so they settled for him loading and closing it. It felt good to be up here, especially at this hour, when the chances of running into anyone were almost nil. Within a minute's walk of the house everything became still, the only sounds those secreted by the woods themselves. Last year, negotiating a price for logs, the farmer had told him about a pair of peregrine falcons that wintered here, how you could catch a glimpse of them if you were patient and fortune was with you.

They walked on in silence, passing through wedges of mellow sunlight, the ground mulching underfoot. Breaking cover from the trees, he called Shane to heel and they crouched low in one of the furrows, watching the rabbit up ahead as it grazed. He could sense his son's unease, that the boy had no instinct for it. Perhaps the familial custom of entering the forces would end with him. In the meantime, it was important for Stephen to see the damage even a pellet could do, and so with orders whispered into his son's ear, he told him to take aim.

He was woken by the shouting. An NCO barked orders to collect their ammunition, to do it quickly. For a moment he forgot where he was, the half-light offering few clues. He had dreamt of Salisbury Plain, of an exercise going wrong, of soldiers being gassed by their own side, turning their guns on each other as he ran away, hiding from Taylor, who was ordering him to shoot himself. Finally he'd fallen into some quicksand, his submergence slow but inexorable.

As he made his way along the passage, someone remarked that it was a beautiful day for a war, and for a moment he thought he might be sick. They gathered their ammunition and helmets, together with some field dressings and morphine. Again they were told about removing all personal items.

And then there was a lull. More waiting, listening to the sounds around them, the moan of the ship's bowels. Outside, it was still dark, a sliver of moon hanging above them in a tilted smile as the ship edged into position, cutting through the gentle swell at a steady eleven knots. Nobody knew what would be waiting for them, though they'd been told things looked quiet.

Up on deck, he got his first view of East Falkland, its silhouetted hills rising from the calm waters of the sound as dawn broke behind him. Ahead, over the island, the last stars shimmered, the pale sky crystalline.

The order came to get to the galley for breakfast, their last fresh meal for a while, they knew. He forced it down, the nausea rising all the time, before heading back to his bunk. He cleaned his rifle again, stripping it down, reassembling it while trying to ignore the tremor in his hand. An hour later, someone came in and told them that one of their Sea Kings had ditched on a flight between ships, its crew of eighteen dead.

Returning to the deck to witness the dawn, he saw that dozens of their vessels had gathered around them. Helicopters flew overhead, Harriers screeched by, searching for enemy positions. Gunfire could be heard in the distance, the occasional explosion reaching them as an innocuous faint rumble.

He watched the youngsters taking it all in, this convergence of an armada, gathered so far from home. This spectacle of war amassing around them. He felt it too: that nothing here could stand up to this. That perhaps their encroachment had been witnessed, from hilltops, from a reconnaissance plane high above them, whoever was here now long fled.

When the clatter of machine-gun fire came, it was still barely a surprise. A Pucara fighter appeared from behind them, its fuselage lit magnesium white by the morning sun. Coming in low, it fired several rockets at the *Argonaut*, before banking hard to attack the *Canberra*, missing on both occasions. Fire was returned from a frigate to the west of them, the shells streaking through the air until the lone pilot was shot down, water erupting as the plane crashed into the sound and, after some cheers, the near-calmness returned.

Their lift-off times were chalked on a board, and finally they were taken to shore, the Sea King skimming just a few metres above the water towards the island, the cold, brackish air now replaced by the heat of the helicopter's engines and the fug of aviation fuel. The rhythmic *wap-wap* of the rotor blades was hypnotic, and he wished he could just sit there for ever, despite the prospect of a missile scything into them at any time. Beside him, the door gunner scanned the horizon for enemy aircraft. When their eyes met briefly, Richard half smiled, trying to convey a sense of shared incredulity about the madness they found themselves amid, but the man's face remained impassive.

The Sea King banked hard to the right, the g-force pressing him down as if some great weight had been thrust on to him, his body no longer his own. Although they had been told there would be no resistance on this side of the island, it still seemed ridiculous to be landing in daylight.

A minute later they touched down on a flat piece of ground that overlooked the bay. Climbing out, he expected a volley of gunfire, an attack of some sort despite what had been said, but nothing came. They set about forming a defensive position until the Sea King was airborne, returning to the ship for their equipment.

As they waited in the freezing air for the launcher and missiles to be brought over, they began digging into the peaty earth, the ground black and sodden, their holes filling in as quickly as they made them. Again it struck him how exposed they were, perched on the side of a bluff in sharp relief. In training there had always been an abundance of vegetation to use as cover, to hide themselves and the system. But looking around, he saw there wasn't a single tree, the barren, featureless ground leaving them reliant on their netting to blend in. In reality, he knew they wouldn't be targeted particularly; the enemy planes, having flown so far from the mainland, would be seeking more substantial quarry.

As they worked, his thoughts turned once more to home: to the woods above Highfield, rich with elm and ash, marking the seasons absolutely, the trees softening the wind to a whisper, filtering the sun's blaze so that it mottled the earth. Even in winter, when the cold clung to everything and ice tapered like bones from the branches, there was still comfort to be found there, the woods cocooning you in their own rhythm, embracing you, your senses mollified by their ancient splendour. But there was something ghostly about this landscape he now looked out on, with its frail sun offering little warmth, the light a sickly grey as it bled on to mile after mile of colourless scrub.

Pausing, he looked out beyond the tumult in the sound, searching the sky for life, but could see nothing other than a gull a mile or so out to sea, the inception of war perhaps displacing the natural order. What resources could such a land yield? he wondered. What exactly was it they were fighting for so far from home?

Taylor, perhaps sensing his reverie, snapped at them to work faster. Over the next hour, the Sea King returned several times, their supply vehicle and missiles slung beneath it in cargo nets like a stork carrying a baby. They were given their food supplies, plus extra small-arms ammunition. Finally, with the trench for the Rapier's cables dug, they worked quickly to make the system operational.

He heard the plane before he saw it, its jet engine screaming along the valley behind them like a banshee, the roar serrated and sickening. Fear pulsed through him as it approached and he froze momentarily, forgetting drills as if they'd never been learned. A couple of the others ran into one another, slipping in the mud, their shouts lost to the incoming thunder. Anti-aircraft fire went up in staccato bursts from the hill next to them, from those who'd managed to set up. Then the ships in the sound opened up their guns, filling the sky with ordnance.

He saw it then, hugging the contours of the land, scything through the air with unimaginable velocity, before it shot over them, its downdraft an intense sirocco, the guttural roar following behind.

And then it was over, the plane, with perhaps only enough fuel for one pass, disappearing around the headland, returning to the South American mainland. A silence of sorts returned and they finished setting up in a wordless efficiency.

They settled into a routine, each gunner taking turns with four-hour shifts in the operating seat of the Rapier, while the others watched for enemy ground forces, unloaded missiles or prepared meals from their ration packs. Between this they would grab some rest, perhaps even a moment's sleep before the cold prodded them awake. Richard would do an occasional shift in the seat, but for now he manned the radio, checked that the generator had enough petrol.

The cloud was low, his body becoming numb as wind blew the rain in horizontally up from the Antarctic. His fears of damage to the system during transportation were born out, as the radar began developing faults, often failing to distinguish between enemy aircraft and their own helicopters. After speaking with Taylor, the decision was made to turn it off, relying instead on visual recognition. This reduced the likelihood of mistakes being made but also dramatically lessened their reaction time, now down to just a few seconds.

As night crept in over the horizon, they would sit there, the seven of them, boots deep in freezing water, shivering, clutching their rifles, waiting for the alarm to sound, or for the enemy's special forces to sneak up on them, death perhaps a silent, barely acknowledged affair. These periods were the worst, thinking that the darkness would last for ever, until, finally, a hem of light would appear along the horizon and he felt his breathing ease a little. On exercise in Northern Ireland, someone had once told him that first light wasn't when you could make out the shape of things around you; it was when the brain could first determine something's colour.

Days blurred into one another now, time only meaningfully marked by finishing a shift on the Rapier or lighting a hexi block to make a brew. The enemy air raids continued, their frequency increasing, the noise of one attack barely dying down before the next began, so that it became the norm. They'd not shot anything down yet, the pilots' deft manoeuvres almost balletic as they sliced the air in glorious streamlined arcs.

All the time the wind chill pushed the temperature below zero, sleet and rain hammering into them in relentless squalls. In the distance, lines of their infantry could be seen trekking across the slopes like veins, and he felt some envy that at least they were moving.

Later, news came that some of their ships had been hit, increasing the pressure on the Rapier crews to protect them. Often, though, the enemy's bombs would fail to detonate, the terrain requiring their pilots to come in low and fast, the fuses denied enough time in the air to arm themselves. HMS *Ardent* had no such fortune, though, struck several times as she limped for cover, finally sinking the next day.

By this time, the Argentines were also using retarded bombs, silent killers that parachuted slowly down around them, so that you saw death approaching, announcing itself in blithe descent. These, as well as the occasional stray shell from their own side, were never far away. It was mostly down to luck in the end.

During lulls, if he was sitting in the Rapier, he would practise by tracking their own helicopters as they brought ammunition and stores ashore. Some days intelligence would filter through of a planned enemy attack, an audacious ground assault via a beach landing, and they'd steel themselves for hours, but it never came. He wondered how he would fare in hand-to-hand fighting, when the man you killed wasn't flying away from you at Mach 2, unseen and faceless. When you could look into his eyes as you ran your bayonet through him. Or as he ran his into you.

Eventually, their air superiority showing, the attacks began to diminish, with enemy plane losses mounting. His unit still hadn't hit anything themselves but had perhaps done enough to spoil the planes' accuracy.

After a quiet few days, the next attack came from the west, the guns from their ships below opening up before their unit could get anything away from the hillside. Skyhawks and Mirages screamed in, fast and low, some banking hard, using the hills as camouflage. By this point he had gained an admiration for their pilots, their outrageous flair and courage as they flew into great clouds of ordnance, pass after pass, gambling on having enough fuel to return home.

Two of his gunners had been flown out for supplies, the bad weather keeping them away for now, and so he was doing an extra shift in the seat to give the others a break. He tried to locate the planes in the tracker, his thumb steady on the joystick as they targeted the *Antelope*, sitting in the entrance to San Carlos Water. One plane was shot down by a Rapier missile launched further along the coast, its burning fuselage hitting the water after an arcing tumble. Another fell to a hail of cannon shells fired from the ship's deck, the plane crashing into its mast before exploding. Although it had managed to get its bombs off first, neither had detonated. Still he couldn't fix on anything, his own frustration mirrored in Taylor's face to the side of him.

Scores of enemy planes came in now, some below their position, unloading their bombs in breathtaking passes. Remarkably, none of them exploded, and although several small fires broke out on board the ships, they were quickly under control. When finally the skies were quiet again, he slumped forward in the operating seat, incredulous that they'd taken no major loss.

They had settled down for the night when the noise tore up the hill like a train in a tunnel, a great wave of heat following it. More explosions came, immense bellows that resounded through him. Climbing from their trench, they watched the sky turn red, realising that one of the unexploded bombs on board the *Antelope* had gone off, starting a chain reaction with the ship's magazines. They stood there, staring in silence at the firework display before them, wondering how many men were on board. Throughout the night, the ship glowed like a blacksmith's forge, the hills around them shimmering.

At first light they saw the extent of the damage, the frigate's shell peeled open like a tin can, its back broken. Word got through that the ship had been evacuated in time, the only casualty the poor bastard trying to defuse the bomb. Later that day, the *Antelope* slipped below the water's surface as they looked on from the hillside.

The problems with the radar still vexed him. To add to this, the tracker head was now faulty, meaning that they had to physically turn it towards attacking aircraft.

The weather continued to pummel them, the bottom of their ditch permanently underwater. To compound this, their boots were horribly ineffective, water seeping into them, the risk of trench foot ever present. They heard of a soldier further along the coast deliberately soaking his foot until he had to be airlifted away to have his sock surgically removed.

Generally, though, they felt things were tipping their way, that combat in the skies was nearing its end, the ground war looming. As he heated some water to rehydrate a vacuum-packed shepherd's pie, he thought of the meals Mary cooked when he was home, trying hard to evoke their flavour and smell. Of Jenny helping her bake on Sunday mornings, the house filled with the scent of pastry and cinnamon. The closest thing they'd come up with by way of a treat out here was to crumble an oatmeal block into some drinking chocolate, achieving a few seconds' decadence.

* * *

A day later, the order came to move. They joined the Welsh Guards of 5 Brigade, who were being taken by boat round to Bluff Cove, closer to the capital, Stanley, to avoid the long march. They were to travel with them on the *Sir Galahad*, go ashore ahead of the Guardsmen; from their new position, they would provide them with cover as they waited to land.

It felt good to be moving, albeit closer to the main fighting. They boarded the ship, the Guardsmen eyeing them with suspicion at first, perhaps, in the absence of any headdress, suspecting them of being special forces. They must have looked peculiar – dishevelled wretches, bearded and filthy, stinking of sweat. The warmth of the ship was welcome, and Richard found a corner beneath some pipes before falling into an exhausted sleep.

Nineteen

Rationally, he knew the silvered thread splayed across the path to be gossamer, the dew-glistened filament of a spider, assembled since he was up here yesterday. And yet it was equally compelling to regard it as a trip wire, the enemy's cunningness disguising it so. Either way, he walked carefully around it, vowing to stay off the paths from now on.

From its bark he could tell that the dog was deep in the woods, ensuring that any wildlife would be hunkered down, and he realised that if he was to see either of the peregrines, he'd have to leave the animal at home. The farmer had told him it was cold enough in the uplands to the north, that the birds could arrive any day now, returning to one of the ancient eyries. He had asked Mary to get him a book on falcons, and although he found its style overly academic, a strong desire to catch a glimpse of them emerged.

For now he reckoned on spending at least half his waking hours up here, some of them without Shane. He would divide the wood's boundary into rough quadrants, working his way into the centre and then out again ninety degrees round, scanning each tall tree for movement before moving on to the next section. But his most likely sighting, according to the book, would be when the birds hunted, observing the fluster of their prey as it attempted to escape. If luck was with him, he'd witness a kill, a wood pigeon or magpie plucked straight from the sky as the falcon scythed into it from above. For now he would scan the ground for half-eaten carcasses, signs that the birds had returned. This surveillance would also allow him to watch for anyone approaching the house through the woods, using the trees as cover.

Within an hour he had reached the tree with the small hollow eight feet or so up its trunk, the bottle of whisky he kept there cool, still half full. After taking a swig, feeling the burn deep in his throat, he scanned the foliage around him, listening hard for the clumsy footfall of a human, before returning the bottle to its hole. Sitting on a fallen bough, he looked up to the sky, the tree-sifted wind heaving gently above him, the mid-afternoon light clean, glass-like. Despite his best efforts, raising the binoculars to his face still took him back to that other time.

There was a delay in the ship setting off, Port Pleasant their new destination, an inlet a few miles short of Bluff Cove, from where the Welsh Guards would march the final hours to the capital.

Once they'd dropped anchor in one of the narrow channels, Richard went on deck. The damp squalls of recent days had passed, the sky for once perfectly clear and blue, the sea as calm as a boating lake. On the hills across the water, sheep grazed in the heather, gulls drifting on the breeze above them. Where the terrain sloped down to the water in crags, a pair of seals had broken the surface, their heads bobbing gently like silvered buoys. He thought how far away the conflict seemed for now, the only sound the lapping of the swell against the side of the boat.

Perhaps his war was almost over, an Argentine surrender ushering in a premature end. His contact with the enemy had been meagre, the true maelstrom of battle playing out elsewhere, his contribution sporadic, insignificant. That others, on both sides, had given their lives in the last few weeks felt beyond comprehension. It was what you signed up for, the prospect of this eventuality – and for many this bestowed nobility on the profession, there being no higher honour than to breathe your last defending your country. But what did you know of such matters in your late teens, when deep down you believed you'd live for ever? What did you know of the politics at play, the bureaucrats who sent people to die? Because that was it: you couldn't pick your battles, regarding some as more worthy than others. Your life was worth as little or as much regardless of where or how you fell, whatever the cause.

Looking around now, the arena of combat tranquil, there was something absurd to it all, the idiocy of war, where monstrous acts were sanitised by lies, the old lie, of it being sweet and right to die this way.

Taylor wrenched him from his thoughts. 'Wake up, Briggs, we're out of here.'

His sergeant was keen to get off the ship, concerned at how vulnerable they were, sitting there in perfect visibility with no escort or anti-aircraft capability set up. There was some debate about whether they could just sail the extra distance, taking the Guardsmen on to Bluff Cove after all, making the march unnecessary, but the decision was made to stay put. An hour later, a Sea King took his unit the half-mile or so ashore, where they watched 2 Para preparing for the final push on Stanley.

As they dug in and set up, the problems with the Rapier persisted. He continued testing the system, making small adjustments, but he could now hear the fault tone in his headset, an intermittent knocking that meant nothing would launch immediately. Again he voiced his concerns to Taylor but was told to get on with it. They had what they had. An electrical engineer had been requested, but none was nearby.

He looked through the optics at the *Galahad,* sitting in the still waters of the cove for hours now. Silence gathered around him, broken only by his smock whipping in the wind. Out at sea, a gull arced beneath the weak sun and he tracked it in the sights, while the others prepared some food behind him. The mood among them had lifted with the small change in scenery, sporadic bursts of laughter rising as if they were on exercise. There was an easiness among them, he realised, a connection that such living afforded. You ate and cooked together, slept and shat next to each other. You fought and died together. Even he felt less alienated for once, as if part of something beyond himself. You did this, the killing, the being killed, not because you were ordered to, not for your country or those you loved at home. You did it for the people around you, your surrogate family, men you might avoid or even despise in other times. Your proximity to each other, the fact that the person next to you might share your final minutes, meant a bond was hewn, one you succumbed to so that you didn't die alone.

* * *

He had barely shouted the alarm when the sickening roar of jet engines blasted by just thirty feet above them, the smell of kerosene thick and acrid in its downdraught. He could see the helmet of the lead pilot as the jet banked, the stencilled letters on the underbellies of its bombs. Some of the Paras fired off rounds from rifles and machine guns in a futile gesture.

He focused on the lead jet, trying to keep it in the cross hairs as it streaked away.

'In cover,' he called out, his heart beating wildly.

'Engage,' came Taylor's response.

He pressed the fire button. Nothing. Just the *tap tap* in his ear of the system failing. He pressed it several times, but still nothing. A few seconds later the lead jet dropped its 250kg bombs on to the *Galahad*, which exploded instantly. The second plane missed its target, but the third hit, before all three thundered away in steady climbs until they were just specks in the distance. The attack had lasted just seconds.

Roars from the explosions reached them with an appalling bellow. The *Galahad* was carrying large amounts of petrol, mostly for the Rapier generators, and once this caught, the fireball was devastating. Men on board ran in all directions, beating at the flames as their clothes caught fire, many jumping into the water. Some were able to climb into life rafts that had been launched. Screams, small and distant, carried across to him, their pitch rising each time, but he could only sit and watch, subjected to anger from the Paras at his inability to prevent the attack, while Taylor cast him a sympathetic look.

He wanted to go down to the shore, to help with the rescue, but their orders were to stay with the Rapier, in case more planes came. By now, smoke from the *Galahad* was rising, thick and black, in great plumes. He trained his binoculars across the water. A helicopter had arrived and was winching survivors away from the flames and exploding ammunition. Another, seeing the life rafts drifting back towards the burning ship, hovered dangerously low, using the wash from its rotor blades to steer them to safety. Beyond this he could see a soldier running along the *Galahad*'s deck in terror, his hair smoking, his arms on fire, skin from his hands flapping loose like latex gloves. Further along, blackened faces appeared one at a time from the smoke, men staggering, falling to their knees. Others scanned the ship for shelter from the fires, stumbling back and forth in half-blindness. Below him, on the beach, men were helped out of the water, some collapsing to the ground before being placed on stretchers. Finally he looked away.

Later, when the silence returned, it began to snow.

They kept their heads down. There was no talk of blame among their own unit; he'd done all he could. The equipment had failed him. Failed those on board. It could have been anyone in the seat, though he could see the relief on others' faces that it hadn't been them.

He overheard accounts from men who had gone down to the shore to assist the wounded. Of faces beyond recognition, skin pustulous and broiling from the heat. Of soldiers who'd crawled along in the ship's blackness, clambering over the remains of others, unable to breathe as they searched for exits below deck. As he tried to find out how many had been lost, he heard reports of limbs being blasted away, leaving smoking, blackened stumps. And of the smell of burning flesh.

The next day, trekking across sun-bleached plains, they came across a dead horse, felled by artillery. Its wounds had begun to yield a plentiful source of food for insects and carrion birds, perhaps some small mammals. They gathered around it, the sheer size of the animal commanding their attention, though no one spoke. They walked on in silence. Richard remembered as a child seeing a dead blackbird, the shock in observing this creature so removed from its own sphere, so inert and fragile. He'd prodded it with his shoe, hoping to see it resume flight. Finally he found enough courage to pick it up, his sadness replaced by a fascination with its structure, its sculpted brilliance. Gently he fanned open one of its lustrous wings, marvelling at the arrangement of feathers, how perfectly engineered and intricate they were. Burying it in a shallow grave, he'd vowed to return, to observe its degradation, perhaps taking the skeleton home, but he hadn't.

He thought about their reaction to the horse, how it had drawn a moment's quiet sorrow from them, as if the carcass was emblematic of all that had occurred here. As they headed into the biting wind, a longing rose in him to see his dog, to lose his hands in its fur as it tried to lick his face. Or to hear the animal's bark echo through the woods, knowing it would soon return to his side.

Twenty

He could hear Sergeant Taylor's voice in his sleep. Not the authoritative and precise tolling that issued orders, but a softer, less certain inflection, as if the man had forgotten who he was. A silence followed, in which one of the nightmares feigned to resume, before Taylor spoke again, awkward laughter following his words. Remembering he was at Highfield, Richard rolled over and tried to place the time and day, the light in the bedroom suggesting he'd slept through much of the morning. He'd come to bed around four, he thought, having sat in the spare room for hours sketching badly the basic form of a peregrine from a picture in the book. If he had any talent for such matters it remained untapped, yet he found the activity meditative, especially when he drank less. The trick, he was learning, was not to think about it too much, to let the pencil glide with the same effortless efficiency a falcon accomplished in flight. Away from the woods, the spare room was the only other place where the agitation eased, his mind largely his own again. Initially he'd found the steady dripping of rain into bowls infuriating, destroying what little concentration he could muster. But in time, and especially after a downpour, there seemed to be a rhythm playing out around him, the rhapsody completed by the scratching of pencil on paper.

He could hear his wife's voice now, which meant it was still before lunchtime. Why was Taylor here, invading his home, bothering him? What unfinished business had he been sent to oversee? If his sergeant came upstairs, Richard vowed to climb out of the window, shimmy down the wall and wait in the woods until he'd gone. If the man couldn't issue an order, then Richard was not obliged to follow any.

But then after a few minutes something incensed him about the man's presence, and he walked out to the landing, went to the loo and then sat on the top stair.

They spent the next few nights of the war hunkered down in a sodden trench as battles played out, exchanges of tracer rounds arcing up and down the hillside like dashes on the night's black page. The sky was star-filled, its grandeur for once making little impression on him. Flares went up from both sides, burnishing the terrain with a pallid blue patina, the dead and injured who littered the land briefly illuminated like waxworks or extras in a film. The *pop pop* of distant firefights reached them on the breeze, as if occurring in the past or the future. Occasionally a scream would carry thinly across the slopes, followed by a sickening wail that spoke of pain he couldn't imagine. Finally, hours later, it would fade to nothing and he thought he might fall asleep, only for it to start up again. They listened one night to a wounded Argentine, pinned down where he'd fallen in open ground, beyond rescue. Between the whimpering he would cry out for his mother – *Mamá, Mamá* – his voice threading through the valley like a ghostly wind. *Can't you just die in silence?* someone in their trench finally shouted.

He thought for the first time about running away, detaching himself from the others, sitting out the war in one of the corrugated outbuildings they'd passed, eking out his rations. Soon the fantasy began to sustain him, and he hatched elaborate scenarios in which he scavenged for food at night, hid during the day. In time, the others would stop looking for him, presuming him lost to battle. When the guns fell silent and he was found, he would claim to have lost his mind or his memory, the result of an exploding shell. Wandering, confused and weak, the night air thick with smoke, he had taken shelter where he could. He'd searched for them without success. Few would believe him, the act of desertion as loathsome now as in the days when they shot you for it. It was still the ultimate display of cowardice, the worst thing you could do to those around you: abandon them in combat. You might as well put a gun to your own head.

In the pre-dawn half-light, one of their younger gunners complained that he could no longer feel his feet. Convinced that he would lose them to frostbite, he began to panic, wandering up and down the line, crying out for help. Taylor told him to shut up, to remove his boots and rub them. Finally Richard got him to sit down, telling him to slow his breathing. The boy's boots off, Richard zipped open his own clothing and placed the gunner's feet in his armpits until they were warm again.

* * *

As a pale sun rose, they were shelled from the enemy's position on high ground, the gorse around them igniting, giving off a rich, sweet scent that tempered the stench of sheep shit. Thanks to the peat, the earth around them sometimes burned, emitting a warm glow that they huddled round when it was safe. With two months of preparation, the Argentine machine-gun posts were well dug in, keeping them pinned down in daylight. Artillery and mortar were also fired from Stanley, the ground shaking, clods of earth raining down like some plague. Sporadic rounds from snipers would rip into the terrain, or ricochet off the rock and scree, until they became used to it: if you heard it, you probably hadn't been hit. The main targets of these hidden gunmen were the officers, singled out by their behaviour, their manner – one bullet, one kill the ideal ratio. Well-camouflaged snipers could instil fear and disorder out of all proportion to their number, their impact often psychological more than lethal. He thought how their taking of lives differed from his own (or at least from how it was supposed to), their telescopic sight giving them an intimate connection with the target, the face studied, the target's eyes as if just feet away. If the hide site had been chosen well, a single sniper could hold up an entire company for hours, even days, masking his shots in the ambient artillery fire so as to remain undetected.

Later he found himself alone with Taylor, the two of them sharing a brew during a lull in fighting. Despite the few years Richard had on his sergeant, the man possessed a maturity that gave him a paternal edge during their exchanges. It came with rank, he supposed, but more than that, his nature lent itself to all this; he was, as others probably said, born for it, destined to lead, to triumph. Not in a mindless, gung-ho sense like some here, men who craved the savagery of conflict. But one who was calmly focused on the order (if such a thing existed) of war, who conducted himself as a foreman on a building site might, or a film director, aware of but untouched by the maelstrom around him. Part of it, yet separate from it.

Richard handed him his tea.

'Still in one piece?' Taylor asked.

It was said without irony. The man wasn't without a sense of humour, but he left the repartee, the bravado, to others.

'I think so.'

'They say with luck it'll not be long now.'

Did Richard believe this? There had been little talk of victory, of significant gains, no sign that things were going their way on the ground. Not that they'd be told anything this far down the food chain; perhaps Taylor had heard something.

They swigged tea in silence for a while until Taylor spoke again.

'Wasn't your fault, you know. I'll make sure they're told about the Rapier.'

In those words Richard could already sense the doubt of others, the need for his sergeant to make a strong case about the equipment. And despite this assurance, he detected Taylor's own misgiving, that the man felt a need to protect him whatever the truth of the situation. For the first time Richard too began to question what had happened. How the Rapier failing seemed to occur most when he was in the seat, as if some frailty in his technique, an absence of conviction in his hand on the joystick, his thumb on the button, was sensed deep in its mechanics. This was what they would say: that he didn't want to be here, that they shouldn't have brought him. He wanted to leave, so let him.

As another night drew in, they were joined by a private, about Richard's age, mid to late thirties, who they all regarded as unhinged, as someone you didn't want to be around anywhere, let alone in battle. During a lull in the fighting, the man pulled out a piece of cloth from his Bergen in which was wrapped a pair of pliers. They looked at him nonplussed, listening with disgust as he spoke of the gold fillings one could find in the mouths of enemy corpses.

In the twilight, plumes of smoke rose along the ridges above them, their own trenches thick with the smell of cordite. There was concern that the enemy would outflank them, concern that they were too well dug in. Still the cold seethed into him, rain needling his face, becoming a blizzard by day's end. He coiled his body into itself, curling up as tightly as he could, until he sensed a numbness spreading to all parts. It felt as good a place as any to die, he thought, with nothing but the wild rain for company.

But then, the following dawn, just as he believed he could take no more, a ceasefire was rumoured. A surrender. The news of a white flag over Stanley. Taylor told them to keep their heads down for another hour or so, to wait for confirmation. There was always one unit who weren't told, a peripheral sniper out of the loop. Someone with the fight left in them.

Slowly, in the hours that followed, the Argentine trenches

were cleared, their passage to the capital opened up. Enemy soldiers trudged down off the hills, giving themselves up, their faces dejected.

A while later Richard stood and took in the terrain around him. The battle site was ravaged and scarred, pocked with scorching craters, as if an asteroid belt had rained down. Gradually men returned from advanced positions, from the final assaults he'd listened to in the night, exhausted, some in shock. The walking wounded were helped back, many with bullet wounds, and it surprised him what it took to put someone down; people generally didn't die from a single bullet, as they might in a film. All around him medics treated the injured, drawing an M on the forehead of those given morphine.

As the symphony of war faded, a silence gathered for the first time in days. He slumped against the wall of peaty earth, lighting a cigarette and exhaling heavily. The sleet had eased now, a wedge of light lancing down to them between the clouds. Sitting there, his body trembling, he became aware of the unbroken trilling of a skylark as it hovered vigorously above them, and he thought he might weep.

He watched his daughter idle back and forth on the garden swing, the rope mewling against the branch at the end of each parabola. Earlier she'd drawn a near-perfect hopscotch court by the side of the house, the game, in the absence of a fellow player, boring her after a few minutes. He thought about the changes he'd witnessed in her, remembering an unselfconscious girl, headstrong and joyful. How he'd returned to find a sadness about her, one that grew when she began attending Stephen's school and her face had drawn the tyranny of strangers. How he'd love to confront her persecutors, or at least their parents, supposedly upstanding members of the town who did nothing but breed cruelty, who knew nothing of war and its sacrifice.

Seeing him at the window, she smiled and waved, almost losing her balance, giggling at her near miss, before returning to the tune she was singing. Listening to her, he recalled the marching songs that had seared themselves so indelibly into his memory during training, call-and-response cadences that helped the passing of long miles.

> A little bit of rhythm and soul,
> Early in the morning,
> The bullets they are flying high,
> You see your buddies fall and lie,
> Such an awful way to die,
> Early in the morning.

Turning away from the window, he supposed it must be the weekend, or perhaps school had broken up for the holidays. Back in the spare room, he remembered how he used to read to Jenny at bedtime and wondered why he no longer did. Perhaps she was too old for that now, or perhaps Mary did it. And with this, other memories announced themselves as a series of images, rippling by like a flip book: washing his daughter's hair in the bath; the day of his wedding; his mother's face rich with pride at his passing-out parade. He felt no particular attachment to these events beyond a suspicion that they could not be recaptured, that they had played out in another lifetime and to someone else.

Lifting a section of the carpet in the corner of the room, he eased a pill from the foil strip and posted it in the gap between two floorboards. It felt good to stop taking them, as if they had stolen something from him, and he realised now that it had been an attempt by his doctor and Mary to control him. Perhaps Taylor even had had a hand in it, though as far as Richard knew, his sergeant had not visited Highfield again. Certainly it felt important not to trust anyone, not to let his guard down. He would be sharp again, able to deal with the danger his family faced from the town. Able to protect his daughter again.

In the absence of the pills, he'd begun to feel strong once more, as if all the physical training had fashioned some permanent fortitude deep within him, his walking pace in the last week leaving the dog lagging behind. His heart raced often these days, though, regardless of how much exertion he placed on it, a rapid tolling against his ribcage that left him faint, the sensation, to his relief, lasting only a few moments. After the most recent episode, he was moved to consider the darkness within the body, how the organs, the muscles and tendons all functioned in total blackness, light only penetrating them in the event of a rupturing wound.

Still he was drawn to the woods each day, relishing how nothing of human extraction occurred there, how his senses relinquished themselves to the sound and colour, to the birdsong that flowed like liquid down from the canopy. He liked to walk for hours at a time, deep into the conifers, the air among the pines heavy and spiced as he neared the wood's core, a spot where light and sound barely breached, where night drew in earlier, departed later. Where he could no longer smell the stench of war. The woods were his alone. Sometimes he would break cover and observe the town from above as dusk extinguished it, the copses behind him trembling with life, winged predators negotiating the trees in near-silence, the treeline a threshold between the world he could bear and the one he could not. Watching the town's lights pulse on one by one below, it was odd to think that he was the only one of its denizens to have fought, at least in this war. Why had no one else from this provincial hovel signed up? Why hadn't this town spilt its share of blood?

He listened to the sounds of the old house, the movements of the others who lived there. Now that winter was done, it had become feasible for him to spend entire nights among the trees, knowing that the falcons were roosting nearby, sharing their nocturnal dominion if they allowed him. He'd already identified several large hollows that would make ideal camps; later today he would take some tools up and fashion a rudimentary dwelling in one of them, careful to camouflage it well on his retreat. His son's fishing line would make adequate trip wires, the camp unapproachable without his knowledge. The dog would come with him, the two of them returning to Highfield only to replenish food supplies. In time perhaps he could even fend for himself, trapping small mammals, foraging as his wife liked to, he and the dog becoming truly wild things, feral and free.

And from this base in the woods he would be better positioned to assess whatever threat was taking shape in the barn. For weeks now he had felt the enemy's presence, his senses sharpening as the medication receded from his system. He had been careless to let them get so close, to outflank him. As with the hapless wood pigeon, oblivious to its blind spot as the peregrine lanced into it from above like a sniper's bullet, he had left himself vulnerable.

Twenty-one

The house was quiet when he woke, the dog furled asleep on the floor. He'd come to bed late, watching from the spare room as dawn bled into the valley, the first birdsong of the day cascading down from the tall trees that fringed the garden. His aim had been to stay awake until there was enough natural light to walk by, then head up into the woods to begin work on the camp. But despite feeling more alert since ceasing his medication, exhausting bouts of fatigue still overwhelmed him when he deprived his body of all sleep, and instead he'd collapsed on to the bed beside Mary without bothering to undress.

He stood and walked to the window, the dog stirring into a long stretch. Judging by the position of the sun, it was around midday, a drowsy scent rising from the garden's flora. Irritated at wasting an entire morning, he called the dog and headed downstairs. The kitchen was empty, signs of hastily prepared breakfasts strewn along the surfaces, the sweet smell nauseating. He made some coffee, rolled a cigarette.

Sitting at the kitchen table, he tried to recall what day it was – the start of the week, perhaps, though what did it matter nowadays? He felt sure it wasn't the weekend, although his daughter's school shoes lay by his feet. He had some affinity with seasonal fluxes, how the tones and light in the woods shifted, the days drawing out still. But the tyranny of time he'd once melded his life to, the precision with which every task, every movement was invested, had relinquished its hold on him. Days, weeks now blurred into one another, an afternoon sometimes passing in an instant, as if his attendance within it were incidental; other times the day felt suspended, its progress barely perceptible, his thoughts playing out the only sense that one moment was moving to the next. He'd prefer not to have thoughts either, lining up as they did in attack formation, preludes to the awful images that appeared, scenes that were as vivid and compelling as reality. Perhaps they *were* real, for who was he to promote one version of the day above another? Maybe he was still in the Falklands and the scenes at Highfield – here now in the kitchen, up in the woods – were the illusion.

It was strange to have some awareness of the changes taking place within him but to have no opinion on them. The other day, sitting upstairs looking at a sketch he'd made of a diving peregrine, he'd realised he was crying, the tears that fell on to the paper his, yet somehow disconnected from him, the sadness, if that was what it was, observed rather than felt.

There was a tree half an hour's walk from Highfield that he regarded as his own, that he pictured one day securing a rope to. A mature beech, its smooth boughs radiated formidably; the lowest of these he'd marked as his personal gallows should the need arise. And yet there was work to be done before then. A camp to build, where he could be alone. The enemy who encroached a little nearer each day to deal with.

The end of the war seemed only to bring chaos. Walking into the capital for the first time, the ground burnished with a light frost, he was shocked at how unremarkable and desolate Stanley was. This was what they had been fighting for, the symbol of the war: a ramshackle town, its streets a sea of rubbish, smoke rising from its buildings. Clothes were splayed everywhere, as if a tornado had whipped them from the bodies of those who lived here. There was a forsaken air to the town as fires burned and vehicles lay abandoned. Weapons were strewn about, faeces littered the streets. As they headed further in, handfuls of civilians appeared, offering them warm applause, some explaining that they'd been held in the community hall for more than a month. A line of dead Argentine soldiers had been laid out along a wall like exhibits, his exhaustion somehow numbing him to it. A tractor towed a trailer brimming with more bodies, while some of the enemy injured lay on sheets of corrugated iron.

Later, when they were certain it was over, soldiers headed to the beach, firing what enemy weapons had been gathered up, playing with them like toys, their laughter at times demented. Others merely sat around and got drunk. On the outskirts of the town, more of the Argentine dead lay lined up along a hedge.

Back in Stanley, choppers droned overhead. A Chinook landed nearby, its twin rotor blades pulsing through him. Many of the buildings had been adorned with red crosses, the vapour of death seeping from beneath their doors. On one of the larger sheep sheds, the letters POWs had been painted in white, and he headed over to it. Inside there were prisoners, many who looked barely out of adolescence, huddled together, crestfallen, avoiding eye contact with their captors. He handed out cigarettes to those who wanted them, while others were selected for interrogation.

Later, someone hoisted the Union Flag over the governor's house and it billowed in the breeze. Further out of town, little white gates and pretty fences gave the illusion that nothing much of significance had occurred there.

As men gathered and shared cigarettes, they heard details of the land battles, close-up fighting where bayonets were thrust into the enemy, like something from another time. Men spoke of the young Argentine conscripts, hopelessly inexperienced, having their throats slit or holding their stomachs in as they fell to their knees. Others were dismembered by artillery, the detail of what a shell could do to human flesh and bone remarked on matter-of-factly. A church service was held on the outskirts of Stanley for their own fallen.

They spent a week shacked up in the islanders' homes, warming themselves by peat-fuelled stoves, feeling returning to their feet and toes for the first time in weeks. The conversation was short-lived, unremarkable. Some units got to head home early, while those left behind set about clearing up the post-war squalor. Richard queued for some of the mutton stew on offer, but within hours his stomach cramped at the food's richness and he spent the rest of the day curled in a retching ball.

A day or so later, he slipped out of town before dusk, keen

to escape the wretchedness of the place. He walked along the road, then cut west across open ground towards the series of hills that had been taken on their approach to Stanley. The landscape here was scarred with gullies where shells had landed, turbid water pooling in them. They'd been warned of the landmines, and with each firm step he dared one to find him. He imagined hearing its soft click, solitary and unexceptional, before shrapnel lanced up into him, saving some poor bastard from the same fate.

He walked and walked, trying to escape the sound in his head. Not the sound of men screaming as their faces burned, or the screech of jets, but the *tap tap* of the Rapier failing. *Tap tap*. As the ground rose, wind gusted by, the whispered voices of the dead riding it.

He'd been walking for an hour, perhaps longer. There were no buildings now, no signs of life. A track of sorts unspooled like ribbon into the distance, and he followed it, uncaring of where it took him.

Out here, alone, he saw for the first time another aspect of the island, one he'd been blind to since they arrived. The grass around him, canted by the wind, had a timeless beauty to it, as if not even war could tame the great prairies. Granite stacks rose like ancient monoliths, their lichen-covered surfaces evoking the uplands of home. The air, now absent of the fog of war, felt purer, and he inhaled deeply. And when the clouds did finally part, the sky was somehow bluer here than at home, despite the weakness of the sun.

The hole was barely four feet deep, hidden from view by the prostrate grass. He stumbled, one foot, then the other, falling awkwardly, his whole body except his trailing right hand now below ground. Gathering himself, he stood and looked at what had broken his fall. The man – an Argentine, although it was hard to tell – couldn't have been a day over nineteen, a boy really, the agony on his face frozen in death, terror held in his hollow blackened cheeks, in his bulbous eyes. Where his lips had burned away, teeth protruded like dentures in a permanent grin. As Richard pushed himself away from the body, he could see that both the boy's legs and one of his arms were missing, apparently vaporised by whatever had struck him. The dog tag around his neck trailed across his chest, its end disappearing down between the exposed ribs, into the heart of him. And off to the side, extending up the wall of the crater, the fingers of his remaining hand still gripped tightly a string of rosary beads.

The noise coming from the barn was intolerable now. It wasn't particularly loud, more an incessant irritation that disrupted his thoughts, an irregular knocking. *Tap tap.* Taylor's voice, although distant, as if it had been thinned by the wind, still startled him, and he leapt from the chair, darted across the kitchen floor, pushing his back into the wall by the window. Why hadn't the dog heard the gate, alerted him?

He held his breath, listening hard in order to pinpoint the voice's location, but when Taylor spoke again, it just sounded as if he was everywhere, his words encroaching in irregular fashion, overlapping one another, his orders confused, chaotic. Richard inched his head out, scanned the yard, but there was no movement. The noise from the barn had stopped now, Highfield silent enough that he could hear his own heartbeat.

* * *

Climbing out of the hole that day, he had vomited until dry, before running several metres and collapsing in a sobbing heap. He lay there, curled into himself, for an hour, perhaps longer, until the sky had darkened, the distant lights of Stanley glinting on the coast. Walking back to the hole, he had gathered as much tussocky grass as he could carry, dropping it gently into the hollow before edging back a few paces. He'd wanted to say something, a few words to acknowledge the moment, but nothing came. Eventually he walked on a little further before looping back to camp.

Before falling into the hole, he'd seen something at the edge of his vision. High above him, a bird of prey, a falcon of some sort, had soared majestically below the deepening layers of cloud, its hunting territory quiet once again. Richard had stood and watched it, this thing of beauty, relishing the trance it induced in him, mesmerised by the easy cadence of its flight. Marvelling at its grace, its otherworldliness, he felt envy at such realms that men could not occupy. He wondered if somehow the bird could comprehend what had taken place here, what men could do to each other, the things they were capable of. Several times it rose high, almost beyond sight, before swooping in a fast dive, falling as if it were some great weight, and he realised it was attacking the gulls beneath. He wondered where it nested in such barren terrain – perhaps on the cliff faces he'd seen to the west.

At one point the bird flew directly overhead, little more than a hundred feet above him, the silhouette resembling an anchor, its pale underside flecked with tawny notches, its body taut and muscular. He imagined it eyeing him, curious at this figure below, perhaps fearful, perhaps not. Perhaps knowing that humans were something to avoid.

He'd watched it drift in the currents until finally it disappeared beyond the hills to the west.

Taylor had not spoken for several minutes now. Perhaps he had left, or was securing the barn himself. It made sense to go out the back door, unseen, head up into the woods, where he could better assess the situation. But this thought led only to more chatter – not Taylor's voice, but some version of his own, telling him how he always ran away, always took the easy option, and so he headed out to the barn.

Back in the house now, he tried to rationalise what he'd seen. Mary was speaking next to him, her words a series of sounds, familiar yet beyond his comprehension. At one point she touched his arm and he thought he might hurt her. Finally she left and he was alone with the dog again.

Taylor had been right about the threat. The enemy, using the barn as a base, had become well established, not only moving in to his territory but infiltrating his family too. On some level this hardly mattered, given his own plans to move up to the camp he was building. But what would stop the invasion spreading there? The man, once in the house, would seek him out however well he was hidden.

In the utility room, he changed into his fatigues and put his beanie on, before pulling the stick of camo paint across each cheek and down the bridge of his nose. Opening the drawer of the old dresser, he took out two boxes of ammunition and the key to the cabinet and, after shutting the dog in the kitchen, headed out to the barn.

In the yard, the air shimmered in the summer heat, the warmth on his face reminding him of some forgotten time, and for a second he allowed the seething white sun to enter his eyes. When his vision returned, he saw swallows scything in and out of the far barn, their rapid swoops and turns a silent mimicry of the Skyhawks and Mirages. Again the voice, bringing him back, urging him to remain focused, not to be distracted this time.

Entering the barn, he allowed the man to turn, his face full of bewilderment as he let his toolbox drop to the floor. He was talking now, something about the changes to the barn, Richard scanning the interior for signs that other people were in there. It was so hot now; the barns had always been cool, even in summer, but he could feel a rivulet of sweat tracking down the side of his face into the hairs of his beard. Fumes caught in the back of his throat like the kerosene from a jet, and he thought he might throw up if he stayed in here much longer. Still the man spoke, his accent familiar now, the inflection like something Richard had heard on the streets of Belfast, and as he reached towards his toolbox a single shot to the forehead was all it took, the noise echoing briefly off the walls.

Something unfathomable had occurred, a thing beyond description, a thing he suspected was to be feared, and yet a great calmness swept through him. He could hear Taylor's voice again now, urging him on, insisting that the threat remained. *Are you going to let everyone down again?*

Richard pushed his boot into the side of the man on the ground, ensuring that no more shots were needed, before crossing the yard into the field and heading down into the town, every now and then checking the skies for movement, thinking that perhaps the milder weather had seen the birds return to the north. Next year he would redouble his efforts to find them.

The breeze of earlier had blown itself out now and the sun fell heavily on his uniform. Looking at the rifle as he walked, he berated himself for not cleaning it more often, promising to do so when he got back to Highfield.

Emerging from the alleyway, he noticed that people stopped what they were doing and stared, while a few scurried into shops or turned on their heels. He kept to the centre of the road, exposed but with a better view of the terrain, and after a hundred yards a car appeared over the brow of the hill, moving towards him, slowing but not stopping. In the second before he put the windscreen in, he thought the driver had mouthed something.

He watched as the car veered into the wall, before continuing on, heading into Market Lane, leaving the screams behind him, his pace in keeping with the song he muttered.

A little bit of rhythm and soul,
Early in the morning,
The bullets they are flying high,
You see your buddies fall and lie,
Such an awful way to die,
Early in the morning.

Part Four

Autumn 2012

Twenty-two

Stephen stood before his sister's grave. They had walked – he and his mother – to the cemetery in silence. Every now and then she'd paused, as if the route had changed and she was looking for clues in the landscape. The people who passed them gave polite nods, one or two looking a little longer than they might have, their minds processing who was before them.

Last night, knowing that they were coming here today, Stephen hadn't slept much, instead watching the shadows that shifted imperceptibly across the walls, his room silvered by the light of a hunter's moon. Through the ill-fitting window came the murmur of the river, its whisper soothing if not soporific. When sleep had finally come, he'd dreamt of Suzanne, a frenzy of flesh and lust, and then, on waking, lingering guilt at how good it had felt.

His mother had announced her intention after dinner last night, more a statement than an invitation, uttered with a casual air that remained unconvincing.

'I'll come,' he'd said.

'If you like.'

They had cut through a part of the town he'd forgotten

was there, an entire neighbourhood his mind had filtered out, Stephen carrying the fresh chrysanthemums, his mother holding a bag that contained a small gardening fork and some gloves. Above them the sky had yet to decide on its course for the day, the expanse of blue converging with a rain front to the west. Beyond the houses the path was jaundiced with fallen sycamore leaves, as if their route to the cemetery had been illuminated, marked with a golden wash. Occasionally his mother stopped, plucking a crisp packet or some other litter from the hedge, placing it in the bag with a disapproving sigh.

Walking like this, with his mother, he'd remembered doing so as a teenager when they lived at Highfield, accompanying her and Jenny on Saturday afternoons when Suzanne was busy and he had nothing better to do. By then, he knew something was profoundly wrong at home, an awfulness that their mother tried to play down, attempts to keep her own panic from them, the walks some crucial vestige of family life.

It was where his fondness for nature, for places still regarded as wild, came from: those days outdoors, the three of them escaping, as their father also had, into the woods and valleys around them. Before then, fishing with Brendan had been something he'd enjoyed, but without an appreciation of why, of how the landscape had begun to nourish him, of the part it would play in all that followed. How he would return to it again and again for solace, walking the coast path at home as a form of meditation, its dramatic beauty, features hewn from ancient ice and fire, granting him the insignificance he sought. One such summer evening, shortly after learning that Zoe was pregnant, he'd climbed a steep section of the path and sat on the tip of a headland looking out to sea. The sky was star-clad, a hazed band of the Milky Way visible to the west. He'd watched a fishing boat flank the coast, its silhouette crimping the water's surface, the chunter of its engine pulsing faintly up to him. Beyond, in the vessel's wake, the sea gleamed a luminous azure, as phosphorescent algae were ignited by the turbulence, giving the boat a shimmering tail as if a million fireflies were following it.

An urge to see his wife and daughter rose in him, the anticipation of talking to them at teatime lifting his spirits despite the proximity of the cemetery. There was comfort in knowing he could be home in five hours, and he resolved to leave here tomorrow. He would spend today urging his mother to move away, before heading back to focus on the hearing and the rest of his life. And on his return he would find a quiet moment, sit Zoe down and tell her about a boy named Stephen Briggs and what had really happened here.

In the years that followed his departure from the town, as new episodes were laid down like strata over the old, life couldn't pass by quickly enough. Anything that replaced the images of that day was welcomed, as if the new experiences would eventually seal his time here in some impervious chamber, like a condemned nuclear reactor entombed in concrete. That had always been his aim: the construction of an existence so removed from his past that the connection was one day severed. A new family, a home on the other side of the country. If he ran far enough, closed enough doors behind him, it could never catch up, never find him. But in recent years, perhaps after Amy was born, it had become impossible not to recall time spent with his father, days that remained unsullied by the man's last hours. Because up until then, they had been a family like any other – navigating life as best they could, flawed and fragile, bound by the shared chronicle of all they'd been through. And yet before returning here it had become almost impossible to evoke the man his father had been, the person left behind on an island in the South Atlantic. The father who had returned was another version of himself – spectral, his presence merely implied, as if his time there had consumed him.

Zoe had once told him about the strangler tree, how it came to exist when a bird carried a fig to its nest, where the seed then sprouted, sending its roots inexorably outwards. One set reached the ground, providing itself with nutrients, while the other slowly throttled the host tree, often killing it, so that only a hollow central core remained. You could see where the original tree had been, but only by virtue of what had replaced it.

The cemetery was quiet. An elderly woman stood several rows away, her back to them, while a man Stephen's age idled along the far wall, scrutinising the gravestones. Dominating the section they were in, a ten-foot statue of an angel rose from its plinth, a crow perched on the apex of one of the stone wings, observing them with indifference. Driving past here a few days ago, he'd almost turned the car round, headed home, the pilgrimage aborted before it began. His mother had been unwell in the past without him feeling the need to visit each time. A phone call would have sufficed, betraying Peter's trust if necessary; the offer to drive up made, knowing it would be declined. He could have broached the subject of her friend's concern, though she'd likely still have dismissed it, as she had so far during his stay. Zoe's mother had developed a form of dementia a few years ago, though he'd been too selfish to properly listen to how it manifested. In his ignorance, he'd bracketed it with the general decline in mental health that came with old age, there being no need to know any more. Presumably his mother's eccentricity would make it harder still to determine where one ended and the other began.

They stood by the grave. His mother knelt down and removed the lifeless flowers of a previous visit, before sweeping away the dead leaves that had gathered. After smoothing out the decorative gravel, she laid the chrysan-themums gently down, adjusting them a couple of times until she was satisfied with their position. Then she began removing the weeds that had encroached on to the stone-work, quietly admonishing herself when the root remained in the ground.

He bent down to help.

'It's OK,' she said. 'I've got it.'

Standing, he watched her inspect the grass, her head a few inches above it, the search intense and methodical, as if something minute and precious had been lost there. Reading the inscription to the side of her, he pictured himself here as a boy, shaking despite it being a warm day in spring, his legs feeling as if they were about to give way. There had only been about ten people standing around the hole that day; most he'd known, a few he hadn't. Men and women from the newspapers aimed cameras at them from afar, which was somehow both respectful and not. It was thought that people from the town might attend, but it came at the end of a week full of such visits, when enough grief had been expended. Or perhaps they'd have stayed away anyway, the ostracism amassing already.

The day, the service itself, had passed in a blur of surreal anguish, his legs tremulous throughout, his heart performing little lurches, nausea rising all the time. No one made eye contact, their faces blanched of colour, stares fixed to the ground as occasional wisps of blossom drifted past them on the breeze. There was a sense that the earth had tilted on its axis that morning, and once or twice he closed his eyes hard, hoping to awake from a terrible dream. He felt the need to keep it together, not merely for himself, but for the others; that if one of them fell apart, they all would, the emotion held in check by the frailest of barriers. He remembered none of what was said in the tribute to his sister, a eulogy uttered by a reverend who himself wore the strain of all that had happened that week, his face as beleaguered as their own. Near the end of the service Stephen had reached out, taking his mother's hand, its touch cold and lifeless, his grip unreciprocated.

And then, before he knew it, he was in his uncle's car, heading to a new life, waving anxiously from the back window to his mother as she was led away by his grandparents, his uncle smoking heavily in the silence.

He looked at his sister's grave. She would have been in her

mid thirties now, a wife perhaps, a mother. He tried to imagine what she might have done with her life, who she would have become. At times in his childhood he'd suspected his parents of loving her more, that the mark on her face meant she needed a surplus, the distribution an attempt to balance matters. He'd even come to resent the birthmark at times, as if it were a favoured sibling itself, an emblem of his parents' bond with her. Whenever his father returned on leave, Jenny would race through the house to him, flinging herself into his arms, delirious with joy. Stephen and his mother would stand back and wait their turn, or as adolescence arrived he would have to be called down from whatever he was doing.

As he pictured his sister now, it was her hair that dominated the image, great tumbles of blonde that never fell the same way twice, a gamut of tones that still burnished in even the dullest light. Their mother would brush it, tie it back each morning, but almost immediately the first few strands worked free, coiling down to her shoulders and beyond. Before he was ill, Jenny would sit on their father's lap at bedtime and he'd gently draw a hairbrush through her curls until she fell into a trance, Shane looking on with envy. Other images formed, of her trying to teach Stephen to play cat's cradle, how he'd get it wrong each time, the string ravelling around his fingers until he couldn't move them, and she'd laugh at his incompetence. His sister rarely seemed bored and was always busy making something from papier mâché or plasticine, or focused intensely on her collage kit at the kitchen table. She played for hours in the garden without ever going far from the house, sometimes helping their mother in the potting shed or greenhouse, her fingers caked in soil, hair wilder than ever. She was a great collector, too, of stickers and badges, the subject matter scarcely relevant, with half her room given to this pursuit, its mirrors and wardrobe, her chest of drawers, emblazoned with years of careful accumulation.

The memories rushed him now, an assault on his senses. The smell of shoe polish on Sunday nights when their mother encouraged them to shine their shoes before the school week. His sister coming into his room shortly after their father had gone to war, looking for the Falklands on Stephen's globe, thinking how impossibly far away they were, her face brimming first with incomprehension and then a kind of wonder.

Perhaps if she had reached her teenage years, she would have endeared herself less, the lustre of her charm fading a little until they were equal in their parents' eyes. But at that time he had to work harder for their love, or so it seemed.

Once, on a family holiday in some seaside town, they were having dinner in a gaudy pub on the seafront when a table near them erupted with shouts and panic. A boy of six or seven had bitten the glass he was drinking from, breaking it in his mouth. As the mother screamed at the blood pouring down her son's chin, the father lifted him, turning the boy upside down, patting his back hard. The spectacle lasted no more than a minute, the family leaving soon after, the side of the boy's mouth stuffed with tissues staff had brought over. At the end of the week, sitting again in the pub, Stephen had inexplicably done the same. Curious at how it was possible, how much pressure could be exerted before it broke, he'd bitten a section clean from the top of the glass, which he held between his teeth as Coke slopped from the fissure on to his lap. There was no blood, no repeat of the display earlier in the week, and his mother calmly removed the piece of glass from his mouth, his father looking on. No one spoke of it on the way home, the silent accusation being that he'd been seeking attention, and although it hadn't felt that way at the time, perhaps he had.

By contrast, his sister flourished in social situations, despite her visible blemish, enthralling those present with endearing wit. This made it all the harder when, at secondary school, she encountered a different kind of reaction. Instead of her precocity ingratiating her, it acted as an additional beacon for those seeking a victim. It was a terrible thing to observe: an ebullient extrovert reduced in weeks to a timid version of herself.

By this time, their father was lost to his sickness, their mother too distracted by everything else to realise the extent of the bullying. Highfield soon became his sister's sanctuary: a bastion, safe on its hillside, impregnable. At weekends, glimpses of her old self appeared – buoyant and enchanting – only for it to ebb away as Monday neared.

He tried hard to help his sister, arranging to meet her between lessons, sitting with her on the bus when he could, but this probably fuelled the tyranny, and after a while she asked him not to hang around with her.

It was years later that he began to see what his parents had attempted, how it was less an inequitable dissemination of love and more about building her up to resist any persecution she might endure. And it had worked on a small scale, when her classmates all came from the same provincial town, had all known her from the age of four. Or perhaps it was just that children's cruelty didn't fully emerge this early.

Spots of rain fell now, an irregular spatter on the path behind them, the stretch of blue overhead all but dwindled.

He'd found Brendan's number in the local paper, under the garden services section. Several times he'd dialled it, only to abort the call before it began to ring. Finally, two pints into the evening, he'd rolled a cigarette and gone outside the Woodman's, waiting until he was alone. Brendan's voice was nothing like Stephen remembered, and yet there was an essence of his friend heard in the terse greeting. After a pause, Stephen spoke, announcing his first name, and a few seconds later his surname – the old one – in case it wasn't enough. Standing there in the night air, he could hear Brendan's breath on the line, sense his mind whirring away.

Finally his friend spoke. 'What are you doing here?'

'Just up to see my mother. I thought we could meet.'

Again just silence, until, 'All right. I should be done by five tomorrow.'

Stephen's mother finished tidying the grave and placed the small pile of weeds in the bag. He noticed that she bowed her head a little, and he did the same, both wanting and not wanting to feel something more than he did.

'There,' she said, standing back to take in the result of her labour. They looked at it together in silence, before starting the walk home.

Twenty-three

The Woodman's was quieter than it might have been. Several young men were assembled around the fruit machine in the corner, so he headed into the main bar, the landlord serving him with quiet efficiency. Sitting down, he looked back across the room. If the man knew who Stephen was, he kept it to himself, his manner neither rude nor friendly, just a look that lingered a fraction longer than it might have. Presumably the whole town knew of his presence now, the news shifting like a pyroclastic flow until it reached everyone.

Embers from an earlier fire smouldered and he thought about placing some of the stacked logs on them. In the end he moved his chair towards the residual heat, trying to disregard the doubt that had crept up on him since arranging to meet Brendan. Suzanne had mentioned that it was her night off, though some incendiary side to him wondered what bizarre dynamic the three of them in the same room might yield. He could picture the party where he and Brendan had first seen her, Stephen thinking how composed she was sitting there alone, untroubled by the two boys leering clumsily at her. Earlier today he'd recalled sitting with her in his bedroom at Highfield, scarcely able to believe his luck as she told him she no longer wanted to go out with his friend, that the more the three of them had hung out together, the greater her attraction to Stephen had become, the momentum irresistible. Knowing that his father was in the next room, he'd put on some music, wondering if anything would happen between them, telling himself it was over between her and Brendan, even if his friend didn't yet know it. Nothing happened, though, Stephen walking her home, their guilt laying claim to any intimacy that might have gathered.

Two years he'd known Brendan at that point, the Irish kid who'd shown him how to fish, how to roll cigarettes, how not to talk to girls. Hardly an enduring friendship, yet it was one he valued, having lost touch with other friends since moving to Highfield.

'You're bad luck, you are,' Brendan used to say to him at the river. 'Never catch a thing when you come.' Despite this assertion, Stephen was never discouraged, never told he wasn't welcome. Perhaps the claim was spurious, Brendan's trips by himself equally unproductive.

It was a little over twenty minutes across the fields between their houses, the tree they often met by roughly halfway. A tall beech with flaring branches, it could be seen from miles away, its presence dominating the skyline as you approached. The first of them to arrive would climb it, ten or twenty feet, squatting on one of its sturdy boughs, observing cars in the distance or an impromptu game of football between kids in the year below them. Sometimes, waiting for each other, they'd score their initials in the bark with penknives, the challenge being to locate the other's letters the next time you were there alone.

Stephen had found the tree this afternoon, its canopy bejewelled with thousands of copper-coloured leaves. Looking around, he'd been tempted to clamber up it, thinking he could just reach the lowest branch and heft himself up. It struck him as immensely liberating, climbing a tree in your forties, losing for a moment the inhibitions of adulthood. He imagined being perched up there, silent and unseen, listening to the wind breathe as it stirred the leaves. Once there, he would look for their initials, perhaps find fresh sets made by their equivalents, kids who knew little of what had occurred here, or who had heard a version, one that lingered like a legend. Instead, he'd just placed a palm against its colossal trunk, feeling content that the tree would outlive them all, its endurance of another order entirely. His mother had once told him about the grand oaks in the top field behind Highfield, how they took three hundred years to grow, three hundred years to live, another three hundred to die. That they were the custodians of history, witnessing and recording all that passed. If one of their number was sick, its neighbours, if clonal, would share nutrients with it via the root stool, a communal nurturance that appeared altruistic. And even in death, their importance to the woodland remained, with fallen, decaying boughs providing homes for insects and small mammals.

Stephen heard the door to the pub open. Brendan wore the look of a man there under duress, his body in recoil, as if gripping itself from within. He glanced over while ordering a drink, Stephen nodding, giving a smile of sorts, Brendan eyeing him as one would a complex and frustrating puzzle. His friend had filled out, his physique that of someone who worked hard on their body, more than merely the result of a laborious job. Stephen had been the stronger of the two at school, though neither would have fared well in a fight then.

The last time they'd seen each other, down by the river when Stephen had returned briefly from his uncle's, Brendan hadn't spoken. Sitting there on the bank, his rod trembling, tightly gripped, he'd refused to look up. Before then, it had seemed their friendship might survive the business with Suzanne, the damage significant, brutal but perhaps impermanent. She had broken up with Brendan the day after being at Highfield, and a week later Stephen had asked his friend if he minded him seeing her, the euphemism gloriously banal, misrepresenting the betrayal that was playing out. In truth, he and Suzanne were already together, basking in a surreptitious courtship. But even after going public, they vowed to keep it low key, to not rub Brendan's face in it or, where possible, let him see them together, at least to begin with. How seismic the fallout had seemed to them, this treachery between friends, love's battle bloody and merciless. And how inconsequential it soon became.

Watching his friend at the bar now, Stephen remembered staying at his house once, before they had met Suzanne. It had got late, the two of them listening to music, smoking out of the bedroom window. Earlier, Brendan's parents had argued, and perhaps in an attempt to show Stephen that this was exceptional, or at least innocuous, Brendan's mother had suggested he stay for dinner. The earlier tension fallen away, it was an engaging hour, Brendan's father dominating the chat, teasing them about their inability to catch any fish, Brendan giving as good as he got, telling his father to stick to music. Stephen realised then how bad things had become at home, how estranged his own father was, how even at weekends, when his mother wasn't at work, they no longer shared mealtimes, Stephen and Jenny taking turns to carry a tray of food upstairs, leaving it outside their father's door, announcing its arrival with a knock. In contrast, meals at Brendan's appeared a time of truce, a symbolic gathering where all that had gone before was forgiven or forgotten, wiped clean with banter and laughter, the regaling of each other's day. Later, Brendan's father had played his guitar in the lounge, working on new songs, Brendan's mother seeing her way through a bottle of wine, the house, much smaller than Highfield, mellowed and warm.

Placing a pint on the table, Brendan undid his jacket and sat down. Stephen held his own glass up, but his friend chose to ignore it, instead scanning the room as if their meeting were a liaison of furtive lovers.

'Thanks for coming,' Stephen said. 'I wasn't sure you would.'

'You and me both.'

'They got rid of the pool table.'

'All about food these days. Not that you'd choose to eat here.'

'Beer's good, though.'

'It's OK.'

'You come in here much?'

Brendan shrugged, his gaze still averted, fingers tapping out a febrile rhythm on his glass. 'You back for long, then?'

'Few days. To see my mother.'

'She still in one of those old cottages by the river?'

'Yeah. It's dark and damp, but she likes it down there.'

Brendan played with a beer mat, turning it over and over between thumb and finger before leaning it against his glass. A cheer carried through from the other bar, followed by a procession of coins clinking into a tray. One of the men began stacking them on the bar, catching Stephen's eye as the landlord exchanged the coins for notes and a row of celebratory shots.

In the silence, Brendan leant over, tossed a couple of logs on the fire, watching to see if they caught. The two of them sipped their drinks in unison, Stephen tracing a finger down the glass, following the frothy trails. He thought that Brendan had aged more than himself, his hair thinning, silvered a little at the sides, his eyes heavy with fatigue. They used to tease each other about who was the better-looking, idle boasts that were both harmless and untested until Suzanne came along. Yet it was his friend's character rather than his looks she alluded to in those first few days, as they tried to anticipate Brendan's reaction.

'I can't talk to him like I can talk to you,' she'd said, and he'd leaned in to kiss her.

'He'll forgive us.'

Looking down at Brendan's hand, Stephen spoke again.

'You're married, then?'

'With children. Boy and a girl.'

'I've a daughter,' Stephen said. He thought about getting

his wallet out, prompting a sharing of photos, but decided against it.

'Mine finish school in a couple of years. Makes me feel old.'

This time their eyes did meet, just a glance, the moment charging the air between them.

'Amy's still at primary school. Not that you'd think it, the stuff she's into.'

'The technology generation. I can't keep up with it.'

'They know so much.'

'The phones mine have.'

'We got excited over CB radios, remember?' Brendan looked up, perhaps unhappy with Stephen's choice of pronoun. 'Your business going well?'

'People always need their grass cutting.'

'I'm a technician, at a university. At least I think I still am.'

'How come?'

'Doesn't matter. Bit of job insecurity at the moment. So how long has it been, do you think?'

'Since?'

'Since we last saw each other. Twenty. Twenty-five years?'

'Pretty simple to work out. Summer of eighty-three.'

'Have you lived here ever since?'

Brendan sighed, as if his sternness required great effort to maintain. 'We moved away for a few years, me and Mum. North. Where she grew up. We lived with my grandparents until Mum found somewhere.'

'But you came back?'

'Just me. Fuck knows why. I met my wife, got some work here. Ended up staying. I don't know, something about the place. My boy goes to the same school we did. You remember that hut we used to smoke behind? It's still there. Kids in the year above him use it. Told him he'll be for it if I catch him smoking.'

'Remember old Kelly?'

'Sadistic fuck, yeah. Long dead, I think. Just as well; you can't touch the kids these days. He wouldn't have known what to do.'

'Didn't you get a beating off him once?'

'Let off a firework in class. Got the cane for my troubles. Hurt like hell, but I didn't let him know it.'

'What about Riley's, on the corner there?'

'The tuck shop? Gone now. Probably 'cos no one ever paid for anything.'

Stephen laughed a little, Brendan finishing his pint in a long quaff.

'Another?' Stephen said.

Standing at the bar, he looked through to the other side, picturing Brendan's father in there, almost hearing one of his songs from that night they'd all been in here, when his own father was on parade.

The men had abandoned the fruit machine now and were sitting in the far corner. Stephen placed the drinks down as Brendan took off his jacket. He rolled a cigarette, offered the pouch across the table, Brendan shaking his head.

'Didn't think you of all people would give up,' Stephen said.

'My wife hates it. I suppose I do now.'

The wood had caught behind them, hissing and flaring in orange shards. Stephen placed the cigarette on top of his pouch, nostalgic for the days when it could be lit inside. For the likes of Stephen, the smoking ban had left pubs drearier places, stark and vast, the eye, in the absence of a permanent and faint fog, carrying to every corner, each blemish and gaudy aspect of decor enhanced. Healthier dwellings, certainly, but generally devoid of character. With nothing else to do with his hands, he was drinking faster than he wanted. The laughter from the other bar was more raucous now, and again he thought back to the abuse Brendan's father had received that night, his own father sitting in a stupor just feet from where they were now.

When Brendan next spoke, the words sounded barbed, accusatory. 'So, were they fucking each other?' For a moment, Stephen thought it was some reference to him and Suzanne.

'Who?'

'Your mum, my old man.'

It had been implied at the inquest, though not confirmed; the papers too had hinted at a relationship. His mother never spoke of it and he hadn't ever asked her. He knew they had become friends in those last months, working together in the barn, Brendan's father arriving before they went to school, one morning a week through the winter and into spring. Stephen would help out too, though not as much as his mother wanted. She was different around Aiden, though, in the mornings before he arrived, her mood shifting, shrugging off the stresses of their situation for a few hours, preening herself in a mirror.

'I don't know,' he said.

'I think they were.' Brendan's voice had shifted a little

now, from his initial barbed tone to something more resigned, the anger barely able to sustain itself.

'Does it matter?'

'No, I don't suppose it does now.'

'I think my mother was lonely.'

After a minute's silence, Brendan spoke again. 'My mum remarried, a couple of years later. Bloke's an idiot but she's happy.'

'Did you stay on at school?'

'I went to college after the summer. It was good to get away, even if only in the daytime. There were reporters everywhere.'

'I saw the stuff in the nationals, but my uncle kept most of it from me.'

'They wanted a piece of everyone, even those without any connection. Not just the witnesses or victims' families, but their friends, people who'd slept with them in the past. People who'd fixed their plumbing or delivered newspapers. Anyone who had a view on it. To start with, they trod carefully, kept a bit of distance. But as more of them came, they all wanted to outdo each other, get that one quote or detail the others had missed. So much of the reporting was inaccurate, the worst kind of sensationalism. More than anything they wanted photographs, of your family, of mine, of the aftermath. Money changed hands, deals were done. People regretted being so cosy with them at the start. They were here for weeks, months in a couple of cases. I heard that some of them returned on the anniversary for the first few years, composing features on how the town was coping. The focus shifted from what had actually happened to how it impacted on everyone. The broadsheets tried to dress it up in fancy terms, but they were as bad as the tabloids. And although they went home sooner, the TV people were the worst.'

'I didn't know. My uncle took us on holiday the first week. And then we didn't have the TV on for a month. I came back for the funerals, but only for a couple of days.'

'Didn't the papers hassle you?'

'There were phone calls, a few turned up at the house.'

'That's what I mean. We were their focus. The survivors. "What was it like to live here?" they'd ask. "How will the town cope?" The *town*. Not us as people. The place itself became a celebrity.'

It was not so much anger in Brendan's voice as a quiet intensity, as though telling this to someone who didn't live here was a release for him, even if it was Stephen.

'We just wanted to grieve in peace,' he continued. 'Everyone knew someone who'd been affected.' Stephen hadn't thought of it like this, the ripples stretching outwards until they reached everyone: mothers who'd lost sons, who'd lost lovers, who'd lost friends. A town that had lost its innocence. 'People closed ranks, but not in a we're-all-in-this-together way, more an unspoken refusal to talk to anyone from outside. And then of course the psychologists arrived. I mean, I think they helped some people, those who would talk. But most preferred the stiff-upper-lip approach, especially after the initial horror faded. If you didn't talk about it, it went away. Only for most people it didn't go away. You can still see it now in some of their faces, the older ones especially.'

'Did you get help?'

'It was offered, and I had a couple of sessions, but I didn't see the point then. My wife made me speak to someone years later, after losing it a few times. Having children helped.' Stephen was keen to light his cigarette now, to feel the smoke deep in his lungs. 'And then the tourists started coming.'

'Who?'

'We noticed it a month or so after. More cars in town than normal, people parking and walking around as if they were lost, pointing this way and that, taking pictures.'

'They came just to see . . .'

'They came to see the town, your old house up there. Even now you get one or two a year. You can spot them a mile off, the fascination in their faces.'

'So why did you come back?'

'I don't know. Why is anyone drawn to the town they grew up in? Why does your mother stay?'

'Because she blames herself. So she can be near Jenny.'

Stephen played with his cigarette, rolling it between finger and thumb, wanting to get another drink. It was quieter in the other bar now, but he could feel the men's eyes on him, their voices hushed, one of them asking the landlord something.

'Are you going to smoke that?' Brendan said.

Outside, the air had sharpened. Light from the moon bled through a layer of cloud, their faces just visible in the beer garden. If the men did come out, inquisitive or seeking confrontation, they might not look round here. On some level Stephen hoped they would, a quiet eruption of violence, people eager to make a name for themselves, his own anger given an outlet. Once it was over, he would walk back to the cottage, show his mother the wounds of a debt they could never pay.

Brendan was talking about his work, some big job he'd landed with the council, how he was taking someone on next month. His son was good at rugby, apparently, trials for a big local club soon; his daughter was musical, something Stephen could see meant much to him.

'Guitar?'

'I wish. Piano. They cost a fortune. Then there's the tuning.'

Brendan mentioned his wife briefly, a local woman, in the year below them, a note of warmth in his voice.

'Did she . . .'

'Lose anyone? No. You ever go up to the house?'

'Day before yesterday, for the first time.'

'Bet it's a state.'

'Why hasn't anyone bought it, done something with it?'

'Would you want to?'

Stephen shook his head. 'But to just leave it . . .'

'They want to bulldoze it, but it's listed apparently.'

'Who wants to?'

'The town. Everyone. Sitting up there, peering down on them. You can't blame them. There were several campaigns, then rumours that it would be turned into a youth hostel. Some kids tried to set fire to it a few years ago.'

Stephen pictured Highfield, the one of two days ago. He tried to edit in features of how it had once been: his sister on the garden swing, swaying back and forth, Shane barking at her feet, their mother smiling at the kitchen window. The excitement the day they moved in. Suzanne up in his room. But all he could see was the small holes in the lounge wall, and the one upstairs.

Brendan finished his pint, tapped his glass against Stephen's. 'Come on, keep up.'

Stephen got his wallet out, tossed it across the table. 'Perhaps you'd better get them.'

His friend gone to the bar, Stephen rolled another cigarette. An opening in the cloud allowed the moon to briefly blaze through, its corona like burning magnesium. He was glad they could refer to it without the need to discuss or compare what had been lost. For now, they were just two men, old friends from school, having a pint, catching up on each other's lives, on the children they'd had. Perhaps they would walk home together, along the river if Brendan's house was that side of town, remembering the fish they never caught.

Twenty-four

The air in the attic was cool and damp. Looking back down the ladder, Stephen could see one of the cats eyeing him curiously. He stood and ran a hand along a rafter, searching for a light switch, a splinter of wood piercing his finger, making him flinch and cry out. Sitting back down over the hatchway, he watched as the prick of blood pooled slowly outwards and trickled down to his palm. Wiping it on his trousers, he took in the dimly lit area around him, its far corners still lost to the darkness. He switched on the torch his mother had given him; the light spilled on to the felt above. A water tank took up much of the space to his left, the chimney's stonework rising behind it. Turning, he saw that strips of rudimentary insulation had been hastily laid, perhaps a decade or more ago, its coverage irregular, broken by pipework and wiring. Parts of the far wall had crumbled, and water looked to be coming in from next door's chimney. According to Peter, his mother's landlord was a reasonable man who could be relied upon to make good repairs to the cottage, even if not always promptly. But as far as he knew, his mother had never been in the attic. He would suggest she call the man, get someone round to have a look.

They had discussed coming up here at breakfast.

'Did you not keep any of his stuff?' Stephen said.

'Like what?'

'I don't know, books, photos.'

'He wasn't one for books.'

'Other things, then. There must be something left.'

'There are some boxes in the attic. I can't remember what's in them. Your uncle put them up there when I moved in. It's just junk, stuff I didn't need.'

He let his eyes adjust to the gloom some more, before shuffling along the joists to where several boards formed a floor. Wedging the torch behind one of the rafters, he aimed it back at himself, motes of fibreglass eddying slowly around him, as if he was in a toxic snow globe.

His uncle had created a single row, a line of three cardboard boxes stacked on top of four larger wooden ones. The damp had caused the cardboard to soften so that the heavier boxes tore as he lifted them. Stephen placed the top ones on the floor, leaving a gap he could kneel in.

A large pad lined the wall of the first box he opened, its cover and pages wilting as he lifted it out. The sketches had been made in pencil, their definition diminished but still visible. The first third was given almost entirely to anatomical structures, presumably copied from pictures: wings, beaks, the peregrine's distinctive feet and talons, sometimes an entire skeleton. Further on, his father had become more ambitious, sketching the whole bird, the drawings crude but not without merit. Some were perched on the husks of dead trees, others swooped in streamlined splendour. What was lacking in depth and proportional accuracy was compensated for by the energy of the pieces, the majesty and essence of each falcon captured.

Further down, there were some of Stephen's school reports, endless references to a boy who, despite having ability, didn't put the effort in to achieve anything beyond mediocrity. Between these was a photo of his father, standing in a line of mostly moustached soldiers, looking his awkward self, ill at ease, uncomfortable with the bravado on display.

Stephen recognised the final object he pulled from the box. The size of a place mat, its cover featured a young boy aiming his toy gun at a fleeing wolf, as snow weighed down the surrounding conifer branches. Inside, the pages had yellowed and stiffened, the corners curling with age. He pulled out one of the 45s from its sleeve, the vinyl still glossy after all this time, a couple of scratches written like gossamer across its surface.

Downstairs, his mother had lit the fire. Both cats were assembled on the corner of the sofa nearest the hearth, their bodies coiled tightly in luxurious homage to the warmth. He drew the curtains, put the tall lamp on and sat next to them. His mother called through that she would make some tea once she'd brought some more logs in. He offered to do this, but the back door closed on his words. Above the fire, Jenny smiled out into the room, her curls backlit by the sun, unfurling to the edges of the photograph.

Looking at his sister's audio book, he longed to hear the crackle of needle on vinyl as it traversed the circular groove, the narrator interrupted firstly by each character's instrument, then by one of the scratches that cut the story short. He would take it home with him, see if it could be restored, before giving it to his daughter. In the attic he'd thought he would ask his mother's permission to have it, but deciding against this, he climbed the stairs and packed it in his bag, together with his father's sketchbook.

He'd walked along the river path with Brendan, the moon silvering everything around them – the trees, the river itself, devoid of colour beyond a metallic sheen, the world burnished in greyscale. They said nothing for the most part, comfortable in the silence that had begun back at the Woodman's, the ambient noise of the passing water accompanying them. Occasionally they acknowledged a favoured spot on the bank from that other time, Brendan remembering more detail of the trips than Stephen: lines that snagged, one of them wading in to salvage their weights, arguments over what bait to use. They fantasised about taking on the men in the pub, a glorious stand in which they triumphed despite being outnumbered. Every now and then, one of them stumbled on a tree root, the other poking fun at an inability to hold their beer now that middle age stalked them.

At one point Stephen had felt the urge to leap into the water, to splash about in its icy turbulence, his breath ripped from him, the act a gesture of something he didn't fully understand. Would his friend have followed, flailing and laughing, the two of them shivering violently until their bodies numbed?

It was strange to think they were both fathers, as if the word should be something out of their reach, its membership beyond them. It occurred to him to ask to meet Brendan's children, though in what circumstance, he didn't know. *This is Stephen. His father killed your grandfather.*

And there was Suzanne, too. A mother. All three of them parents, life blazing on regardless. If it was true that none of them was unscathed, then it was also the case that their lives had value.

They'd parted last night where the river curved north, Brendan's house half a mile further on.

'I'm sorry,' Stephen said as they stood by the stile.

'It's OK, she liked you more.'

'Who?'

'Suzanne.'

'No, I mean . . .'

'I know.'

Mention was made of meeting up again, though Stephen suspected they wouldn't. There was no handshake, no hug, just quiet nods in the half-light, Stephen watching the outline of his friend vanish along the path.

Twenty-five

It was never known where his father had got the weapon he used that day, Stephen's mother unable to shed light on the matter at the inquest, recalling only when the guns had first appeared. Acquiring such firearms at that time wasn't difficult, legislation dictating how they were to be stored but little else. The airgun had always been around, the more powerful guns turning up without ceremony one day, housed in a cabinet his father had built for them. They were all legally held, a licence issued long before they moved to Highfield. The doctor who'd supported the application gave evidence at the hearing, citing that there had been no concern with Stephen's father's mental state. He was a serving soldier: what more fit and responsible person could there be? There was nothing remotely unusual about such a man having a private collection, a cache even. Compared to some, the inquest heard, it was modest.

The day itself had begun in drizzle, low cloud furring the slopes of the valley. By lunchtime the sun had burned through, the sky a glassy blue, muted only at its edges. People in the town set up their stalls for the market, hints of the coming summer on the breeze. Above them stood the redbrick clock tower, its dullish notes ushering in the afternoon of another unremarkable day in an ordinary market town in middle England. At Highfield, Stephen's mother had left for work, Brendan's father finishing off in the barn.

The gun his father removed from the cabinet, the inquest was told, was an M1 carbine semi-automatic assault rifle, its ammunition kept in a drawer in the utility room off the kitchen. Stephen remembered focusing hard on the weapon's specifications as the man read them aloud, losing himself in the detail by way of distraction. Designed in the US during the Second World War, the expert said, more than six million were built, the aim to replace its less wieldy predecessors. Relatively lightweight, weighing just 5.7lb when loaded, the gun was 90cm long and could fire 900 rounds a minute, its bullets travelling at 600 metres per second. Accurate up to 200 yards, rounds could nevertheless travel two miles or so, stopping only once they struck something. It was said they could easily penetrate the steel helmets and body armour worn by Japanese soldiers of the era, and while the M1 lacked the firepower of subsequent assault rifles such as the AK-47, its size and weight made it ideal for sustained close combat. Ideal for his father.

There had been no requirement for Stephen to attend the inquest, his uncle suggesting he didn't. They'd driven up, the two of them, just three weeks after burying his sister. Stephen sat with his mother throughout as they listened to hour after hour of background testimony and witness statements, the day still recent enough for it to sound like a piece of fiction.

The first phone call to the police station that day came just after lunchtime when a man in combat fatigues and a woollen beanie, his face smeared with camouflage paint, was seen walking through the town with a rifle. This prompted an initial though routine response, the assumption being that it was a prank or an exaggerated account. When, ten minutes later, a woman ran screaming through the streets, more calls were made, the desk sergeant under the impression that an accident had occurred.

Despite the nature of the descriptions, it was still some time before the tactical firearms team was notified. Almost ninety minutes passed from that first shot until the team, based forty miles away, arrived in the town. By the time they assembled outside Highfield with the knowledge that it was no false alarm, the local telephone exchange had recorded almost two thousand calls, a fact, the coroner said, that hampered both the police and ambulance personnel as the system laboured under the deluge.

After leaving Highfield, Stephen's father had made his way down the field into town, emerging from the alleyway on Cross Street in full view of afternoon shoppers and passing traffic. It was said he wore a blank look, one of cold indifference, his movements measured, unhurried. A woman in a car described seeing him walking towards her down the middle of the road, his eyes vacant as he raised and fired the gun. The first shot shattered the windscreen, missing her and coming to rest in the boot; the second – though she swore to not feeling anything initially – shattered her left clavicle, the car turning sharply into a wall. Pretending to be dead, she lay slumped forward until she sensed the danger had passed, the car radio playing all the while.

Turning right on to Market Lane, Stephen's father came

across the second person he would kill that day. Suzanne's uncle, Ron Jenkins, a painter and decorator, was working on the exterior of the town's bakery when he heard the two shots and the screams that accompanied them, the thud of the car hitting the wall. Walking hurriedly towards Cross Street, a small tin of paint in one hand, brush in the other, he was shot twice, once in the neck, the second bullet penetrating his chest, causing bleeding into one of his lungs. Ultimately it was the bullet to the neck that would kill him.

Stewart Dawson's mistake was to leave his young assistant in charge at the garage, something he did on occasion if work was slow. A mechanic in the town since finishing school thirty years earlier, he'd built up his business steadily, gaining a reputation for the quality of his work, even if some in the town grumbled at his prices. He was divorced and single; his weakness, besides visiting the Woodman's every day after work, was for horses, and once his trainee was up to speed, it was a mere five minutes across town to place a few bets, checking the results later on Ceefax between working on the cars. Scrutinising his betting slip as he left the bookmaker's, he was oblivious to the unfolding carnage, rounding the corner of Chapel Street into Stephen's father's path.

Derek Stapleton could have banked the bookshop's takings at any time that day, his wife suggesting he go in the early afternoon lull. The soon-to-be grandfather, who had once let Stephen's mother have an account in the shop, was known to stop in the Bell – the town's other pub, two streets over from the bank – for a quick brandy, sometimes two. If he was planning to have a drink that day, it was to be on the return journey, Stephen's father bringing him down with three shots to the chest outside the bank, the cloth money bag still gripped tightly in his hand as he lay at the side of the road.

Alan Caruth was probably the best known of those to die. A councillor of twelve years, he was hopeful of becoming mayor one day. A former town planner, Caruth was instrumental in keeping new housing developments on the outskirts to a minimum, his passion for retaining the town's charm well known. Returning from a meeting with prospective developers, he parked in the street behind Market Lane, walking to the office rather than taking the one-way system around town. The second of the two bullets to enter him severed his aorta, causing fatal bleeding between the lungs and the chest wall.

By now the police were getting a sense of the severity of events, though none of them had reached the centre of town. Witnesses a few streets away, on the fringes, spoke of hearing a car backfire, or thinking that truanting kids were letting off fireworks.

The youngest person to die was Peter Barnes, a twenty-three-year-old estate agent who'd moved to the town a month earlier to begin a new job. He'd rented a flat over the bookshop and had popped home between viewings, as he sometimes did, to let his young Jack Russell out, walking it on the green by the town hall. It was said he tried to hide behind a bin, its wooden exterior impotent against the shots, the dog licking his face as he lay on the grass.

It was in these morbid narratives that Stephen got a sense of the randomness of death that day. How mundane decisions, a last-minute alteration in plans, determined who lived, who died. Accounts emerged of lucky escapes, near misses. A woman walking into Cross Street before those first shots, realising she'd forgotten a friend's birthday, stopping at the newsagent's on the corner. In the following days, people began examining their movements in detail: the traffic that had delayed them, the phone call as they were leaving the house, the virus that had kept them off work. Perhaps for these few it became life-changing, this glimpse of death that had been a single street or a few seconds away. And of course there were the others, whose phone didn't ring as they left home, whose route to their final spot was unencumbered or insufficiently delayed. Suzanne had spoken of the guilt many felt at surviving, their good fortune at first inexplicable, then a source of reproach. Why had they lived that day when others hadn't?

The inquest heard how screams were spreading along the town's streets now, emanating outwards like concentric ripples from Stephen's father. A picture was established, not of entirely random firing, but one in which those who appeared suddenly in his vision or moved directly in front of him as he walked back to Highfield were targeted. The exception to this was a young boy, a six-year-old off school, out with his mother despite having a chest infection. Bored in the chemist's, he'd wandered out alone, the bell on the door alerting his mother, who called to him to wait. Standing on the pavement a few metres in front of Stephen's father, the boy had looked at him, curious rather than scared, it was said, as the gun was raised and aimed for a few seconds before being lowered.

By this time, the first sirens could be heard as local police sped through the town. As the hour unfurled, they were always a step or two behind, responding to each incident, arriving a few minutes after Stephen's father had left. As the sergeant told the inquest, though, they were not armed and could have done little to stop him.

Three more people would die before his father reached Highfield.

Gary Draper was a courier for a mail order company, the only victim who didn't live in or have connections with the town. A father of three, the inquest heard, he was a man of simple tastes, devoted to his family and the local football club. Traffic had held him up in the morning, his arrival in the town an hour later than scheduled. The only witness, an elderly woman walking her dog along the path that flanked the main road, spoke of the van braking hard, skidding behind her, causing her to turn around. A man with what she first thought was a large umbrella was standing still in the road, the bonnet of the van a few feet from him. She described the next few seconds as lasting for ever, the only noise the steady chugging of the van's diesel engine as the two men stared at each other.

William Burke's car came around the bend seconds after the shots into the van. It stopped a few hundred yards short of the scene, perhaps seeing the danger ahead. Watching in disbelief, the woman saw Stephen's father approach the car, its driver panicking, unable to find reverse until it was too late.

The only woman to die in the town that day was Sheila Hannigan. A mature student, recently engaged, she had returned home to share the good news with her parents, staying a day longer than planned at her mother's request. She'd caught the bus into town, to withdraw some money from the bank, and had walked down to the humpbacked bridge to pass some time until her return journey. There were no witnesses, her body discovered as police followed the trail of carnage out of town.

Where there *were* witnesses, accounts differed of Stephen's father's precise movements, the number of shots fired, the exact order of events lost in the madness. But as their statements were read out it was clear that he had uttered something each time he raised the gun. Three words: 'In cover', followed by 'Engage.'

Initially ambulances were not allowed to attend to the injured for fear of coming under attack themselves. They were held back behind a cordon until Stephen's father's whereabouts were established. The dead were also untouched until later that afternoon, blankets and coats placed over them by those brave or foolish enough to break cover, one woman in particular, Jeanie Harris, comforting several victims in the moments before they died. (In the days that followed, the places where people fell would be marked in chalk, the spectral outlines of bodies adorning the streets until, finally, they were washed away in the rain.) Details of the injuries inflicted were catalogued, entry and exit wounds, the latter often doing more harm. The hospital, some twelve miles away, that treated the injured had little experience of wounds of this kind, its staff having seen shotgun injuries but nothing from a high-velocity rifle.

By this point, Stephen's father's name was being widely

mentioned, the police's focus turning to the house on the hill. When the firearms team finally arrived, the lane was quiet, the road off it closed from both sides by local officers. Making their way cautiously up to the top, the team dispersed around Highfield, taking up positions with good views of the house, some of them in the barns, others behind the oil tank, Shane barking all the while. It was at this point that they found Aiden lying dead in the smaller barn, a single bullet wound to the head.

Listening to all this, Stephen imagined himself in class, the bell going on what would be his last ever day there. He'd got on the bus, sat next to Brendan, who still wouldn't speak to him. He thought of his mother, a couple of hours into her shift at the nursing home, the phone call asking if she knew where her husband was. He remembered the policewoman who'd stopped him at the bottom of the lane, the body by the humpbacked bridge, covered with a blanket. How long had it taken for death to come to the dying? Seconds, minutes? Hours?

Attempts were made to initiate dialogue with Stephen's father, to negotiate his surrender. The police were aware that they were facing a former soldier, armed and murderous, but had no real idea what weapons they were up against, Stephen unable to help them out beyond the number of guns. Procedures and protocol – the rules of engagement – were discussed in length at the inquest, the precise circumstances in which officers were permitted to open fire, precedents that had been set in previous shootings.

When the bullet broke the glass of the lounge window, heading towards the police, it had already passed through his father's brain. It then ricocheted off the room's stone wall before exiting the house, the officers replying with a burst of fire. They had no way of knowing that the gunman was dead, the sergeant still attempting to communicate with him through a megaphone once the shooting had stopped.

It was several minutes before anything else happened, the air around Highfield smelling faintly of cordite, washing that Stephen's mother had put out fluttering in the breeze, the silence broken only by the keening of a dog's bark.

They would finally enter the house an hour later, after a mirror attached to a pole had shown Stephen's father slumped against the far wall of the lounge, the rifle leant against him, as if propping him up, the wall behind brindled red. At his side lay Shane, issuing a snarl between whimpers.

But it was in that near-still air, before they knew he was dead, that one of the curtains in Jenny's open window twitched, just a few inches or so, enough movement behind it to draw a single shot from the barn.

Twenty-six

They washed up together, his mother drying what he stacked. The kitchen was cold, warmth from the fire not reaching it, the cats only venturing in to eat. There were a few storage heaters positioned about the cottage, heat trickling from them, most of it lost to the draughts through ill-fitting doors and windows. Stephen imagined the landlord offering to install radiators, perhaps even double glazing, his mother declining, not wanting the fuss, or preferring the penance of the cold. He'd watched her fall asleep in the chair last night, her posture barely shifting beyond the loosening of her jaw, head canted a few degrees to the side. When the cat left her lap, he placed the old tartan blanket on her, pulling it up over her arms, then sat and watched her sleep for a while.

Winter would arrive in a few weeks. Stephen pictured the breath misting from his mother's mouth as she busied herself around the cottage, fingerless gloves and scarf a permanent feature indoors in these months, she'd said. On bright days she would move washing around, turning it on the windowsills, eking out every drop of sunlight. He thought of her breaking the ice on the bird bath each morning, topping up the feeders, sparrows and tits watching keenly from a distance, flitting in once she'd left. He hoped Peter called, if not daily, then frequently enough to be counted upon, though Stephen hadn't seen him since the log delivery, suspecting he was being given time alone with his mother. They ate together, his mother and her friend, he'd come to realise, at least once a week, the arrangement informal, occurring when meals lent themselves to sharing, or perhaps when sufficient time had lapsed. A companion, he supposed the old-fashioned term would be. A friendship that didn't need to delve too deeply, to look ahead or to the past, its strength in its comfortable silences.

Peter had lost his wife a decade ago; his children were the best part of a day's drive away. They'd moved here in the nineties, to retire, having holidayed nearby when they first met. The town's legacy was known to them but hadn't diminished their affection for the area.

'It must be nice,' Stephen had said, 'to have some company,' his mother changing the subject, ill at ease with the inquisitive tone.

After washing up, they went through to the lounge. One of the cats had unfurled itself along the sofa, so he took a cushion and sat on the floor while his mother manoeuvred a log to a more central position in the fire. The TV was showing coverage of an explosion in Baghdad, its aftermath, the camera jerking frenetically, attempting to capture all the horror in one sweep, as if a child were operating it.

'We always seem to start the wars these days,' his mother said.

There was no sense that she felt lonely, yet a surge of guilt swept through him at all the long evenings alone she had endured, would endure.

'I was thinking, you could get the train down to stay with us. Or perhaps the bus.'

'Did you find anything?' she said, easing into the armchair. 'Where?'

'In the attic.'

'Not really. Blankets and stuff, that old sewing machine.'

A flicker of annoyance passed across her face, whether at the realisation that there were useful things to be had up there, or at him rummaging through them, he couldn't tell.

'It should all come down, go to a car boot sale.'

'There's stuff I remember from the house. Ornaments, pictures.'

'Don't know why I kept it. I'll ask Peter to get rid of it.'

'Is that everything? From then?' His mother didn't answer, seemingly lost to thoughts of the boxes' disposal. 'There must be something more, of Jenny's. What happened to all her toys, her clothes? Did you not keep anything?'

With an exaggerated sigh, his mother stood and went into the hall, where Stephen heard her going through the old chest below the coats. When she returned, she was holding a pink knitted hat and a small notebook, which she handed to him.

'Only these.'

The wool was a little grubby and had unravelled in places. He wanted to remember it, to picture his sister wearing it on snow-clad days, sculling back and forth on the swing, but he couldn't.

'Did you make it?' he said.

His mother nodded. Bringing it to his face, he inhaled deeply.

'It just smells of the cottage now,' she said.

She held out a hand, but he placed the hat on his lap and opened the notebook. The colour had faded from most of the petals, though he recognised speedwell and dandelion, perhaps cow parsley, their stems arcing down crimped pages, some of them identified by his sister's precise handwriting. Again he tried to recall Jenny collecting the flowers, pressing and gluing them into the book, but if such a memory had existed, it was lost now.

'What did you do with the rest of her things?'

'I think they went to a jumble sale.'

'You think?'

'I don't remember.'

He looked at the mantelpiece. 'Are there any more photographs? I have a couple, from Uncle Michael, but there must be more.'

'The drawer at the top of the bureau. In an envelope.'

He found it among some paperwork and sat back down to look at the photos, frustrated at his mother's discomfort. There were more than a few, perhaps twenty or so, the early ones black and white. He featured in several, scenes from their old house, Jenny in a paddling pool in the garden, transfixed by something she was holding, another where an eight- or nine-year-old Stephen held his sister in ungainly fashion, eager to show his strength. Although he had no recollection of the images themselves, they triggered a wave of deep-seated memories, hazed and incomplete, but tangible nonetheless. As the photographs moved into colour, it felt even more real, an actual piece of his life, albeit one consigned to the furthermost archives of his mind. In one picture – perhaps taken by a grandparent or friend – the four of them sat proudly on a beach next to an elaborate sandcastle, its four crests bejewelled with pebbles and razor shells, glinting in the sun. Each of them wore a smile, the kind that wasn't forced, and Stephen strained to hear the gulls above them, smell the brackish air breezing on their faces. Later, his father had buried him in sand up to his chest, Jenny crying as she realised the tide was coming in.

'Where was this?' he said, showing it to his mother.

'Wales, I think.'

'Can I take it? I'll get it copied.'

She nodded. As he returned the others to the bureau, she took back the hat and the flower book, placing them next to her on the arm of the chair.

'Would you like tea or something?' she asked.

'It's funny how you can't say it. Even now.'

Shaking her head, she returned to the fire, scrutinising its structure as if calculating where best to place the next log. 'Well, I'm going to make some anyway.'

'You still blame me, don't you? For her being home.'

She seemed to tremble slightly, her back still to him, but said nothing.

'It was years before I understood it,' he continued. 'How despite everything, to you her death was somehow my fault.'

His mother sighed, her words finally wrenched from some weary place within her, their utterance almost but not entirely without accusation. 'She should have been at school.'

Jenny had come into his room the evening before that

day. There was a trip organised for her class, to a museum or somewhere, which meant an entire day in the company of her tormentors. Unless she could sit at the front, the bus journey alone would mean prolonged harassment. The two of them spent ages composing the note, careful to mimic precisely their mother's looping handwriting, alluding to a high temperature, how it was hoped Jenny would be back the day after. They gathered some bread and cheese for her lunch, to hide in her room, and at breakfast the next day carried on as normal. Their mother was distracted anyway, Brendan's father due any time to start work in the barn. Waiting until she was in the bathroom, his sister snuck upstairs and hid in her wardrobe, Stephen calling up that the two of them were off to get the bus, feigning a conversation as he walked across the yard.

Once at school, he'd taken the note to Jenny's form tutor, the man eyeing him with suspicion as he read it. Walking back along the corridor, Stephen wanted to find his sister's class, to confront the girls making her life miserable, to see fear in their own faces as he stood over them. For what could avoiding them for a single day do, other than postpone their treatment of her? She had to either win them around, he'd told her in his bedroom on that last night, or stand up to them, show she wasn't afraid.

It would be a one-off, the note, he'd said: he wouldn't do it again, his sister hugging him with relief once he'd agreed. He knew that by the afternoon, with their mother at work, their father indifferent to anything they did, no one would be any wiser.

As Stephen got on the bus that morning, the others

charging down the aisle, fighting for the back seat, the driver had asked after his sister, a warmth in his voice.

'She's poorly,' Stephen had said.

There was a separate inquest into the police's tactics, a month or so after the initial hearing, Stephen's uncle attending. While critical of the officer who'd killed Jenny, it acknowledged that they'd found themselves in an impossible situation that day. Nine people lay dead or dying, scores more injured. The gunman, a former soldier, they knew at that stage, was hidden from view in his own home, armed with at least one powerful weapon. As the siege unfolded, a neighbour told them that Stephen's mother would likely be at work, the children at school. Calls were made to confirm that nobody else lived there.

The bullet that Stephen's father fired into the roof of his mouth went through part of his brain before penetrating the top of his skull – the police, as it passed over them, taking greater cover before returning fire. If a clear sight of the target now presented itself, the order was given that they should take the shot. For hours the inquest debated the semantics of the protocol – what constituted a clear sight, what alternatives they had – deciding in the end that the officer believed that their lives were endangered by the movement in Jenny's window. In his statement, he said that something resembling the barrel of a gun had been extended beyond the curtain, a claim that none of the others in the team could verify one way or the other. Nothing was found near her body, save the book she was reading.

The bullet entered the left side of her chest at an angle of around thirty degrees, lacerating the right cardiac ventricle before exiting at the base of her shoulder blade and coming to rest in the far wall. As blood pooled into her thorax, the pathologist said, she would have lost consciousness in seconds, death following a few minutes later. One of the police statements made reference to Shane stopping his barking for a few seconds at this point, Highfield still and silent, the only movement a gentle swaying of the curtain.

No charges were brought against the officer, although he was suspended from the firearms team pending further training.

Stephen stared at his mother's back, anger at what she'd said rising in him. *She should have been at school.*

'If anyone's to blame . . .' he started, his mother turning round, her eyes eager for him to let it go.

'Why? Because I was a nurse? Because I should have looked after him better?'

Despite the tone, her words had an air of self-rebuke to them, as if years had been spent in consideration of this. In truth, he hadn't meant that, his criticism focused more on what had happened between her and Brendan's father, which had acted as a tipping point.

'Were you having an affair with Aiden?'

His mother issued a laugh of sorts, a scoff. 'You think that was it, the reason?'

'Perhaps.'

'Well I wasn't. It wasn't. Why would that be enough?'

Her denial, despite the emotion in the words, sounded

genuine. Did he believe her? There seemed no reason to avoid the truth after so long.

She was shaking her head now. 'He came into the barn when I was in there with Aiden.'

'Dad?'

'Yes.'

'What happened?'

'Nothing. He looked confused, seeing all the changes, the two of us working in there, but no one spoke and he went back indoors. I followed him inside, told him we were lucky to have Aiden helping us, given all the problems, that he should be grateful, but he ignored me.'

He thought about her words for a minute, how she'd seen his father shortly before it began, something he'd not considered.

'What was he like? Couldn't you have . . . ?' He could see she'd long carried this thought too.

'What should I have done? He was doing strange stuff all the time. I had to go to work. I left Aiden packing away his tools. I told him not to come back the following week unless I called, that it would be all right once things had settled. I could see he felt let down that I hadn't told Richard about him.'

His mother's naïvety seemed extraordinary. Surely she should have better appreciated the situation, how emasculating this would have been for his father. But then Stephen too had known that Aiden was working for them, that it was something to be kept from his father if possible. What gave him particular exoneration? In the end, he settled for a more collective criticism. 'Why didn't anyone see it coming?'

'How do you see something like that?'

'We should have done more to help him.'

'You mean I should have.'

'Why didn't the doctors?'

'It was different then, these things weren't understood. There were no treatment programmes like today, no courses. They gave him some pills, but I think he stopped taking them.'

'Do you wish it had been me?' As soon as the words were uttered, he wanted to take them back.

'What do you mean?'

'It doesn't matter.'

'No, go on.'

He'd meant his question to be neutral, philosophical perhaps. 'Instead of Jen.'

Neither of them spoke for a while, each crackle of the fire amplifying the silence.

'Why now?' his mother said finally. 'Why have you come here bringing it all up now?'

'It needs to be said. Nothing was ever said.'

'Perhaps it's only you who needs it.'

She went into the kitchen, one of the cats following her. He looked hard at the photo of his sister above the fireplace, wanting to shout or smash something, or even to cry, something he'd not done for years now. He wanted to summon his father, to hold him or shake him, he wasn't sure. Perhaps to speak to him would be enough, to reach out to the man in those last days, show him all the beautiful things he still had.

* * *

Despite half anticipating her refusal to serve him, it was hard to reconcile the act with the girl he'd known, with the woman he'd almost risked his marriage for a few days ago. She had shaken her head as he approached the bar, a barely seen gesture announcing the revised state of things, while the handful of regulars watched with interest. He thought how pained her face seemed, richly ambivalent with the array of emotions his return had stirred. How simple it would have been to use all that had happened to justify – to himself at first, to others if necessary – a more serious transgression the other night, as if the world owed them a night together, the moment postponed for more than twenty years. Who would deny them that, an infernal passion, fuelled by anger and wine and decades of reflection? What glorious exorcisms might have occurred? What awfulness?

'I'm sorry,' Suzanne said, looking along the bar to the landlord, indicating the source of the instruction as well as her frustration at complying with it.

'It's OK. I wanted to say goodbye, that's all.'

'Homeward bound?'

'In the morning.'

If sadness or relief were felt at this, she remained impassive.

'They said you were in here last night, with Brendan.'

'It was good to see him.'

'No blood shed, then?'

'It's been good to see both of you again.'

His words, as so often they did, felt trite once they'd left him. Judging any parting display of intimacy to be a potential source of jeopardy for Suzanne, he instead offered her a warm smile.

'Take care,' she said.

Outside, the air brimmed with woodsmoke and the bite of winter. He thought he might try the other pub in town, before deciding against it; his mother, he realised, had begun to appreciate having him here, though she'd never acknowledge it. More and more she would follow him around the cottage, fussing over him, possibly bemoaning his imminent departure. Perhaps she'd lost the most of all of them that day. A husband and daughter, a friend in Brendan's father. And in choosing to stay here, she'd lost a son too.

He'd barely left the car park when he heard someone approach from behind.

'I thought you should know,' Suzanne said. 'They're at the house, some of the men from here. One of them had a can of petrol.'

By the time he'd climbed the hill to Highfield, he felt sure exhaustion would do for him, his lungs worked to the limit of capacity. Having initially thought that Suzanne meant the cottage, he'd run the whole way back there, only to witness through the kitchen window his mother quietly attending to something. It had taken another fifteen minutes to get here, the short cut up through the field burnished with enough moonlight to show the way. This time the gate was ajar, though there was no sign of anyone. Perhaps they'd lost their nerve, the drunken bravado in the pub receding as the night sky bore down on them, exposing the pointlessness of their plan. Yet what did it matter, the final destruction of an already derelict building whose presence served only to remind a community of all they'd lost? The fact that it had taken his return to the town to garner enough rage for such an act seemed the only incongruous aspect.

Crossing the yard, he recalled again the kind woman who'd helped him collect his schoolwork that day, his mother's clothes; how some aspect of his own unfathomable grief had played out in her eyes and at one point he was sure she was going to embrace him. At the time, watching her pack the old suitcase, he'd felt guilty indulging the fantasy that she could be his mother now, there to take him away to some innocent new life, a family adopting the poor child left behind by tragedy. There would be a new brother or sister to get to know, the events of the past few days soon forgotten.

When his uncle had told him instead that he would be living with them, he had still felt relief, firstly at not having to remain in the town, but mostly at not having to live alone with his mother, whom he saw as a symbol of the horror. Perhaps she too regarded their parting in favourable terms, preferring the severance from all reminders, allowing her to grieve alone and completely. Once he'd left, she never missed a birthday, a card with a cheque or book token tucked inside arriving in plenty of time. And for the first few years she would phone as well, spending a few minutes in conversation with her brother before their own awkward exchange. At no time did Stephen's aunt presume to replace his mother in the few years he lived with them, her approach one of considered nurturance: there if he needed someone, while preparing him as best they could for adulthood, for independence. His cousins, who'd long since left home to take up dazzling careers, returned to stay periodically, initially eyeing Stephen with a wary curiosity that eventually turned to pity. The day he moved out, renting a bedsit after taking a job in the nearby fish market, there was a hint of relief in all their faces, that despite a fondness for him, their own vague connection to that day had been removed a little more.

He recognised the first of them to emerge from behind Highfield, one of the lithe young men across the bar in the Woodman's when he'd met Brendan. Early twenties, perhaps younger – certainly with no direct memory for that day. His anger would be vicarious, handed down like a folk tale, a collective narrative into which he could now weave a final chapter. Or maybe he was affected directly, Stephen's father taking from him a parent or grandparent, this deed a personal revenge long regarded. As two other men emerged from the shadow of the house, he could see the soft flicker of light in the upstairs windows, its silent expansion hypnotic, as if the glow rendered Highfield a winter snug. He tried to recall from his last visit the presence of any containers, something that held rainwater in abundance that he could disperse. And yet to tackle the fire he would have to pass the men, the delight at this fact clear on their faces as they held their ground like sentinels. As the stand-off prevailed, the one carrying the petrol can, a man nearer Stephen's age, issued a crude and unoriginal threat along the lines of his not being welcome, that he should go home, take his mother with him.

'This is my home.'

He could hear the fire now as it moved hungrily from room to room in search of combustible matter. Smoke surged from the hole in the roof into the darkness, the fluorescent tape around the chimney stack excited by the heat.

It was his sister's room he wanted to preserve – the rest

could burn – but already the flames had claimed her remaining curtain, which disintegrated in seconds, the window frame itself now charring. He pictured her jungle wallpaper blistering into itself, the floor ablaze, flames licking up to the lone bullet hole in the far wall.

The men seemed in no hurry to depart, likely calculating that whatever crime was being committed, its sanction carried little if any heft. And it was doubtful that those witnessing the fire from the town would rush to report it. When the boys had gathered outside his mother's cottage that day, throwing stones, firstly on to the roof and then into Stephen's face, his fear had been complete, the temptation to run away only overcome when, on seeing his bloodied cheek, the gang dispersed. But now it was with calm resignation that he ran not across the yard and down through the field, nor up into the woods behind Highfield, but into the wall of fists and boots that relished his arrival.

Twenty-seven

The cottage felt stiller than normal this morning, as if it too was bedding down for winter. He helped his mother put away the breakfast things, then went upstairs to pack, his head still thrumming to some callous tune of last night's violence, his body replete with pain. She had remarked matter-of-factly on the state of his face, offering without sympathy or surprise to find something for the swelling. As she stood over him, gently pressing a tea towel laden with ice cubes into his head, he was reminded of a fall from his bike as a boy, a nasty landing that took several layers of skin from both knees. She'd cleaned the wounds of grit, a pragmatic rather than soothing giver of treatment, and applied a sparing layer of antiseptic cream before dressing them. And all the while, as she attended to his adult injuries, he'd wanted to cry at the injustice of it all, the care his mother would now need.

He'd finally drawn her on the subject last night, once the tension had fallen away, before he'd gone to the Woodman's.

'I thought you could come for Christmas,' he'd said.

'I don't know, what with the cats.'

'Peter will feed them. Or bring them with you.'

'They don't travel well. It upsets them.'

'A cattery, then.'

'I'll be OK here.'

'But you're not, are you?' He could see her turning his words over in her mind, still wary of their earlier clash. 'Are you going to tell me what the tests were for?'

She sighed. 'It's not what you think.'

'So tell me.'

'They found a small tumour, in my brain. It's probably benign, but the more it grows, the more it'll make itself known.'

He felt instantly sick, the word appalling, part of a monstrous lexicon that had the power to take your legs from under you. And of all the parts of the body, surely this was the worst, the hub of who you were, the attack all the more personal. But she'd announced it with such stoicism, as if it were merely an annoyance, a disruption.

'When were you going to tell me?' He heard the hint of bitterness in his voice, like a child being told that his parents were going somewhere without him.

'I don't know. Perhaps I wouldn't have had to. I've got to have another scan next week. They'll know more after that.'

'And then what?'

'They don't know. Surgery perhaps. Radiotherapy if they can't remove it all. The specialist says the odds are good.'

He crossed the room, tried to hold her, the arms of the chair, his mother's posture, making it awkward. Finally she moved across a little, put a hand on his shoulder, and they stayed there for several minutes in silent embrace. When his arm became numb, he pulled away and stood.

'You need to move near us more than ever now,' he said. 'So we can look after you.'

She looked bemused by this, as if his suggestion was ridiculous or impossible.

'Look after me?'

'Yes, now that you're unwell.'

'Peter will cook me some meals.'

'You need your family at times like this. You don't owe this town anything.'

At this, she turned to the window and looked out. 'It's terrible about the trees, isn't it?'

'The trees?'

'The man on the news said they're all dying.'

From the bedroom window, Stephen watched as half a dozen long-tailed tits flitted around the bird table, their feeding finally interrupted by a jackdaw careening in, banishing them to the next garden. Further along, Peter was planting some bulbs in one of the beds behind Shane's grave, standing upright every now and then, easing his back. The dog hadn't been the same afterwards, living out its final days in a sullen lament. Unsure if it was dangerous or not, the police almost shot it that day, a sympathetic officer finally cornering the animal, cajoling it into one of the vans. It surprised them all when his mother agreed to have it back, a colleague from the nursing home looking after the dog during her bouts in the psychiatric hospital. Once home, she walked it in the early morning and at dusk, slipping in and out of the cottage largely unnoticed, the animal living another year or so. Stephen liked to think she went along the valley and up in the woods to where his father had been laid to rest, Shane perhaps bolting when he got the chance, running back to an empty Highfield, his allegiance Pavlovian.

A neighbour chatted idly with Peter over the line of wilting buddleia, perhaps exchanging strategies for their flora, discussing what would survive the frost when it came. Beyond them the sky was rinsed of colour, the morning sun made frail by banking stratus. Stephen finished packing, left an envelope of money on the bedside table and went downstairs.

His mother was cleaning the old Belfast sink, working a brush hard into its corners, a bottle of bleach nearby, the smell smarting. He observed her for a moment, imagining the thing that grew inside her, realising that she saw this too as reparation, as a reasonable sentence. With a complete absence of self-pity, she'd remarked last night that there would be some small comfort in knowing the thing that would ultimately kill her.

Sensing he was there, she spoke. 'Would you like a cup of something before you go?'

'I told Zoe I'd be home to collect Amy from school.'

At the front door, she seemed surprised when again he held her, embarrassed almost, as a teenager might be with an older relative, their embrace the evening before seemingly a one-off. Her body felt delicate between his arms, as if an ounce more force would see it break and crumble before him. She patted his back before pulling away.

'They set fire to the house last night,' he said, his tone apologetic.

She seemed to consider his words briefly before dismissing them. 'Perhaps you could bring Amy up soon.'

He thought to repeat the invite for Christmas, but instead merely asked her to say goodbye to Peter for him. Just as when he'd arrived, one of the cats wove itself between her feet, a simple devotion he'd begun to appreciate. At the end of the row of cottages he turned to wave, but his mother had gone inside.

On the outskirts, he parked where the school bus used to drop them off, just yards from the granite memorial listing those from the town to fall in the Great War. The track was rudimentary but passable, his boots clogged heavy with mud before long. Cocooning him were hedgerows still rich with fruit – rowan and haws, blackberries and sloes – gangs of sparrows chattering deep within them. As he followed the path out of the valley, the cloud began to retreat, autumn's mellow tones diffusing around him.

In the garden of the Woodman's, Brendan had told him about one of the injured, a man now in his fifties, who still had a bullet from that day lodged in his head. Entering through his ear, it came to rest millimetres from his brain. After a scan, doctors deemed an attempted removal too risky, and so, almost thirty years on, he lived with the residue of that day in every sense, knowing that the bullet could shift and kill him at any time. And as well as the holes in the walls at Highfield, Brendan had spoken of several in the town, if you knew where to look, small hollows that bore witness to an insane hour.

Where the trail levelled out, arcing limbs from a line of elders had formed a short tunnel, the river below quietened for a moment as he walked through it. Broken sunlight slanted to the ground around him, the landscape he'd always regarded as restless now becalmed. Finally the path opened out to a grassed clearing that overlooked much of the valley. Through his binoculars he could see Highfield opposite, the early sun caught in the shells of its remaining pebble-dash walls, a thread of smoke from last night's fire furling upwards. He could see movement around the grounds, likely the same firefighters he'd heard approaching as he scrambled home like some wounded wretch. Perhaps it would be demolished now, rendered too unsafe to be left to the elements. A patchwork of trees radiated out from the house, their canopies bronzed, the evergreen conifers crowding the few oaks. Below, the road home followed the river west until, a mile or so out of town, they parted at a row of houses, one of which he supposed was Brendan's.

Beyond the houses, the last curtain of mist was receding; above it, in the woods, was the spot where his father's ashes had been strewn to the wind. An image of the man came to him now, a young version, perhaps before Jenny was born, a smiling, contented version, home on leave. They had been in the driveway of their old house, his father washing the car, Stephen doing the same to his sit-in toy version that had been a birthday present that year. Neighbours walked by, smiling at the spectacle, the cul-de-sac a docile, innocent place, the sun blazing as it always seemed to then. They shared the bucket of soapy water, Stephen mimicking his father's rhythmic motion around the wheel arches, the confluence of grimy water spooling over the kerb, down into a drain.

He would see Amy later, her face a beacon across the

playground, as if all the day's light was refracted from it. Was this the same for every parent at the school gates, the instant recognition of your child in a sea of faces? He could hear Zoe telling him of its evolutionary origin, its prevalence in the animal kingdom, the benefit of such an attribute to survival. Sometimes his daughter would run the last bit to him, breaking free from the others, giddy, barely able to get the words out quickly enough as she related some event that was both commonplace and extraordinary. Driving home, he'd watch her in the rear-view mirror, some days seeing a vestige of his sister, half expecting his daughter's face to be blushed on one side.

Was he a good father? It seemed unfair that such things could be measured only by others, and with hindsight, the legacy of fatherhood determined when it was too late to have an effect. No one really told you what you were doing right, or wrong.

For much of his childhood his own father had been an apparition, even before he was ill, the long absences, the need for solitude when he returned each time, veiling the man. Did that make him a bad father? Certainly Stephen, as he got older, had relished his being away, the freedom it offered, his mother's reins long and loose. The prospect of his father being at home more once he'd left the army had been unsettling, perhaps for all of them.

Stephen often wondered if he had only intended to kill Brendan's father that day, but that once he had, he became someone else. That some terrible flashback had taken hold of him, the forces in operation, as his mother said, little understood or given much credence in those days.

Again and again he remembered the witnesses who spoke of how empty his father's eyes were, glazed and dead like those of the rabbit they'd shot up in the field, as if the human in him had flown, leaving an abomination, a monster – or as Stephen preferred to think, nothing at all, only the husk of the strangler tree remaining. Yet even now he still thought of his father as a gentle man, a good person whose hard-wiring had been corrupted by the things he'd seen or done. When Stephen was still at primary school, they'd played their own game of 'war' when his father was home. On the front room floor, two lines of defences were established from tin cans and pebbles, whatever was to hand, behind which were positioned Stephen's plastic soldiers, some of them embedded more than others. Armed with a small fir cone each, they would take turns launching assaults across the carpet, the victor the one to knock over all of the enemy.

Returning here had made the victims of that day vivid again, as he pictured them again and again approaching the last few minutes of their lives. They still appeared in his dreams at times, their faces gleaned from his imagination and snippets from the inquest, shifting silently towards him, the walking dead. He rarely dreamt of his sister any more, and when he did, she appeared more as an archetype these days, a representation of the girl he remembered, her face unblemished, its features sometimes merged with or replaced by his daughter's. Standing in her room at Highfield the other day, he'd wondered what her final thought had been, whether she had heard that final shot a fraction of a second before the bullet entered her. Had she watched their father coming and going, leaving the house, gun over one shoulder, returning an hour later, the vanguard of all the mayhem to follow? And then, as the police arrived, did she think to break cover, suspecting on some gloriously naïve level that their presence was a result of her missing school?

Going through it all, he rehearsed in his head how he would tell Zoe, trying to anticipate her reaction. It had been easy to let her think his father was instead a victim of a mass shooting she'd vaguely heard of. It explained his reluctance to ever discuss it, to ever return to the town. It explained his mother's estrangement. It was unlikely that she'd check the details, look up any of the original coverage. But why had he been so afraid of telling her? In case she thought that his father's actions were hard-wired somewhere deep in his own DNA? Or just because the association was too much of a burden to ask of anyone?

He thought he might disclose his past at the upcoming hearing, as mitigation of sorts, though it was difficult to see it being given weight after so much time. And what guarantees could he provide that a repetition would not occur, especially if his face still bore the marks of last night?

More than ever he needed the distraction of work, his life thrown out of all kilter in its absence, it being the one thing that allowed the vividness of the past to dim. He'd already missed a research trip to the Azores with the oceanography students, and next month he'd been due to visit the marine science centre in Gothenburg, collecting samples on their research vessel. And yet it was the less glamorous manifest-ations of the job he most mourned the loss of, the comfort of routine, banter with colleagues, a sense that he belonged.

The longer he was away from it all, the more likely they'd regard him as superfluous.

He regretted hitting Ferguson. With luck, they would send him on some course, issue a written warning, if he showed sufficient contrition. Whatever anger had festered in him, something in his visit here had seen it dissipate. He would become a better father, a better husband, give up smoking at New Year. He would like for Amy to have a brother or sister, so that she wasn't an only child.

Perhaps they would all come up here for Christmas, the three of them, not exactly a surprise visit, but one with insufficient announcement, his mother given little time to find a reason to cancel. He would show Amy the woods around Highfield, see if there was a horse in the top field, tell her about the aunt she never knew who liked to dance barefoot in her bedroom until she was giddy, who took an age to tie her shoelaces, refusing all instruction on how it was best done, whose laughter began as a stifled giggle before erupting into an uncontrollable and infectious guffaw. He would ring his mother more, perhaps Peter too, to learn the things she wouldn't tell him, the prognosis. There was a friend of Zoe's he could ask about the disease, what was to come, what the odds she spoke of were. And he would come up when he could, once the hearing was out of the way, just to be around, company of sorts.

The wind was gusting a little now. He scanned the valley, searching for movement, his eyes tracking back and forth in restless repetition. Eventually something slipped from the mosaic of trees opposite, sculling upwards before settling into a steady glide. He found the bird in the binoculars, its form shifting silently across the wooded background like a satellite traversing the night sky. Every now and then it would vanish, reappearing where the canopy became more vivid. It was undoubtedly a raptor, probably a juvenile buzzard, perhaps a sparrowhawk, though the distance between them allowed him to imagine it was a peregrine. He hoped it would soar above the crest of the hill, up into the first thermals of the day, so that he might witness its awesome stoop, its body emblazoned with sunlight. Instead, the shape was again lost to the trees and didn't return.

Q&A with Tom Vowler

How challenging did you find it conjuring the damaged mindset of a man scarred by war?

Very. For what means do we have to replicate such horror beyond reading and listening and imagining? I suppose Richard is a reluctant soldier, an outsider who struggles deeply with the blind obedience and machismo of military life, and in that sense I found great empathy with him. He finds it hard to connect with his comrades, the vagaries of soldiering beyond him. And then from nowhere war breaks out, which in some ways, despite its attendant horrors, allows him to feel part of something for the first time. Of course the damage is done nonetheless, his sensitivities divergent with all he witnesses, with the guilt he feels. Astonishingly, more veterans of the Falklands have now committed suicide than died in action, though things have changed considerably since then. I remember reading a quote during my research, that you could teach men to kill but not to see death.

What made you choose the epigraph from John Banville's The Sea?

There's a nod to Banville's lyricism here, an affection for language and the effect/affect it engenders in itself. But of course all three of my central characters carry a heavy cargo of trauma, their pasts burdening each of them, whether it be for a year in Richard's case, or several decades in Mary's. Stephen's attempt to sever the links to his childhood involve relocating to the coast, where the rhythms of the sea instil in him a small sense of calm.

Your writing is imbued with nature and landscape, and the way it plays into your characters' experiences. How important do you think this is in characterisation?

I'm always suspicious of a narrative without a keenly felt world, where the story could be transported anywhere without losing something. Certainly I use landscape – generally the natural world rather than an urban setting – to create atmosphere, to give texture, but also to reflect characters' inner realms, the people in my books products of the world around them rather than merely inhabitants. Landscape and characters are mutually dependant, they amplify each other, inform one another. Landscape too, can become a character in itself, its complexity and chronology granting it a stake, allowing the reader to invest in it as they might the people or the story. Proust regarded landscape as four-dimensional, the fourth being 'time', the terrain having a past and a future as well as the present. For me we are wedded to the land around us – be it city or hamlet, coast or upland – for work, for play, our cultural and social lives shaped by it. Perhaps modernity, with its rise in technology and consumerism, has seen treatment of place in fiction neglected, yet whether it's a scarred, battle-riven grassland or some sun-bleached clearing in a wood, my own books will always carry this strong sense of place.

What inspired you to use such a strong bird motif in this book?

This came late in the day, when I was exploring how Richard's post-traumatic stress might manifest. It was at a time I was becoming utterly seduced by J.A. Baker's remarkable book, *The Peregrine*, with its paean to both language and the natural world, in particular the eponymous bird of prey. Reading this immersive, chimeric book shone a light on the path my character's obsessive nature might take. In giving him Baker's fascination with the peregrine and affection for the natural world, I was able to employ a much closer narration, one that allows the reader an intimate insight into Richard's unhinging, which is mirrored in his pursuit of the falcons as he withdraws from life.

And so a trio of fixations began to coalesce: Baker's quest to observe the birds, my character's mimicking of this, and my own fascination with *The Peregrine*, which I'd savour each evening by the fire. I wouldn't go so far as to term my novel's relationship with Baker's book as intertextual, but I certainly owe it a huge debt. I had found my soldier's voice. Also, both

Richard and Stephen are enamoured with the realm of birds, its otherworldliness, which, at times, they long to inhabit, to escape to.

The nature/nurture of childhood and repercussions of the past are central themes in your books. What is it that draws you to these topics, putting family dynamics and personal relationships under such a powerful microscope?

To borrow a former mentor's metaphor: one's primordial swamp will always rise up into the work. Much of this is unconscious, the themes and issues an author writes about perhaps selecting them rather than the other way around, the process rarely as autonomous as we like to think. I hope my books have a deep emotional resonance; certainly I mine my own brushes with trauma during composition, delve into my experiences of love and loss when breathing life into a character.